SEVEN WAYS TO KILL A KING

MELISSA WRIGHT

Copyright © 2020 by Melissa Wright

All rights reserved.

No part of this book may be reproduced in any form or by any electronic or mechanical means, including information storage and retrieval systems, without written permission from the author, except for the use of brief quotations in a book review.

Cover Illustration © Luisa J. Preissler www.luisapreissler.de

Title Treatment by Silver Wing Press http://SilverWing.Press

Character Art by Dominique Wesson

SEVEN WAYS TO KILL A KING

For my Turtles

RAVENSGATE

BLACKSTONE

IRONWOOD

STORMSKEEP

KIRKWALL

PIRN

SMITHPORT

UNNAMED
SEA

Storm Queen's Realm

PROLOGUE

Cassius's eyes trailed over the figures crossing between the warehouse and the Blackwater. Their fingers were stained with pitch, and their clothes were stiff with salt. His duties for the harbormaster required distance, stealth, and a watchful eye. He was to track the goings-on quietly and report on men his employer didn't trust. It was a perfect cover for Cass's true concerns.

"Shoo!" a woman whose vigor belied her age said.

He couldn't help the smile that crawled across his lips as Nan snapped a towel toward an old dog scavenging for scraps. The woman's hair was drawn back to the crown of her head and pinned in a meticulous knot. Cass remembered the color it had once been, before he'd spent years watching it lighten and become streaked with ash. A fresh apron was tied over Nan's long skirt, but beneath it would be tall laced boots and at least one knife.

Three sailors laughed and hooted down an alleyway. It was far too early in the afternoon for their revelry to end well. But that was not Cassius's affair. The men would be the harbor patrol's headache when the time came.

Nan held up a hand to shade her brow, as if gazing out to sky and sea, but her gray eyes hit Cass's instead. She made a gesture questioning if anything had seemed suspicious, and Cass replied with the merest shake of his head. Nan winked and turned, headed once again into the depths of the Blackwater Inn. It was a Myrina day, a day when all eyes would be on alert—a day for the queensguard to mind their watch.

Smithsport was bustling nearly all day long in the summer months, but the lull between the morning's business and the evening's revelry felt the most dangerous of all. It was the time when Princess Myrina of Stormskeep, the daughter of the true queen, went out and about as the scullery maid, an orphan girl affectionately known as Bean, the same as a dozen other maids and servers in Smithsport alone. It was the time Cass's attentions, his duty, became most difficult of all.

A side door to the inn opened, and Myrina's dark hair came into view. From a distance, it was hard to be certain, but he thought the sun lent it the tint of mulled wine. It was tied loosely into a knot at the nape of her slender neck, and a large swath fell over her face. Cass could remember Miri's hair, too, before the dyes, when it had been as blond and wild as a lion's mane. She swung a bucket toward the street, and the dirty water splashed over the stones.

Cass slipped farther into the shadows. When Miri straightened, the stray dog ran toward her, a spring in his step because he recognized her as a woman with food or attention. Miri's face came up as she glanced at the street, probably checking for Nan or Thom or anyone who might rat her out, and then she reached into a pocket, drew out a scrap, and handed it carefully to the beast before giving him a quick scratch behind the ear.

She straightened again, her shoulders rising in a deep breath. The air was not entirely fresh so near the port, but it absolutely beat what waited inside. She brushed the hair from her face and turned, and Cass leaned forward to watch her go—to not miss one moment more than he had to.

The door shut, and a shadow shifted—another of his queensguard at watch. The figure glanced at Cass then away. It felt like judgment. It felt like Henry.

"Seven hells," Cass muttered, turning back to scan the street. He wasn't sure what was wrong with him, but it was getting worse. He was fairly certain it was the tedium. This was not what he'd been trained to do. Standing watch without a lick of friction was getting under his skin. If Cassius needed anything, it was action and to get away from the sea.

A broad man in a worn cloak crossed at the corner of the street, catching Cass's notice. The hood alone might have given Cass pause, but the weather in Smithsport did not always account for the way men dressed once they'd been soaked by salt and sea or traveled from far-off lands. What made Cass uneasy was the squareness of the man's shoulders, the bearing that spoke of a soldier and a man who trained with swords. Cass straightened, settling his belt more firmly at his hip. He would follow the man, even if it was nothing. Because surely, it was nothing.

Cass's pulse thrummed in his veins, arguing his own reassurance. But it was midafternoon in Smithsport. He had no reason to think she was anything but safe. Besides, there'd not been a single call—

Suddenly, the call of a bird cut through the air. The first was short and sharp, then the second was longer.

Cass's feet were moving before he'd had a moment to think, his blood suddenly cold. The man in the cloak stepped onto the planks of the Blackwater's porch, his hood falling to reveal a half helm carved with images of a bear.

It was Cass's enemy, the enemy of them all, striding into the single safe haven of the princess and those loyal to her. It would be the death of her and the death of Cass and his brothers-in-arms.

Cassius was bloodsworn, loyal to the queen and her family. But the queen no longer ruled. The Lion Queen of Stormskeep had been murdered, slaughtered before her throne. Her body had been burned to ash. To be a sympathizer was treason and to be queensguard a fate worse than death.

But Cassius of Stormskeep had sworn his protection. He could do nothing else.

CHAPTER 1

Myrina Alexander was born to do great things. It said as much on the tapestries that had lined her nursery walls. She slapped the sodden mop onto the rough stone floor. Its frayed rope caught and pulled as the dirty water puddled into crevices before she'd managed much cleaning at all. She'd still not mastered a few of the most challenging skills of her new life. Through the wall behind her rose the muffled yammering of men who'd drunk too much ale in the rooms she'd been kept safely away from since she was a girl. She was out of sight, away from notice, and alone in a storeroom that needed a good cleaning now and then.

"Great things," she muttered as she yanked the mop to work it free. The handle was long and narrow but nothing at all like the glistening swords woven into those childhood tapestries of a girl battling man and bear. When the snag gave, all the force she'd put into it landed solidly in the ribs of a sturdy figure behind her.

The figure cursed, and she turned to gape at a hulking form she'd had no idea had moved into the space behind her. He was not quite man or bear but something in between and far more dangerous. Sense should have had her calling for help or at least informing the man that he'd no business in the back rooms of the Blackwater, but she could only gape up at the dark eyes and bear half helm of a kingsman of Stormskeep.

A huff of air came as Nan careened into the corridor and nearly slammed bodily into the opposite wall. "There you are," she said through clenched teeth, and though the words appeared to be aimed at Miri, it was clear to Miri that Nan had been searching for the kingsman.

Nan cleared her throat, tugging her apron back into place, and gave a practiced simple-farm-woman smile to the guard. "Apologies for the trouble, if it pleases you. I'll see that the girl is right proper whipped." Nan's fingers curled into a tight fist at her side, but Miri's had gone into the loose, ready stance she'd been taught as a child.

But it was no time for that. Miri forced her fingers to curl into her threadbare skirt and dropped her gaze to the floor before scuttling toward Nan with a silent prayer and tightly pressed lips. Miri's head snapped up when the guard snagged her shirt, jerking her roughly toward his form. She winced away from him. His sour breath smelled not unlike the cook's day-old onion stew.

The kingsman drew her nearer, and Miri let her dark hair fall over her cheek. All color bled from Nan's face. Though her neatly pinned bun was undisturbed, a smear of something dark stood out on her neck. Miri wondered what she'd missed and how many other guards were beyond the wall behind them, outside in the city streets—and whether it was the end for her and Nan.

"Reeks of a life well lived." Even if his words were ugly, the kingsman's voice was low and careful. He was not a man who'd been drinking ale and had stumbled into the back rooms by mistake. The kingsmen were intelligent. He would know she was no mere whipping girl. Thomas had been right—Miri had no business being let out into the world, not when the guards had access to every establishment in the kingdoms.

Nan stepped forward, jaw going into a hard line. "Oh, she'll pay well enough, I assure you." Nan came just shy of snatching at Miri's arm and falling into a tug of war that could cost them both their lives.

Miri glared at her beneath a lowered brow.

Nan drew a thin rod from the pocket of her skirt, and for a moment, Miri didn't think either of them was entirely sure whether Nan intended to use it on her or the guard.

The kingsman let out a snort, apparently not at all concerned for the latter, and tossed Miri roughly to the ground. Her knees hit the stone tiles with a crack, her thin flesh splitting over bone. She bit her tongue and her words and bit back every shred of rage she'd ever felt for the men of the king's guard and what they had done. Nan grabbed Miri by the knot of hair at the nape of her neck and muttered a curse as she dragged her to her feet.

When she was pulled into the next corridor, Miri chanced a glance at the guard. He pushed over a tall shelf, scattering its contents onto the damp floor, then kicked through the mess and knocked over a metal bin and a basket of wooden utensils. Miri drew a breath through her nose, and Nan shoved her into the next room.

Three corridors later, Nan slammed the door shut behind them, barred it with a wooden slat, and turned to lean against it. She placed a hand over her heart as she slid like liquid to the floor. Miri uncurled her fists from their grip on her skirts and straightened the material before pushing the tangled hair from her face.

"Gods, girl," Nan whispered up at her, breath coming in broken heaves. "That was close."

"What are they doing here?" Miri knelt before her protector, who'd cared for her and hidden her since she was a child. "Why are they in Smithsport?"

Nan ran the back of her hand over her forehead and, voice low, said, "King's business. There are at least a dozen down by the dock." Her soft gray eyes held an apology. "We didn't get word in time. I'd no sooner heard they'd been spotted before this one was scampering about. Came in under the cover of a wagon, hidden in supplies like stowaways right through the town gates. Getting sneaky, they are. Thomas knocked an entire barrel of ale in this one's path, made a mess of the thing, but the bear wouldn't be put off."

"So that's what happened to you." Miri reached forward to wipe the muck off Nan's neck, but she brushed her attentions away.

"Come on, help me up, Bean. We've got to get you somewhere safe."

Miri took hold of Nan's arm and helped her to her feet. "Not much of a plan. You know we're trapped back here."

Nan gave her a sly smile and whispered, "Don't think much of your old Nan, do you, Bean?" She yanked a drapery cord by the far wall, and a filthy animal pelt fell silently to the floor.

Miri waved away the dust and stared openly at what appeared to be a trap door. Nan had been holding out on her.

"Aye," Nan whispered. "Now up you go."

&.

MIRI HAD CLIMBED through the trap door and into a small dark chamber nearly an hour before, by her estimation, and had been listening to the rustle of foot traffic and wheeled carts overhead.

Nan had closed and locked the entrance behind her, swearing she would soon be set free. "Listen for Thom," she'd promised. "He'll be along."

A brief scuffle and shouting overhead had followed shortly after. Then came the clink of a metal sword, and sweat had prickled on Miri's skin. Those noises had settled into the more common goings-on, though, and the sweat ran in rivulets down her back instead. She was a dirty, damp mess, and she was fairly certain the barrels tucked in beside her held something far worse than old ale. She wondered how long the stale air in the spare space would hold her and whether she would be able to break out if Thom never came. She wondered what the kingsmen were looking for.

A hollow scrape sounded above, and Miri ducked as loose dirt fell into her tangled hair. She cowered against a barrel, but there was little room to move away. A narrow beam of light speared the space as an overhead plank was shifted aside. Then she heard Thom's knock: three short raps.

She signaled back, two quick taps to the barrel with her knuckles, the second louder than the first. The plank was shoved aside. Miri closed her eyes against the glare, blinded after so long in the empty dark, and was met by Thomas's words.

"Come on, girl. Time to move." He reached into the open space to grab Miri's shirt, glancing quickly at the man beside him.

Miri rose, knocking her head against the low ceiling, then was tugged from the pit into the fresh evening air. It was early, well before sunset, and Thomas Blackwater was unceremoniously shoving a princess of Stormskeep into a dirty barrel.

She resisted momentarily, but he *tsk*ed at her, and she remembered her place in the ordeal. Being caught could get them all killed, not just Miri. She squatted into the barrel and was turned on her side as it was set quickly to rights. As she struggled to shift in the cavity, the figure with Thom disappeared as he slammed the lid into place.

"Quiet, Bean," Thom murmured through the wood. "It'll be over soon."

The barrel was jostled as she was thrown aboard a wagon, and then came the muffled crack of a whip and a call to the horses before her barrel rattled against the others and the wagon's deck below. She bit down hard on a curse and prayed she would not be stuck inside long enough to be taken to port.

The ride was miserable and painful and loud and hot, but it was not the worst she had been through. Miri had experienced much worse, and that low point sat well beneath her current situation. She would get through it so that she could live another day. Myrina Alexander had things to do—great things.

CHAPTER 2

The wagon stopped well before they'd had time to reach the port. Her barrel was unloaded carefully by at least two grunting men, and silence settled into the darkness once more. Miri counted her heartbeats, desperate to be free. Her legs ached to push her to standing and run. Her hands trembled to do anything other than clutch at her skirts. Miri couldn't remember why she'd ever argued with Nan to leave the house. She couldn't recall what had seemed so important about having something productive to do or being near actual crowds. She wanted to take it all back. She wanted to go home.

Three soft taps sounded on the lid of the barrel before the wood was slid aside. Miri gasped in the fresh air and was fished out of her barrel by a cloaked figure who was too tall and narrow to be Thom. She fell clumsily into the man and recognized the familiar scent of sweet ale over that of the sea, salt, sweat, and fish. He was another of Thom's men, another who was loyal to her—one more who could be killed for keeping her safe.

The man said nothing as he tugged Miri into a run, rushing them through a darkened stable. Horses nickered and groaned as they passed, then came the ragged complaint of a single goat, which meant they were passing through the smith's outbuildings. She was nearly home.

The cloaked man drew to a stop at the back of the stable and glanced at a shadowed figure at the edge of a neighboring barn. The two gestured some signal, then Thom's man turned to wrap his cloak over Miri's form.

"Ever faithful," he whispered.

His words chilled her to the bone. Then he was gone.

Miri could see the familiar outline of Nan and Thom's homestead from her place in the doorway. She could walk, very casually, across the space, and come out of the entire ordeal fine. All she needed to do was to take the first step.

Her eyes met the shadowed figure by the barn as she considered the gestures he'd made toward the cloaked man and the words that had been whispered into her ear. *Ever faithful.* They were not Thom's men. They were hers. And Myrina, daughter of the Lion Queen, would not be cowed by dirty, thieving kingsmen.

Her boots landed softly on the hay-strewn ground, and the evening light cast a strange hue across the path. Nothing in her would cave to the desire to run. She would not show fear in front of the men who had saved her. They were her guard, even now, after everything.

At least three other forms waited somewhere in the shadows. There would be more. Whatever had happened to their brethren, their families, or themselves, her mother's guard—the ones who'd lived—had stayed true to their word and their duty. Miri wanted nothing more than to be worthy of the price they had paid. She was afraid she might never get the chance.

She crossed through the garden gate of Nan and Thom's back lot. She passed the barns and the shed, her boots hitting the wobbly planks outside the back door a moment before it rushed open.

Nan yanked her through the doorway then slammed it shut to draw Miri into a too-tight hug. "Maiden save us," she whispered into Miri's hair. Her breath came out in a rush. "But you do smell a bit of a nanny soaked in ale."

The tension in Miri's chest released with a broken chuckle, and Nan eased her grip to look at her face.

"All well?"

Miri managed a shrug. "Seems to be, aside from the drunken goat stink." Her throat was dry, and she wanted to drink a pitcher of water before dumping a second over her head. "Why are they here?"

Nan's expression went wretched. "Looking for sympathizers, I'm told."

A sick feeling swam up from the pit of Miri's stomach.

Nan shook her head. "Rounding them up to take to the square."

For the festival. Miri fell heavily into a kitchen chair. "They're going to celebrate it. Make a show of them at the festival of moons."

Nan leaned down to put a hand on Miri's shoulder. "They'll be protected, Bean. They always have been."

But that wasn't true. Sympathizers had been captured time and again. They'd been dragged behind wagons, tied onto gates, and burned by sorcerer's fire. *How many more will be killed? How much longer can I let them get away with it?*

Miri stood, the action bringing her too close to Nan, but she held her ground. "I have to stop it. I won't risk another murder in her name. I won't let—" The word stuck in Miri's throat. She couldn't say her sister's name and could barely think it. "They will not keep her captive another day." Miri let the vow ring in her voice. Let Nan see it clear in her gaze. "I'm going to put an end to this. And it has to be now."

※

"You aren't going to try to stop me?"

Nan's eyes were soft, and in them were all the memories of

the years Miri had been under their care. "I wish with all of my heart I could." Her hand came up to cradle Miri's cheek. Her fingers were cold and the wrap covering her palm soft and tattered. She smelled of fresh dough, sweet ale, and the citrus oils Thom's men brought from across the sea. "It was only a matter of time. You were never my child. Not my sweet, fragile Bean. You're the daughter of the Lion Queen. I know what waits inside you. As much as I might want to hold you here, honor prevents me."

Miri put her hand over Nan's, her own fingers still trembling while her heart was a feral beast in her chest. Nan never spoke of the Lion Queen or dared to whisper of Miri's true birth. Since she was a child, she had been Bean, a poor cousin's orphan come to earn a living to keep off the streets, hidden away with scars of a tragic past, too damaged for marriage, unfit for society. Miri watched the sadness wash over Nan's features. She was the woman who had protected her when no one else could. But something else was there too: pride and duty.

"My family is sworn to the throne," Nan said. "The true throne. To the rightful queen and all who are hers." She straightened. "It is not my place to command you, Myrina, but to follow your command."

Miri opened her mouth in a rush to protest and vow that she would never command or make demands after everything they had done.

But Nan continued, "To keep you safe."

Miri's heart felt a stab of guilt. What was happening was her fault. It was her fault that they were all in danger.

"To that end, we have always known you would leave us. One day, you would no longer be our little Bean."

Nan's thumb brushed over Miri's cheek, but Miri had not shed a tear. Miri hadn't cried since *before*—not since the darkness while fleeing Stormskeep and not since seeing her mother killed.

"What has been in your heart all these years is too strong to be hidden, sweet Myrina. While I may wish for your safety and that you remain out of harm's way or foolish plans, I cannot stop you. All I can do is offer my support."

Miri swallowed, but before she could speak again, a clatter came at the door. Her hand shot to her waist, but the hidden blade would do her no good against a dozen kingsmen or—if it was truly a hunt for sympathizers—the king's sorcerers. She didn't know why she bothered to carry the weapon when killing a man would draw the guard faster than anything else, but that didn't stop her from reaching or from wanting to fight.

Nan's hand fell to Miri's shoulder, steadying her. "It's Thomas. But the guard will not be far behind."

A massive cloaked form shouldered through the door, bringing with him the scent of smoke and sour ale. Thomas was not much of a drinker, but it was hard to supply the ale house without being covered in the warm yeasty scent. The sourness had not come from proximity to spills, though. It was for keeping guards away.

Thom shoved his hood down, face grim. "They'll be along soon. Best get going, Miri."

"I can't—" Miri's words caught in her throat. She was close to arguing that she couldn't leave them when they were in danger, but staying would only mean a more certain death. Her eyes flicked between Nan and Thomas. They had both known her intent. Neither of them meant to stop her. She pressed her lips together. It was time. She was truly, finally, going to go and repay her debts. "Will you be safe?"

Nan gave her a soft smile. "We've made it this far, dearie. Nothing can hurt us now."

The words were light, but Miri heard the emotion behind them. The thing that could hurt them was Miri. She had to stay safe, at least until she was out of their hands and they could no longer accept blame. They'd done more than enough through the years.

"Is everything ready?" Nan asked Thomas as she tied on a clean apron.

He nodded, gesturing with a thumb over his shoulder. "In the stable. Hurry along now. Say those goodbyes."

"Pshaw." Nan pushed Miri toward the old man. "'Tis you who's put off saying what needs to be said for too long."

Thomas gave Nan a look but tugged Miri into a massive hug. He squeezed her tight against his barrel chest, and his cropped beard scuffed Miri's cheek. "You'll do well, little lion. You always have." His words were no more than a whisper, but they hurt far worse than Nan's had. Thomas had always held his feelings close to his vest, so his show of affection seemed larger and more severe. It seemed like an end.

"Off with you," he said, spinning Miri out of the hug to rush her through the kitchen door.

It was a short sprint to the stable. The windows were shuttered so that the last few stalls were dark. Nan followed them, the sparse light from her lantern casting across Charlie's scattered hay.

Miri reached up to pat the horse before she grabbed his bridle, but a figure shifted in the shadows, and her hand froze in midair.

"Hurry," Thomas said to Miri, leading her forward with a heavy hand on her back. "We're not sending you on Charlie. He's too old, and the beast knows the way home from any tavern within a six-day ride."

The shadowed figure shifted aside, allowing them past as Nan's lantern light crawled across the barn floor and the edge of the stranger's cloak.

"These are Wolf and Milo," Thom said of two geldings that came into the light. "They'll be taking you on from here."

Miri was nudged toward the nearest horse and unceremoniously tossed astride. She nearly gasped at Thomas, but every sound she might have made seemed to be tangled in the mass of emotion that vined from the pit of her stomach to her throat.

"You'll be watched after well," Thomas said, and Miri had the strange sense that the words were less a promise than a threat.

That was when she realized the cloaked figure was meant for the other horse. "What?" she snapped, surprised at the loudness when her words had finally broken free.

Thomas patted her leg. "You're no fool, girl. You know as well as any of us what can happen to a woman traveling alone through the neighboring kingdoms."

She opened her mouth to protest again, but he was right. Miri did know. She'd thought of it before, of how each of her plans would require an ally to be properly seen through to the end. She understood strategy as well as the laws. But she'd gotten used to her guards being at a distance, not riding at her side.

Nan reached past Thomas to squeeze Miri's hand. "He's bloodsworn, Bean. He'll do naught but protect you."

The figure went still—though he'd barely moved before—and Miri's hands went slick with sweat. He was not merely a queensguard. He was bloodsworn, a member of the queen's personal guard. If they were caught, he would be killed after lengthy torture on the square in front of cheering crowds—like the others.

Nan's hand slipped out of Miri's fingers, and Thomas gave one final squeeze to Miri's leg. The cloaked figure leapt onto the dark horse beside her, his scruffy, square jaw momentarily coming into view.

Nan whispered, "Hood up, dear. And Maiden protect you."

The man beside her kicked his heel into his horse's flank, and Thomas smacked the one he'd called Wolf—the one beneath Miri—on the rear. Both horses shot forward just as the doors to the stable opened, and Miri and her bloodsworn raced into the night. Nestled behind Miri were packs of food and supplies, what would be the last mementos of her time with Nan and Thom. Before her, patches of darkness stretched from the edge of town into a forest that was as black as a starless night. She was heading into the beginning of the end.

CHAPTER 3

The horses drove through the thick forest at speed, their steady hoofbeats the only sound that reached Miri through the roaring in her ears. The drumming was muffled background noise to the memories from so long ago that were assaulting her: running, darkness, terror, pain, the wetness on her cheeks that was her mother's blood and her own tears, and the way her sister had screamed.

"Bean," her guard said sharply, and Miri jolted to realize it was not the first time he'd said it.

In the darkness, he grabbed her reins, pulling the horse to a juddering stop. The gelding, Wolf, let out a soft grunt and tossed his head. The horse was out of breath, while Miri's was tight in her chest.

The guard leaned in close. "Bean," he said again.

Miri nodded, her grip easing on the reins. She had herself under control.

The man let loose his hold on Wolf's reins then drew his horse a step away before dismounting. In one swift motion, he pulled the bridle and saddle to the ground then raised a hand to smack the bay on the rump.

"Wait," Miri whispered, glancing at the darkened forest for a sign... of what, she wasn't sure. "What are you doing?"

The guard's head turned, and his hood fell, but his features were unclear in the darkness. She could just make out that he was giving her a look.

Thom had said that she could not go on Charlie because Charlie knew the way home. He'd meant for them to ride farther than just the forest between the town and the cliffs. "Thom said—"

"Thom did not know our plans. Keeping them secret is the only way to assure you're safe." She opened her mouth to argue, but the man stepped closer. "He was only providing for whatever route we chose to take. We are not bound to any paths aside from those free of kingsmen."

Miri's mouth went dry at the reminder. Then she realized what his words meant. "We're going to the port."

"No," he said levelly. "The port isn't safe. Too many kingsmen are searching the ships."

She gritted her teeth. "I'm no fool. There is only one way out of this town, and if it's not by ship—"

"I did not say it was not by ship. I said the port isn't safe." He was silent for a moment then added, "We do not have time for this. Dismount."

Her fingers tightened on the reins, and for a heartbeat, Miri had the urge to kick the beast hard and run away. The man meant to take her down the cliffs, load her onto a ship, and escape to sea. A spare bit of moonlight glinted in the man's eye, and Miri knew he would be too fast for her. He would catch her. He could force her, if Thomas had ordered it. But she took a breath, because that was wrong, and she knew it. Thom had protected her since she was a child. Miri trusted him with every part of her being. If he'd sent the guard to protect her, that was what the man would do, even if the cost was his life. He was sworn to it.

She threw her leg over the back of the horse and landed

softly in the tall grass. The man before her was bloodsworn. He was not Thomas's man. He was hers.

Metal glinted in the moonlight. It was the edge of a sharpened blade, and Miri's hand went to her hip, fingers around the handle of her dagger before the man's words registered. He'd said, "We need to cut your hair."

She stared at him, her eyes finally adjusting to the sparse light filtering through the canopy. It was dark in the forest but not as dark as Miri had ever seen—not as dark as the places she'd hidden. "Why? No one knows me."

His voice was low, as quiet as Wolf's and Milo's purring breaths. "It will be easier if you present as a man."

She understood then, suddenly and with a sickening jolt in her gut. "They don't know I'm a woman. The men on the ship." Gods, that meant he didn't trust them. It meant they were not his men.

His mouth drew down at the corners, a strange and familiar motion. Miri stepped closer, turning so that when he looked at her, his face reached more of the light. Her hand came up to her throat. The curve of his jaw had gone square and stubbled, his nose was straight and sharp, and what had once been a boyish crooked smile had formed into a hard line. His face was full of the angles of a man, but it was him.

"Christopher?" she asked, her voice a hoarse whisper.

His dark eyes flicked to the forest then back to Miri's own. "It's Cass now."

Cassius, she remembered. That was the boy's middle name. But he was not the child she'd grown up with, not the boy who'd played at swords in the gardens at court. He was a man, broad and brooding, and by all appearances resigned to his duty at the cost of his life. Thomas had not sent Miri off with merely a queensguard. He'd sent her off with one who'd been raised by the Lion Queen herself.

"Gods," Miri whispered. *How long has it been?* The memories crashed into her, the way they always did, drowning her in heartbreak and remembered blood.

"That life is gone now." Cass's voice was still low but filled with resolve. "Please do not say it again."

That name would get him killed. He'd gone into hiding, like her.

She nodded slowly. *This is all my fault.*

He raised the knife once more, but Miri held up a hand. The fear and sickness had given way to something else. Cassius was a queensguard. To him, her word was law.

"I'm not going by ship."

He squared off to face her. "How else do you expect to escape?"

Miri's hand twitched but did not tighten to a fist. "I've no intention of escaping. I've run from this long enough. *Too* long."

He stared at her, possibly reconsidering his oath. He let out a breath and tucked a thumb into his knife belt. "What, exactly, Bean…" He let the word linger, a reminder of who Miri was and who hiding had made her become. "Do you intend to do?"

In the close darkness, Miri waited, letting him see the tilt to the corner of her mouth and the seriousness in her eyes. "I intend to kill the bastard king."

Cass's mouth went slack, but she needed him to understand it was not just the single treachery she would repay. Her mother's rule had been stolen by more than that king. The Queen's Realm had been split into kingdoms to be ruled by seven men. It had been treason—and murder.

All of it would be repaid. Miri didn't mention what they had done to her older sister or how she would try to break the true heir free. Some wounds had still not healed, after all those years, and as long as an Alexander, particularly her captive sister, the heir apparent, remained hostage, the cut would feel fresh.

Miri took a steadying breath before she climbed back onto her horse. "Not just the king of Stormskeep. Every one of the treasonous curs will die by my hand."

CHAPTER 4

Miri had been right. Her word was law. Cass had not been in a position to argue her demands, though he'd certainly managed to make it known his opinion was counter to hers. He attested that a better course of action awaited and what she was suggesting seemed rash, but in the end, he'd done as she'd asked. He'd abandoned his strategy in favor of hers.

But nothing about Miri's plans were rash. She'd been plotting since she was no more than a girl.

So, she had not dressed as a man and dropped over a cliff into a dangerous sea to be hauled away from those threats in a raggedy ship by men who feared her. Her long hair was, in fact, still intact, though she'd twisted it into a quick plait as her guard pointedly took his time resaddling his horse. She'd had her hair chopped in the past, when she escaped as a child and gone to live with Thom and Nan in the bustling town of Smithsport. It had been a traumatic and grueling journey, and she did not relish the idea of ever again being hidden in a damp, dark box on a boat, blood streaming from her busted nose, and having the sense that she couldn't breathe. Her chest had been so tight and her heart so torn that she was convinced she might never draw a full breath again.

But that fear was not why she chose not to go on Cass's ship. She was nearly sure of it.

Miri would, she decided, be agreeable to swapping her mess of skirts for the slim pants that would be inside her pack. She had been taught to sew, among many other things, but she'd long had a complicated relationship with skirts. She understood their purpose, the reason behind royal dress, and the pomp and the symbolism. It was a sort of power of its own and a separation. But that did not mean it made it easier to jump astride a horse.

The years that had followed her most complicated attire had seen her in threadbare rags, not because Nan would not have wanted her in better clothes but because it had been Nan's duty to keep Miri from notice.

She had succeeded in that duty, and enough time had passed that it was easier to manage. The attack on the castle had come when Miri was young, before she'd grown into those gangly limbs. Her face had been narrow and thin, to the constant dismay of her nursemaids, and she'd favored her mother's side of the family in the shape of her eyes. But Miri's face and figure had filled out, her cheeks taking on the soft curve of her father, a far less recognizable royal. Once time had passed and she'd lost more of her resemblance to the Lion Queen, Nan had begun to let Miri's hair grow, allow her to come along on occasional trips to the market, and let her work in the back rooms of the Blackwater.

The horse beneath her let out a soft nicker, and his ears pricked, and Miri adjusted his path to regain his attention.

The kings of the realm had thought Miri dead like her mother, and no one paid much mind to a lowly cleaning girl, but that had not stopped Nan from dyeing Miri's lion's-mane hair with plants that Thom's men had brought from a continent away. They'd done everything they could to protect Miri. She would not let them down.

"Bean." Cass's word was a bit harsh, and Miri became aware she'd been ignoring him again, unintentional though it was. When she looked back at him, she realized, too, that it was nearly light. They'd ridden through the night.

Cass frowned. "The horses are in need of a rest. Shall you share with me precisely where we're headed?"

His tone said, *Aside from the killing of kings, of course.* Miri eased up on her posture, letting the horse slow to a walk. "Pirn first. Then Kirkwall." She wanted most of all to conquer Stormskeep, her true home, but that would be no easy feat. That left six other kingdoms—six other castles to invade and escape. Smithsport's king had a castle on a small isle on the sea, but he was a sluggard and a fool. He would be an easy mark and little threat, so Miri would leave him for later. She didn't want to start a slaughter where she lived. There was no reason to put Thom and Nan at risk if she were to fail in her other attempts.

Though it was *more* risk, anyway, because the two had already risked their lives, the Blackwater, and everything they held dear.

Cass cleared his throat, bringing her attention back to him. The look he gave her said he'd not meant to launch her into explanation of her assassination plot, but Miri wondered if what else she saw there was surprise that she'd actually planned the thing through.

"Shall I find us an inn?" he asked.

She gave him a look. "There's no inn for a day's ride."

He inclined his head just a bit then turned his horse to follow a trickling stream.

Miri remembered something else she'd learned as a child: just because you held rule over someone did not mean that person could not find a way to dictate your course of action. She clicked her tongue to urge her horse into a walk behind Cass. She had the feeling she would face more than one battle of wits with Cass, and it was not the time to waste her energy.

Silver River ran from the mountains at Blackstone to a small inlet near Smithsport. It was one of only two large rivers that allowed boat travel to the sea, but the land between there and Pirn was riddled with lakes and streams. Their path would be dependent on crossings, weather, and whatever troubles might arise on the road. The forests and trails south of Pirn were not particularly known for bandits, but times were tough in the entire realm. Reaching the seven kingdoms alone would not be easy, killing aside, but Miri had no other option but to get it done.

Her guard surveyed the land, slowing to a stop near a bend in the creek. He glanced at Miri as her horse came to rest beside his. "We'll break here for the night. I'll heat some water."

Miri felt her eyes widen. She did not smell so much like a drunken goat that washing would be his first request, surely.

Cass's lips tightened, his gaze averting from her face. "Nan sent new dyes," he said. "For your hair."

"Of course." She hoped her cheeks had not colored. New dye was not a terrible idea, in case anyone noticed that Nan's charge had suddenly gone missing while kingsmen were about scouring for sympathizers.

Miri stepped down from her horse, relishing the stretch of her legs. Her stomach reminded her she'd forgotten to eat, lost in her mind as she'd been, and she wasn't sure exactly what was in her pack. She patted Wolf on the neck and scratched near his ear as she slid the bridle free. Though she wondered briefly whether horses trained well enough to ground tie would draw suspicion, she doubted very much that they would see many passersby in the spot her guard had chosen. As she moved to grab the saddle, her hand bumped Cass's on the leather.

"I've got it," he said. "You can clean up before dinner." He turned before Miri could gauge his expression, but she was fairly certain she spotted the edge of a smirk.

Miri looked down at herself and yanked the hem of her woven vest into place. Her hands were soiled, her skirt hem had come loose, and she truly did need a good wash. She rummaged through the pack, slightly unsettled at how little she had to her name, and gathered a set of clean clothes and one of the small pressed soaps into her arms. She glanced around the camp and sighed. Cass meant to dye her hair, and Nan had sent the clothes of a trader. Her life as the other Bean was truly over. That poor orphan girl in need of a helping hand was no longer an anchor of habit.

Miri walked to the creek and kneeled to splash water over her arms. The coolness of it cut through her ruminations. As a child, Miri had traveled the realm with her mother to oversee her rule of the territories that had since been called kingdoms. The men who had been merely lords—responsible for seeing out the queen's orders—now ruled as kings. They took what riches each kingdom had, not for the good of the realm and its people but for themselves. They had killed the queen. They held Miri's sister captive.

The time for thinking was over. She'd had years and years to plan. It was time to act. Miri stripped down to her sleeveless shift and soaked a strip of cloth to rub at the smudges over her skin. The soap smelled of sweet orange and some flower Miri couldn't identify, and she felt a pang of loss for Nan. They would be safer if she was away in the midst of searching kingsmen, but she would miss Nan and Thom.

She slid the slim pants under her shift, followed by thick woolen socks and high lace-up boots. She splashed her face last, wincing at the cold, then glanced over her shoulder to make certain she was alone. Cass stood at the edge of a thick copse of trees, breaking branches into the fire.

As she turned back toward the creek, she drew the filthy shift over her head to replace it with a clean shirt and leather vest. Running a hand over the hem of her underclothes, she felt for the small metal locket sewn inside. It was the only memento of her other life—the life before Thom and Nan and Bean—and all that truly mattered for possessions.

But the hidden memento was not the only lingering reminder of her past. Miri was reminded every day, in a thousand ways, like knife blades to her heart. Even there, in the unfamiliar wood, she rode with a queensguard at her side.

By the time Miri rinsed the clothes and hung them to dry, Cass's fire had produced a steady bed of coals. A small black pot hung near the edge, smelling very unlike the sweet-scented soap. Miri stifled a groan.

Cass looked up at her, brushing his palms together once before moving to stand.

Miri frowned and pulled her hair over her shoulder. "Cut it to here," she told him. "No sense in dyeing the extra."

He nodded solemnly, and Miri realized that was maybe the first actual command she'd given him. He'd not argued, at least, which was a step up from her earlier changing of his plans.

She settled onto a log as her guard came to stand behind her. His work was quick, his blade sharp, and the locks of her hair dropped to the ground. Cass gathered them, crossed to the fire, and tossed the hair into the flame before taking hold of the pot. The camp filled with the sudden stench of singed hair, but it was mild in comparison to what waited inside the pot.

Cass spared Miri a glance as he crossed again to stand behind her, but she could see the fumes had made his eyes water. She leaned her head back, and he drew her hair into a mass, away from her vest, to smooth Nan's latest concoction over the locks.

"What color do you suppose she sent?" Miri asked.

"Dead seal, by the looks of it."

Miri snorted a laugh but choked on the noxious smell.

"How long do we have to leave this in?"

Head tilted back, she opened her eyes to stare up at Cass. His voice had been low, one hand wrapped around the base of her hair as he trailed the fingers of his other hand through the locks. "I'm not sure," she said. "Depends on the mixture. Nan usually pins it up and wipes my head in oils if it's going to be a while." She reached up to cover her mouth. "Oh, Cass, did she warn you to wear gloves?"

He bit down a grin, but his eyes still laughed at her. "I've coated my hands in that oil. But thanks for the notice."

She smiled as she reached blindly for her pocket to draw a hair pin free. She handed it to him, and he twisted the length of her treated hair to pin it to her crown. He was not practiced at it, because it felt lopsided and wobbly, and though his expression showed that he was focused on being careful, the knot pinched a bit more than she liked.

When he was done, Cass wiped the dye from his hands then slid his fingers over her hairline to coat it with oil.

"That should do it," Miri said awkwardly, suddenly realizing how much, exactly, she would be relying on him.

She cleared her throat, stood to stretch, and remembered that she had no idea what Nan had sent for food. She glanced again at Cass as he stood wiping the oil from his hands with a cloth, his head lowered but his gaze on her. His shoulders were broad and his forearms muscled. His bearing was that of a man who knew his way through a fight. She wondered how his hunting skills were.

She also wondered precisely what Cassius of Stormskeep and the queensguard had learned in his tutelage. "How well did you know my mother?"

All the blood drained from his face.

Miri nodded. He was one of Henry's, then, as she'd suspected. He would have been training to become a personal guard to the queen, not just her family or the throne. "I'm sorry for what you've gone through," she said.

Miri turned and kneeled to rummage through the other packs. Her mother had taught her to look a person in the eyes when she apologized to them, but Miri's emotions felt tethered by thin wire. She wasn't certain, on the run once again and leaving those she cared about, that she could think about the boy Cass had been and the loss he might feel for someone so dear to her.

He was quiet behind her and too still, and Miri rubbed her

brow with the back of her wrist. It came away slick with oil, and the pin in her hair was already threatening to fall loose. "It seems we've enough for a few days' ride. Bread, dried meat, and a bit of fruit." She glanced up at the trees. Gods, it was dawn, and they were in the forest, heading to kill a king.

Cass shifted behind her. "I can hunt. You should get some sleep."

She pulled a braided loaf from Nan's meticulously wrapped cloth, a little sick at the realization that Nan would have prepared the packs while Miri was stuffed in a barrel—and worse, that Nan might have been planning to ship her off on a moment's notice all along. Miri turned, tearing the loaf to pass half to Cass. "You don't have to. I can make do."

He stepped closer, ignoring the proffered bread. "We have friends along the route. There's no need to rush into—"

At her glare, his words cut off.

"I said I can make do."

His mouth went into a hard line, but he leaned closer. "We'll stop first at a small inn near Silverton. They'll have word of the king's men."

Miri drew back from him at the mention of the kings and that their men were not just causing trouble in Smithsport. She wanted to scream, *What in seven hells have they been up to now?* But she didn't. She and Cass might have been isolated in the forest, but it was clear by the expression on his face that it was not the best place to speak of treason.

And when she shoved away thoughts of her mother, Nan, and Thom, treason was about all Miri's heart had room for. "Fine," she said coolly. "Silverton, tomorrow's eve."

CHAPTER 5

Miri woke feeling as if her head weighed a solid stone. She groaned, rolling onto her back to face a noonday sun through a canopy of trees. "Seven hells," she muttered, remembering the dye she'd left in her hair. She glanced over the clearing to find Cass strapping a pack onto the bay horse. Grateful to see he'd left a pot on the fire, she sat up. At least she wouldn't be dipping her scalp into a cool stream to rinse the dye. She rubbed her face, and her fingers came away oily and with a leaf that had been stuck to her temple. The knot of hair was likely a crooked lump on the side of her head and plastered in bits of shed underbrush. She reminded that herself sleep deprivation was no way to win a war.

Cass crossed the camp to hand her a waterskin and a hunk of dried fruit. "You'll want to ready yourself. We should discuss our stories in case it comes up while we encounter other travelers."

Miri took a bite of the fruit and stood. "I've had six threads in place since I was a child. I know them by heart." She took a long draw from the waterskin before glancing at Cass. "Do you honestly think I'd walk into this blindly or that my protection has not been mapped out?"

His expression did not change. "I honestly think that your threads—as prepared as they were—did not include me."

The fruit went sour in Miri's mouth. He was right. She'd always planned to go on her own. Everything Nan and Thom had lain into place was centered on Miri and Miri alone. But that wasn't true. *They'd* sent her with Cass. They'd known they would all along, surely, because once she thought about it, he fit seamlessly in each of her cover stories.

A wind picked up, rustling the green leaves. Cass's eyes were hazel, his lashes dark. The light of day made everything so much more real and finite.

"Fine," she said. "My brother."

He took her hand in his and slid a thin band onto her finger. "Husband," he said.

Right. Because having a brother would not protect her as much as being wed. She kept forgetting the laws had changed and that the safety of Smithsport would soon be long gone. "Husband," she echoed. "And what of you?"

"I know your threads as well," he said. "I'll merely slide in as your newly acquired helpmeet."

That would make it easy on Miri, and he could serve his dead queen. Miri turned from him, relieving the tightness of the circle of gold on her finger by the pressure of her thumb. It had slid right over her knuckle but sat like a collar on her finger. That was why she hated those kings, for what they'd forced her life to become. They had bound her to lies and hiding. She walked to the fire, lifted the pot by its handle, and carried it to the creek to wash away what was left of that other girl.

By the time Miri rinsed her hair and returned, Cass had smothered the fire and saddled her horse. She handed him the pot, which had grown cool, and his gaze only briefly flitted to her hair, which was loose and dark chestnut, the way Nan's had been years before.

"Let's go," Miri said. It was nothing but a command.

THE SILVERTON INN was a small two-and-a-half-story establishment that served food and drink and provided stables, baths, and beds to travelers who followed the Silver River on their journey between kingdoms. Its exterior was modeled after the Pirn style, simple white cottages with decorative trim, and the building had a cob roof that rose to a central peak over rough walls boasting narrow windows in even rows. Cass led Miri toward the rear of the inn, apparently familiar with the layout and location of the stables. He was met at the entrance by a boy no more than twelve who had dark hair cropped close to his head. The two exchanged words as Miri glanced casually toward the back of the inn to note the exits.

It was a habit that was not borne of her fear of kingsmen. It was how she'd been taught to live. A princess must always have a route for escape. Her mother's planning had been all that had saved Miri in the end.

"My lady," Cass said from beside her.

She jolted, staring down at his hand raised to assist her from her horse. "We're traders," she mouthed. "I should know how to dismount a horse."

His answering smile was forced. "We're newly wed. I should offer regardless of your skill."

She inclined her chin sharply and slid down from the horse before taking hold of his hand. His head nearly shook, but apparently, he thought better of it. Cass tossed the boy a copper and slipped his free hand on the small of Miri's back to lead her through the straw and divots scattered over the ground.

He was terrible at pretending. She was a trader, not a lady of the royal court. He squeezed her hand, and Miri smoothed the frown from her face. If she were honest, she'd seen the way the newly wed acted. It was a good deal worse.

Cass led her to the door, but carefully moved Miri aside before he let go to open the sturdy affair. His glance was sharp and met briefly by the barkeep, then it softened as it returned to Miri. They walked in quietly, took a table by the wall, and were met immediately by a middle-aged waitress with warm amber skin.

"Welcome to the Silverton Inn. What'll you have?"

"Food and a room," Cass answered.

A clatter and thud came at the back entrance, followed by a curse in a young boy's tone. The waitress didn't even glance over her shoulder. "That'll be your bags, then. I'll be sure to have them settled carefully into your room."

The woman turned from the table and made a comment to another patron as Miri's gaze slid over the room. The place was large and open, poorly lit for the late afternoon but stocked with candles and lanterns that would likely be burned come suppertime. They'd made good time, probably because of Miri's insistence that they need not stop for regular breaks, and had beat the evening crowd. Cass had assured her the inn was not usually full, but Miri could tell the space had held its share of travelers. Empty tankards, stacked upside down and right-side up, lined the back bar. The tables were dark wood, thick, heavy planks stained with age and scarred from use. Chairs and stools scattered the space, and a large fireplace filled half of the back wall, charred marks crawling away from it toward the ceiling and across the floor.

"Someplace you've been often?" Miri asked.

"On occasion."

Her gaze snapped to his at the evasion she heard behind the words.

He sighed. "I've been working for the harbormaster, on and off. Sometimes his business takes me north."

He'd had a job. She kept forgetting that, losing the idea that the few who were left of the queensguard, like her, had to hide as well and pretend.

"It wasn't that bad." His voice was low, the words an apology, and Miri tried to clear her face of whatever it showed.

"Of course," she said. *Of course.*

The waitress returned with two mugs and a carafe of water. "We've a spring out back," she said. "Or, if you'd like, warm mead. At supper, the boys'll be bringing in some brandy sharp enough to shave your face."

Cass smiled at her. "Water for now. But maybe we'll be down for a late dinner to partake in the brandy."

The woman wiggled her eyebrows at Miri while wiping a hand on her apron. "It burns, but don't I recommend it, though. Stuff'll make you forget your manners and shout at the rafters." The woman gave Miri a solid pat on her shoulder as she turned and whooped a call toward the ceiling. Somehow, it made Miri feel more at ease.

"Do you drink, Cass?"

His eyes moved to the barkeep, a barrel-chested man with gray streaking his beard. "Not when I'm working." Cass leaned back, drawing his hands from the table as the waitress settled a platter of food on it.

"Thank you," Miri offered, but the woman was already headed toward the muffled shouting in the back room. It sounded like a delivery of some sort.

Cass purposefully picked up his knife to spear a hunk of meat. "Eat, Bean," he said.

The reminder immediately drew Miri back, and she settled her shoulders into the casual posture of a trader. It wasn't difficult after a long day's ride. They'd spent the previous night huddled against a low embankment. Cass had forgone a fire because of their proximity to the town, and though it was well past spring, Miri had felt the chill of the earth through her thin blanket. She'd slept fitfully most of her life, so that was nothing new, but she was certainly ready for rest in a real bed.

When they finally climbed the narrow stairs to their room, Miri had the sinking feeling the inn was built more for drinking than for rest. Cass turned sideways to pass through the hallway, his palm resting against the handle of a blade at his hip. They ducked through the door into a room that was a few yards wide and held little more than a cot, a side table, and a wash basin. Miri stepped past Cass as he bolted the door, then she climbed onto the bed to peer out the small window into the darkening trees. A few figures shifted between the stable and the inn, and Miri made out the form of a tall, slender man in a dark cloak. She wondered if it was the queensguard who'd yanked her out of the barrel only days before and how many were left. *Six? Ten?* The kingsmen had been sniffing them out for years, rabid dogs in search of the last scraps of meat.

Miri turned to ask Cass whether her mother's men had followed and if more were at watch, but Cass had drawn a cloak from their packs and was settling it onto the floor. Miri glanced beneath her at the muddy boots that stood in her bed, and her lips went tight. She was fairly certain the bed was only wide enough for one in any case, but when Cass lay flat on the uneven wood planks between the bed and the wall, she said, "You've slept far less than me. Take the bed for now, and we'll switch later."

He'd been staying up watching her. She knew full well that it had not been as safe in the woods as it felt.

Cass stared up at her, his expression disproportionately harried. He was in need of a good shave but otherwise did not appear to weather the outdoors as poorly as she did. His clothes did not look especially well made but were not as rumpled and stained as hers. She'd been a mess since she'd met him, and his mouth had been twisted into similar expressions nearly the entire time.

Miri squatted on the bed, coming closer to hear muffled words. Cass wasn't preparing to sleep. He was eavesdropping. "What is it?" she whispered.

He frowned at her, and she closed her lips, sliding farther down to lie on her stomach, her hair spilling over the side of the bed. The mattress smelled faintly of hay and sweat beneath a hefty dose of lavender. Miri pressed her chin into her shirt, lifting the material to cover her nose.

Cass snorted quietly. Their faces were close as they both listened to the voices rising from below.

"Sixteen strong, they was, sorcerers demanding blood for the kings."

"No, I tell you, they took the miller's daughter and three from the orphanage outside of Pirn."

They were stealing women and children for blood rites to pay for the magic the kings spent like water from a spring. Blood was blood. It didn't matter whether it came from a child or an elder, a woman or a man. The sorcerers chose by fetish, not need. There was only one person whose blood was stronger, and that was the queen. Her fate was tied to her people's and to long-ago bindings.

Someone with a lower voice made mention of the kingsmen in Smithsport, but the sound was overtaken by the rattle of carriage wheels outside. Miri's eyes met Cass's in the dim light from the window. She wasn't entirely certain how much danger they were truly in.

She lowered the material from her face and whispered, "Why now?"

Cass's expression betrayed nothing, which meant there must be something hidden beneath. If there'd been no talk of the kingsmen's plans, he could have said.

The *why now* echoed in her thoughts because it had not just been the kings who'd decided to move. Miri had left as well. She meant to save Thom and Nan from danger, of course, but they'd been in danger before. They'd had close calls and near misses many times over the years. This time had been different. Miri knew why, in a place locked deep within her heart. She'd only been avoiding it and denying the truth.

It was the festival of moons. It was her sister's name day. She would be turning the age that an heir could take command of her own guard, and she could be free to choose a husband, should she wish, to begin her duties of a second-in-command. It was Lettie.

Miri's fingers curled into a ball against her chest. She felt the pain as if she'd been stabbed, as if summoning the name had drawn a dagger from thin air and plunged it through her heart, or as if a sorcerer had stolen her blood.

Miri tucked her chin and rolled to her back, unable to breathe. Lettie would be celebrating her twentieth name day in a dungeon or a cell—or however they held her. Miri could not be brought to imagine the things her sister's captors had done. She could not know because the kings who had exploited every weakness in the queen's defenses had taken great pains to avoid information getting out about how the queen's heir was held. As king, Nicholas had gone as far as to lock his servants in the keep to prevent a single secret from escaping. And at the festival of moons, Leticia Alexander, tall and thin, stunning in her beauty even as a child, would turn from princess to active member of her royal line, and the kings who had slaughtered their mother would be forced to kill her too—to remove her from succession and quell any last supporters who still held to the old ways.

"They'll do it at the festival," Miri whispered to the air above her bed. "They'll drag her into the square dressed in Lion silks. They'll draw her braid behind her shoulder and wrap her wrists in leather and chains."

She felt the stillness of Cass and that he did not seem to even draw breath. She wished she'd never spoken, but she couldn't seem to stop. The kings were only holding Lettie hostage to use as leverage against the sorcerers who were tied to queen's blood. Once she rose into her full power as heir, Lettie would have to be removed from their game.

"They'll kill the others first to make her watch as her people —our people—are tortured for their crimes. For being loyal to a true heir. For being loyal to the throne." Miri swallowed against the lump in her throat, unable to keep the images at bay. She could imagine the unhealed lash marks, the torn fabric, and the open wounds, festering from too long being untreated and from the filth of a prison cell. She could hear their screams and the rage in her sister's tone. Leticia was a Lion, regardless of her caramel hair and sharp features. But ferocity would not save her against the seven kings—not against sorcery and deceit. "They'll wait for her and leave her until the festival's dawn. As the sun rises on the square, when the revelers are slow with drink and no longer care, they'll drive a spike into her neck. They will let her bleed out and let her life drain slowly onto the marble steps that honor the queens before." Miri closed her eyes. "Did you know that? Did you realize that by that day's dawn, Lettie will be queen?"

She would no longer be a princess or an heir.

Their mother had been murdered. Lettie was next.

CHAPTER 6

Miri's words had finally ceased, and she'd fallen asleep with the sound of Cass's sharp intake of breath echoing through her mind. Cass had known her family. He had been raised as a bloodsworn, highest of the queensguard, taken in as a boy, and situated nearer to her family than anyone else. Henry, head of that guard, would have felt like a father to Cass, and the Lion Queen was the most vital part of his life.

Duty, honor, and reverence—Cass would have been taught that his life was forfeit for that queen and for any of them. Her mother's word was law. The queensguard motto swam in Miri's memory: *Ever faithful*.

It was true, even now. The Lion Queen was dead, one daughter was in chains, and the other was in hiding, and the queensguard still stood by their oath. She would remember that and remember that Cass had lost too.

Miri and Cass had been trained in the art of cunning and war, but it had not prepared them for the torment of grief, trauma, and true loss. Lettie had been trained to be queen, her skills more specific to negotiation and strategy, but she had not had

Nan to watch over her since their mother's death. She did not have the guard. Lettie would have no one.

Miri opened her eyes to the narrow room at the Silverton inn. A faint orange glow was just beginning to tint the glass. She would not leave her sister to die at the hands of those kings or be strung out on the Stormskeep square. She might not have had the power to reach Lettie while she was trapped inside the secure walls of the castle keep with the sorcerers' bindings in place for the past several years, but the moment they brought her out, Miri would set her sister free, even if it caused the death of them both and even if those deaths had to be by her own hand.

She turned to find Cass leaned against the wall on the floor beside her, his knee drawn up and knife in hand. He was spinning the blade between his fingers, mindlessly shifting the pattern in which it spun. His fingers stilled at Miri's attention, and Cass slid the dagger into a sheath near his boot.

"You don't have to wait for me," she said, minding the level of her voice. If they'd heard the others below the night before, surely their own conversation would carry. "You can wake me anytime. I'm not a queen."

His expression was flat, but a reply waited beneath.

"Say it," she told him. "I'll not have you biting your tongue to spare my feelings."

He shook his head. Miri lifted to an elbow, giving him a level stare. Cass sighed.

"What are you playing at, Miri? You know we'll never get past the guards. You know we can't just waltz into the nearest castle and—" He made a vague gesture Miri supposed meant *kill a king* then shrugged a shoulder. "We should return to Smithsport. You should get on that ship and sail to somewhere safe."

Any grace he'd earned by his pained breath the night before was forgotten. Miri leaned close. "My sister is captive to those murderous bastard kings. If you think, for one moment, I prize my safety over hers—" Her words cut off at his look, because

Miri knew all too well the sacrifice Cass was willing to make. He'd only wanted to save her and make her see that the path she was taking would be the death of them all. "I release you from your duty," she said.

Cass's brow lowered dangerously.

"If you don't want to help me, then go. It's better to find out here and be done with it. I'm more than willing to do this alone."

He shifted so near that his breath brushed her skin. His words were a quiet vow. "I do not answer to you, *Princess*. My duty is to the queen. Her word is my law."

The way he'd said "princess" felt like a slap—or worse, like he'd been calling her Bean, like she was nothing and she had no control of what he would do.

He was right, and she knew it, and the notion made searing heat fill her chest. She wanted to roar like her sister and scream and tear. His eyes flicked over her face and caught the flare of her nostrils and the color in her cheeks. She hated him for it. She hated everything.

Her fingers curled into her palms, and voice cold, she said, "I have traveled the seven kingdoms since the year I was born. I know every palace. I know every route. I have insight and reason, and I'm good with a sword." She knew those kings—the men who'd killed her mother—with a familiarity that hurt. Her eyes cut into Cass's, and the room took on an eerie early-morning glow. "I will tell you what else, Cassius of Stormskeep. I will die with my hands covered in king's blood. And I will die more satisfied than any fool who escapes to the sea."

His jaw went tight at the way she'd said his name, but Cass only inclined his head. "As you say," he whispered. His dark eyes grazed hers as he made to stand. "And so we ride into death together."

CASS HAD NOT RETURNED to their rooms for nearly an hour, so long that Miri had begun to wonder if he'd abandoned her. Maybe he'd decided she was a fool after all. She wasn't surprised. It did seem like a daunting affair, even to her. But Miri could do nothing else. She had no other option.

A light knock came at the door, and she hesitated, wondering whether she should hide or answer. The room was small, and quite suddenly, she felt trapped. Her hand settled on the dagger at her belt, but the voice of the person that called through the door was soft and feminine.

"Good morning, miss. Your husband asked that I should offer you breakfast. Would you like to come down or sup in your room?"

Miri stood to cross the room, which took fewer than half a dozen steps, and drew the door open a crack. At first glance, she thought her visitor was the waitress from the night before, but the woman's hair was a bit lighter and a bit shorter, and she wore a large brass ring through her ear.

"Thank you," Miri said, opening the door wider to take a cake from the plate. "This is plenty, but I would like a bath."

The woman smiled, and a mischievous twinkle lit her eye. "Of course you do." She leaned in conspiratorially. "You go on down. Bathing room is by the kitchen—second door—and I'll wrap some of these cakes up for you to go. The boy's readying your horses."

"Thank you," Miri said again, and the woman winked as she turned.

Miri stared after her for a moment then gathered her things to go below. The inn felt empty, and Miri wondered if Cass had chosen it because of that or if his surreptitious glances at the barkeep had kicked off an elaborate scheme. She remembered traveling as a child and how the guard would arrange for places to be emptied of staff, citizens, and anyone the guard might not be able to easily control. She didn't think Cass had that kind of power, but the new kings had been brutal, and Miri knew that many more secret loyalists were about than anyone would willingly admit. The kings who had been lords had not garnered love and support from the territories they'd once been tasked with overseeing.

Miri's bare feet were quiet on the narrow stair. The only sounds were the muffled horse calls from the stables and a clatter from the kitchen. She crossed in front of the doorway to the kitchen, glancing in to see a massive, window-filled space, a wide iron stove, and counters covered in flour, pots, and bowls. Two women stood before a counter, backs to the door, as they kneaded dough, and the barrel-chested man stood by the windows, a steaming cup on the sill before him. None of them seemed to notice her. Soon the inn would be filled with the inviting scent of freshly baked bread and the sting of lye.

Miri turned into the next doorway and glanced toward the hallway behind her as she followed the thin wooden door into the room. When she pushed it closed behind her, she heard the sound of something small being dropped into water. She spun, abruptly aware she was not alone.

Cass stared back at her, his naked legs curled into a wide metal tub, muscled torso bare. The waitress from the night before dropped two towels onto a table beside the tub.

"Well met, miss," the woman said.

Miri felt her gaze shoot away from Cass's bare flesh. His abdomen was tight where it dipped into the murky water. It was the wrong thing to do, and she was being rude to the maid, but she couldn't seem to gather her wits.

"Wife," Cass said smoothly in greeting before the silence stretched on.

The coolness in his tone, as if the situation were entirely fine, cut through Miri's horror. "Good morning," she managed.

The woman inclined her head slightly then turned from the room. Miri pressed her eyes closed. A few muffled shouts echoed from the stables, followed by a familiar nickering and pawing of hooves. Then she heard the cascade of water falling from Cass's form as he stood from the tub and rinsed the soap off. Miri turned to face the door, refusing to open her eyes.

She heard his footsteps as he walked to the mirror, then came the clatter of a razor and a bowl. Curse him, he was going to shave while she waited. It was likely that he was only torturing her, reminding Miri that her whims were not his law. She would be damned to seven hells if he thought she would be cowed. She bit down against her instincts of civility and crossed to the stool. Cass might not have to listen to her, but he bleeding well knew he'd no business alone with a naked princess, not if he meant to leave his honor as a guardsman intact.

Checkmate, Miri thought as she unlaced her vest. She did not turn when she heard Cass gathering his things but waited until he shut the door. If he wanted to play the game of rules and law, he'd chosen the wrong opponent.

Miri undressed slowly, checking her hem for the lump of her mother's hidden pendant before she stepped carefully into the tub. She was well and truly settled when she realized he'd used the last of the hot water from the bucket beside the tub. She opened her mouth to call for the maid but remembered the look from the woman's sister in the hall—the smile when she'd said, "Of course you do," to Miri's request for a bath. They thought the two newly wed had planned a midmorning tryst. Miri ground her teeth and stepped out of the tub, splattering water across the stone floor as she made her way to grab the pitcher by the mirror. Cold water it was, if it meant not giving Cass the satisfaction of winning.

She was dressed in her trading clothes, hair wrapped in a tight braid and what might pass as a skinning knife at her side, when she walked into the cool morning air. Cass was waiting for her by the stables, and the apparent conversation he was having with a broad-shouldered man cut off as she crossed to meet them. The man disappeared into the shadows, and Cass approached Miri as the boy brought their saddled horses nearer.

Cass threw him another coin, and the boy nodded, handing over the reins to go.

Cass raised a hand for Miri to help her onto her horse. She looked at the proffered palm for a moment then at Cass's clean-shaven face. She let her eyes linger on the small patch of scruff he'd missed by the edge of his jaw then smiled as she took his help to mount her horse.

Miri remembered once being offered a hand by a boy at court and her mockingly sweet response of, "But who would help you, Lord Hammond, once the rest of us are ahorse?" Lord Ham Hock, Lettie had called him. Gods, but they'd been cruel. What Miri wouldn't give to go back to those days and recapture every single moment and live them again.

She would warn her mother and say anything that might have made the difference. But her mother had known. Miri remembered, too, how as a girl she'd mentioned one of the men who now called themselves kings.

"I don't like the way he looks at you, Momma."

Her mother had patted Miri's hand, the reassuring motion belying the resolve in her mother's tone. "I know, my little bean. That is the look of a thirst for power. You're right not to trust it." The Lion Queen had not liked it either. She had known the men were out for her blood.

But Miri's mother had never thought they would use the sorcerers. No one had imagined what had happened could truly be done.

Miri drew a breath, suddenly aware of Cass's eyes on her. She gave a small nod. She had hold of it. She was fine. Cass nudged his horse forward toward the trail—toward King Casper of Pirn.

CHAPTER 7

"Tell me again where we're going." Miri's words were mild, but a vague playfulness fluttered in her gut. She was bored. Surely, that was all it was. But sparring with Cass had felt good. Banter and social company were something she'd rarely had since she was a girl, and it kept her mind occupied with something other than their impending death.

Cass's chest swelled in a sigh, but he played along. "A stately manor on the outskirts of Pirn."

"Will it be lovely?" she asked. "Rich and glorious, ostentatious in a way that I have never seen?"

Cass gave her a sidelong glance, as they both well knew the palaces and cities the princess had visited. The manor would be nothing of the sort. "My lady, you will be struck speechless at its very presence."

His tone said *with any luck*, and Miri swallowed a snort. She nudged her horse faster. "I cannot wait. It's been quite some time since I've been dumbstruck. I hope this manor is up to the challenge."

Cass's fingers resituated on his reins, and she wondered briefly if he was thinking of her reaction when she'd walked in on his bath. Frowning, she realized she'd certainly left him an opening there. She was out of practice.

"I'd like a sword," she announced abruptly.

That earned her a full glance.

She nodded. "I'm falling out of practice, here on the trail, and it will feel good to get some exercise after the long rides."

"My lady—"

"A trader should know how to properly use a blade."

Miri could tell he wanted to argue that he'd given her a proper blade, but he only nodded. "We'll find one in the market at Pirn."

It would be an unidentifiable one that she could drop and would not be tracked back should they need to run. Miri's eyes fell to her hands and the worn leather of the reins against her pale, dirt-smudged skin. She drew a deep breath and took in the forest, which was made of tall, narrow trees that were well into the season. They were far from the nearest town and several days from Pirn. The wait was going to kill her if the actual plan did not.

"And throwing blades," Miri said. "At the market. It's been so long since I've tried my hand at that."

Cass gave her a look. She ignored it. Nan had hidden Miri's throwing knives after an unfortunate incident involving a bag of grain and two chickens.

"It's probably a skill you don't forget."

Miri's words were more for herself than anyone else, but Cass slowed his horse.

"What are you doing?" she asked.

He sighed again. "Seems like you're ready to take a break. Why don't we stop for lunch?"

The words were not really phrased as a question, but Cass drew up short before he'd slipped a leg over his mount. His head snapped toward the horizon, and he scanned the trees.

Smoke—Miri smelled it too.

Cass turned his horse, urging Miri to follow, but before he could kick up a run, she said, "Wait!"

His answering expression was grave.

"It's not a campfire," Miri said. It was something else—something rancid and smelling faintly of old, damp straw. "We should help. It may be someone's barn."

Cass didn't speak but let his gaze warn her instead.

"They're burning people out," Miri whispered. She stared at him for several moments, the idea of it making her sick. She should not go—Cass was right—but she couldn't let the kingsmen keep hurting people in her mother's name.

It was foolish. The smart thing was to run the other way. If she wanted to save her sister, she should stay as far away from the kingsmen and their trouble as possible.

She knew what happened when citizens rose against them. She knew how the kings would make everyone pay.

Miri kicked her heels hard into Wolf's flanks and jerked the reins out of Cass's reach as she sped past him. She was done, tired of allowing good people to be murdered.

As Miri rode into the clearing at full speed, ducking under limbs and brush, the pillar of smoke rose through the trees like a beacon.

Cass caught her just as she broke through the line of trees, bits of earth flying from their horses' hooves as he grabbed the reins to jerk Wolf to a broken halt. She might have fought him, but her attention had caught on the figures in the distance. Half a dozen kingsmen held a struggling woman and a bloodied man in their grasps.

Cass laid a hand on Miri's forearm, and she met his steady gaze. His posture was pure anticipation. His other hand was on his reins, loose and ready to wield a blade. An understanding passed between them. Miri would have to decide. Face the kingsmen at risk to Cass's life and hers, or abandon the man and woman to their fate of being dragged to Stormskeep and tortured for their loyalty to the long-dead queen.

She didn't know what to do. There was no right answer. There was a chance she and Cass couldn't overcome so many trained kingsmen on their own. And if they did, they had little chance to escape before others were warned. If Miri saved those two people, she would be sacrificing a chance to help so many more.

A shout rang out in the clearing as a spiral of fire rose through the air.

It wasn't half a dozen kingsmen—it was half a dozen kingsmen and a sorcerer.

Miri's blood ran cold. "Go," she whispered.

Cass turned to sprint back into the woods. The horses were sure-footed and well trained, and Miri and Cass had both ridden since they were young. They should have made it. They should have gotten free.

A black-cloaked figure stepped from behind a tree and grabbed Miri's leg as she barreled past. Cass slammed into them just as Miri's form was ripped from the saddle, and Wolf reared and spun in the tangle of limbs and reins. Cass's arm drew Miri onto his horse, and he leapt from the horse the moment she had a grip on his saddle.

Cass's body seemed to ram headlong into the kingsman as Miri grappled for Milo's reins. She jerked the horse to a spinning stop just as Cass rolled over the form of the kingsman, black fabric and leaves dancing through the air in their wake. After only a brief struggle came the sickening sound of blade through flesh, then Cass crouched over the prone form, eyes on the forest around them.

Miri held her breath, waiting to see if someone had heard and if more were coming. Cass's eyes met hers, and Miri could see she was meant to run, but she didn't.

The snap of a twig made her wish she had. Her gaze flicked to the trees, hands and heart trembling with the need to run, and she saw the black cloak of a tall, slender man. Cass straightened, and the two of them exchanged hurried gestures before Cass turned to stride toward Miri. He closed the distance to grab the saddle and pull himself up behind her. She startled, shifting forward, but Cass spoke low in her ear.

"We need to get out of here. Terric will take care of our trail."

Miri tried to look at Cass, but he was pressed too close against her, and she couldn't see to gauge his expression. "We can't just leave him—"

"Go," he whispered into her ear. When he apparently realized she meant to argue, he reached around to her grab the reins himself. "This is our duty, princess. This is *his* duty."

Miri's eyes shot to the cloaked man, who was already starting his work. *His duty.* It was to protect her and—if need be—to die in place of the queen or her family. She thought she might be sick.

☙

MIRI LEANED FORWARD. Cass's chest was pressed against her back. Her guard was apparently unwilling to listen to anything she might say. The queensguard would die if he were caught, but if they stayed, Miri and Cass would die along with him. He was following a queen's order, not Miri's. She couldn't stop it.

The horse raced through the trees, his gait smooth, but Cass and Miri were ill fit in the narrow saddle. Miri pressed her legs tight to stay ahorse, hands gripping over the edge of the saddle leather and into Milo's mane. A short, sharp whistle came from behind her, then Wolf ran back through the trees, nostrils flared but eyes not wide with terror. He'd been trained well. He came to a stop beside them, and Cass took hold of Miri's waist to throw her astride. He wasted no time before they were off again, at a full run through the forests of Pirn.

They didn't stop until well past nightfall, when Cass was satisfied that they had not been trailed. They'd crossed a dozen creeks, only to cross again, and gone through thick brush and sand in order to confuse their path. But they hadn't been followed. Terric had taken care of that. Gods, she hoped he was alive. She hoped he had not been caught.

They would know soon enough. As soon as they made it to Pirn, rumor of the kingsmen would pass to their ears. It would be a wonder if Miri's rash action had not set the king's full guard on a rampage through Pirn.

Miri and Cass set their camp at the base of a small rise, and Cass tied the horses nearby. He lit a fire, snapping the wood with more force than might have been necessary. His fingers were still flaked with the kingsman's dried blood.

She was a fool—a sodding fool.

Cass leaned down to blow on the flame, and when the light flared, it caught his expression. Miri had thought him angry, and certainly, he was, but something else simmered beneath his displeasure. Terric was a queensguard and had been his friend. Miri hadn't just risked cost to herself. If Terric didn't make it, it would cost them both.

Her fingertips curled into her palms. She sank to sit on the cool ground, heedless of the settled dew.

"I'm going for meat." Cass gave her a look, one that seemed to imply she should stay precisely where she was until he returned—possibly longer.

She managed a curt nod.

Then he was gone. The horses let out quiet breaths and tore occasional clumps of grass from beneath the trees. Shadows shifted outside the fire, and after a time, the faint sounds of the forest returned. Miri tried not to drown in her thoughts. Her hands could do nothing to occupy her mind, for her heart had no interest in finding the occupation. She'd been there before. She'd made mistakes and chosen wrong. It had always made her feel exactly that alone.

By the time Cass came back through the trees, cold had settled into Miri's bones. She'd added a few sticks to the fire, but it hadn't helped.

Cass dropped the body of a small rabbit onto the ground across from her. Its form was limp and molded to the curves of the earth. He knelt before it wordlessly and shifted the rabbit to puncture its fur.

"Have you thought about it? About what you're going to do?" His low voice felt loud in the darkness. His long fingers curled tighter around the animal's neck as he pulled the pelt slowly down its form.

Miri knew what he was doing, but she would not be scared away, and she let him see it in her gaze.

"You're not capable of killing a man with your bare hands." His words were flat and without malice.

She didn't bother arguing that she would have a sword. She knew how the struggle of fighting went and that it was never truly how one planned. "I have killed," she said quietly.

"Chickens. Maybe a doe." He met her stare. "It's not the same."

"It's not different." It was. Killing to eat was not killing to kill. Wild game was no man. It was only a meal.

Cass was trying to scare her because of what she'd done and because they were getting closer to Pirn and the nearness of executing her plan. But there was no turning back. She had no other choice.

It wouldn't be easy. And yes, she'd drawn a bow on a deer and watched the light fade from its eyes at her strike and known it would never again fawn. But she'd never killed a man. Of course, she'd imagined it. Countless times, she'd envisioned holding each of those kings by the scruff of his neck, tugging his head back, and holding a blade at his throat as she whispered, "The Lion Queen sends her regards."

She deserved to be scared. But she would not be turned away.

"There wouldn't be sympathizers if the kings were doing even a remotely decent job." Cass's eyes shot to hers, but Miri kept on. "That man and woman would not have lost their home, their barn, and their freedom if the treasonous bastard lords who stole the throne knew a thing about how to rule. People are starving. Trade suffers even now. A good day's wage will barely buy a hock of meat." Miri bit down hard against the words. Cass didn't need that lecture. He understood better than her.

Things were falling apart. Those men had not taken her mother's rule because the Lion Queen had done poorly at it. They'd stolen it for greed and because it had seemed like that power was something to envy. Since that day, the people of the realm had suffered. For years, it had only grown worse.

Cass shoved the empty shell of the rabbit, tied to a stick as a mass of strange pale forms, into the fire.

He stayed knelt across the fire from Miri, his eyes on the flickering flames. Miri thought about the words they'd overheard at the inn, the children and girls taken by the kingsmen, and how their blood would be used by the sorcerers at the king's command.

When the meat had finally cooked through, Cass shifted it away from the flame. It was several moments before he lifted the spit from the fire and came around to settle beside Miri. He didn't speak as he offered her first share. Miri tore a small hunk free, and the meat was hot against her chilled fingers. He took the spit back, looked at it for another few moments, then slid it toward the fire. He glanced at his boots, settled the heels firmly into the earth, and wrapped his arms loosely around his knees.

Miri took a bite of her portion, but the hot grease felt thick in her throat and made her stomach turn.

They didn't speak until the fire burned low.

"I'm going to Pirn." Miri's voice was barely a whisper, but her words were no less a vow. "And I'm going to kill that bastard king before the next moon."

CHAPTER 8

Cass hadn't argued with Miri again, but he'd made it clear that he did not support her plan. She was risking her life—a life he was sworn to protect and utterly responsible for—so they were at odds with no hope of reconciliation on the matter. The night the kingsman had been slain, Cass had sat quietly in the darkened woods, waiting for his brothers-in-arms to show. No one had come. Miri had not been able to see Cass in those shadows, and he'd been grateful. He'd watched his brothers—bloodsworn and queensguard—die before. He had no desire to see it again.

He prayed Terric had made it out and that the kingsman's body was never found. If it had been, they would know soon enough.

Cass had planned their next stop at a manor outside of Pirn, but with the kingsmen so thickly afoot, he decided to take the princess farther into the city and find safety among the crowds—if he could keep her fool emotions from getting the best of her sense, anyway. Her drive was well and truly dangerous for so many, not just herself.

As he silently rode beside her, Cass remembered Miri as a child. She'd been a mannered, intelligent little lion, bejeweled and beribboned, and a beast with a sword. But the fight had gone out of her for a while.

The escape had been hard on all of them, along with the endless grief of not just losing family but also losing their way of life and everything they held dear. They'd even had to give up their names. Miri had barely spoken that first year. Cass wasn't much older than she was, but those few years had made a difference. He couldn't deny that he would give anything to be able to see Henry again and to have back the family he lost. But he'd understood they were gone and that there was no going back. He couldn't even return to his previous family without putting them at risk.

Miri had grown under the watch and protection of what was left of the queensguard. They'd been scattered and hiding through the realm, but the Lion Queen had put plans into place. She must have known the betrayal was close and sensed something the others hadn't. Cass had wondered so often why the queen had not warned her guard and whether she'd confided in Henry. But there was no way to know once they were gone.

So Cass, one of the few who'd eluded massacre, had watched Miri turn from princess to lost girl to the creature she'd become. He'd seen her with sword and bracer behind Nan's barn or hacking away at oat sacks in the stable. She'd thrown knives and punches but only when she thought she was alone. Miri had always possessed skill, but the motions as she grew had been filled with violence, anger, regret, and the helpless rage that he'd felt for so long as well. What had happened had broken her and was breaking her still.

"We'll be riding into Pirn soon," Cass said. "Perhaps slide up your hood to keep the sun from your face."

Miri had barely spoken to him in the three days since their encounter with the kingsmen. He wasn't sure whether the silence stemmed from his disapproval of her plan or her guilt that she'd risked Terric. She slid the cloak hood up regardless, knowing full well his concern was more that she might be recognized than have too much sun. But Miri was not the little girl she used to be, and though she would certainly draw a man's eye, it was not because of a resemblance to the Lion Queen. Her hair had been dyed dark, her face was smudged with dirt, and she was in the clothes of a woodsman.

"When we arrive," he said carefully, "I'd like to discuss your plans in detail."

Her gaze, suddenly sharp, shot to his. She was ready for a fight.

He inclined his head. "So that I might do what I can to assist you."

Her expression cleared for a moment. Then she said, "I'll not allow you to do it for me. I have to do this myself."

Cass looked ahead, toward the widening gaps in the trees, the low rolling hills, and the first signs of worn paths. "I cannot do it for you, in any case. I wouldn't succeed. I know those who've been better suited to the task who have tried."

Miri did not ask who or what had happened. She was clever enough to know it was a trap. And clearly, those attempts had failed. "I'll not use a bow," she said. "Nothing so obvious. If they realize what's happened, the rest will immediately protect themselves."

He tried not to let his interest show, but gods, she'd truly planned it through. It was not some rash attempt—only foolish and destined to fail.

"When possible, I plan to play those who are already inclined to suspicion and hatred against one another."

He felt her glance at him, but Cass didn't look away from the horizon.

Miri shrugged. "I've enough experience at that, at least."

She would make it look like an accident or as if the attack came from one of the other kings. It would give her precious time for another move. "And when things get heated? When they begin to protect themselves and their borders?"

"Then I will work with what they give me. I don't expect it to be easy, Cassius."

He tried to ignore the way it felt to hear her say his name and to be so near to her after so long standing in the shadows as her guard. He'd wanted to break protocol in Smithsport, but he'd been expressly forbidden. It didn't matter that he'd known her since she was a child or that he might be able to offer comfort. It mattered that the two of them together—a queensguard and a princess of Stormskeep—might draw recognition where one of them would not. She wasn't Princess Myrina any longer. She was Bean. And Bean was not in the habit of accepting social calls.

※

THEY CAME into Pirn late in the day, to a private residence that accepted them as weary travelers looking for a few days' work. Cass felt uneasy about risks to Miri's cover, but the queensguard did not hold traitors within its ranks, let alone a soul who might consider loyalty to treasonous kings. Henry had provided his bloodsworn with knowledge of those who could be trusted, should anything go badly, and things had gone nearly as badly as they could go. The queen was dead, Henry was gone, and the true heir was locked in a fortress tower.

"Evening," the stable hand said as Cass handed over their reins. "What a pair of beauties."

Cass smiled, patting Milo on the shoulder and brushing off a fleck of mud. "They've had a rough bit of riding. They'll be grateful for a break."

The stable hand gave Cass and Miri a once-over but managed to resist noting that they looked quite the same. Cass chuckled and handled the man a coin.

"I'll have your packs sent up," the man said and clicked his tongue to move the horses toward a stall.

Up, apparently, meant the second floor, as the entire layout of the manor's first floor consisted of a massive kitchen, a ballroom, and a maze of halls and corridors. Cass had managed to quickly request dinner in their room as they'd passed through the kitchen while they were led by a young maid to the small suite that would be theirs.

"The third floor," the girl said, "is only for the lord of the house, but you may freely use the bath and the study down here."

Miri made a small sound of relief behind him at the mention of a bath, but she was too busy eating a cake she'd been offered in the kitchen to address anything else.

"Thank you," Cass told the girl. "I believe we will both be ready for a bath and good rest. Please see that we are not disturbed after dinner."

The girl gave him an appraising look, but Cass only smiled politely before slipping her a coin. They could think what they wanted about the newly wed pair, but he needed to pin Miri down on the details of her plan. And seven hells, they did need a bath and good rest.

"The steward said you'd be expecting a package. It's been brought up—oh, and here are your bags."

She backed away as another young girl paced the corridor, passing Miri and Cass with her gaze downcast—not avoiding a look, Cass thought, but annoyed at the weight of her burden. She hefted the packs higher as Cass opened the door, and the girl made quick work of settling them before leaving.

Cass thanked both, passed them two more coins, and sagged in relief when he finally shut the door.

Miri stood in the center of a very small parlor, staring down at a twine-wrapped parcel. "You were expecting a package?" she asked incredulously.

He crossed the distance to draw the handwritten note from the parcel. *You are never alone.* Cass felt something squeeze in his chest, and Miri leaned closer to read the note.

Her honey-brown eyes slid to his face. "They were expecting you?"

Her words were only a whisper, but Cass found he could barely speak. He shook his head softly. "There are only a few of us, but Thom had sent word ahead. Everyone was ready, should they be needed." He saw in her gaze the hope that they meant to help in her plot. "To hide you again," Cass explained. "To help us escape."

Her chest fell with her expression, but Cass nudged her. "Open it."

Miri eyed him suspiciously for one moment before leaning over to tug the twine free. Beneath the plain paper were new clothes—woven shirts and leather vests in the style of Pirn—and a small satchel Cass suspected was filled with coin. Miri peered inside then asked, "Where do they get the money?"

She knew it wasn't hers. The queen's stores had been taken with her throne.

Cass settled onto the small fabric bench to unlace his boots. "Many in the kingdom were well looked after. They miss what has been taken, the same as you or I."

Miri's fingers stilled on the fabric, but she didn't speak. Cass wondered whether she meant to argue that no one felt the same as she did or if the tension in her body was merely because of the reminder of her mother.

He sighed. They had ridden into the city of Pirn, where she planned to avenge her mother's death, and Miri could not even face the thought of the woman, let alone the emotion that came with it.

Cass rose from the bench, boots forgotten, and moved to stand beside Miri. He slid a hand to the small of her back. The motion drew her gaze to his. "We both need a bath and some decent food. Then you and I are going to sit at this table and map out every single detail of your murderous plot." His voice was quiet, but the tone was clear. "Do you agree to those terms, my lady?"

Miri stared up at him, and Cass was grateful he'd not called her *Princess* or *Bean*. He could see the struggle behind her gaze and understood that she'd held her plans tightly for so long that letting go to anyone would be difficult. He hoped she trusted him. He hoped she didn't die.

Miri's brow drew together at his expression, but eventually, she gave him a small nod. "I agree."

CHAPTER 9

Miri woke in the small apartment to the sound of a cart in the street. She blinked in the broken darkness, her brain still foggy. The room was dimly lit in strips by sparse moonlight through the glass. It was not that she'd grown used to the sounds of the forest, but at Nan and Thom's, the sounds had been so different. The air had been filled with noisy patterns of ships coming into port, sailors eager for a stretch of land, and the gulls that called to sea and sky.

Miri had made it to Pirn. It was all so real.

She shifted beneath two layers of warm blanket to find Cass's lean form positioned carefully on the floor at the foot of the single bed. He was by all appearances asleep, but Miri had learned to take nothing of that sort at face value. They'd stayed up half the night, meticulously walking through the first step of Miri's plan. Cass had grilled her on every detail and second-guessed her every move. Her patience had worn down, as had their candle, but Miri felt more secure since she'd had a solution for nearly every one of his proposed flaws. Cass was queensguard. He'd been trained in such things. Miri felt a pang for Henry because of all the small ways in which Cass mirrored the head guard's mannerisms and tone. She pushed the thought away, creeping carefully down her mattress to slide a blanket over the edge of the bed and onto Cass's still form. He cuddled into the quilt, into Miri's warmth, and she settled flat on the bed again.

When the sun rose, they would eat a good breakfast and go to the market at Pirn. Then, two days later, Miri would scratch the first king's name from her list. If she lived, they would escape to Kirkwall, and there, she would knock another from his throne atop a lengthy flight of stairs. Seven kings. Seven murders. Seven men between Miri and her sister's freedom—between Miri's death or freedom for them all.

A sigh came from the floor at the foot of her bed. "Go to sleep, Bean. We've plenty to worry about on the morrow."

Miri bit down a chuckle at his tone and rolled to her side. Gods help her, but she was worried less than she'd ever been. It was not death she was afraid of. It was being trapped, unable to act on her vow. Finally, finally, one way or the other, Miri would be free.

※

THE MARKET at Pirn was a loud and bustling affair. It felt like certain chaos, but beneath it all was a pattern, order, and the apparent familiarity of everyone involved. Miri had not been in a crowd that size for years, and her heart raced with the excitement and terror particular to facing something new. She clung to her satchel. Cass was pressed to her side. They'd eaten a breakfast of honey and biscuits and dressed in clothes that had been provided by a nameless benefactor. Cass's face was once again clean-shaven, and his clothes were of a nicer cut. The garb looked nothing like the uniform of a queensguard—decidedly so. The cut of the fabric rounded over his shoulders, and the shirt was loose and pleated and tied with string. He wore a wide belt and, though it was warm, a long thin cloak that hid most of his blades.

Miri had a weapon, too, though she couldn't imagine it would do her any good should a band of kingsmen find her. Cass had fitted her with a boot dagger, and two more were strapped to the back of her belt. If nothing else, it made her feel safer. And because she was the Lion Queen's daughter, her hair had been bundled away beneath a soft brown bonnet with a ridiculously oversized brim. She pushed at it as they moved through the crowd, hating the way it obstructed her vision. Cass slipped his arm around her waist, tugging her to him when she inadvertently bumped into a curly-headed man with a basket full of salted pork. She glanced at him then tripped over a broken stone in the path.

"Seven hells," Cass muttered, drawing her between two stalls to bend the visor back. Miri stood looking up at him as he folded the material over itself, his mouth drawn and eyes pinched.

"Sorry to be so difficult," she said coolly.

His hazel eyes met hers. "You stick out like a bad apple. It's hard enough to keep an eye on the crowd." He meant by himself. Miri frowned as Cass added, "When we get to the blacksmith, let me do the talking."

"Because you're my husband." She crossed her arms, incredulous.

"Because you've never bartered as someone who holds no power. *Bean.*"

She scowled at his reminder then swatted his hands away from her bonnet. "As you say," she offered. "But I pick the sword."

Cass took hold of her hand and drew her with him as he made a path between stalls of woodcraft and pottery, weaving past carts of oils, wine, cast pots, and caged chickens. A vendor tried to sell Miri a scarf, and another offered wax. Cass kept on, appearing to pay it all no mind, though Miri could feel the tension in him. She kept up, one hand tight in his, the other managing her cloak, until the scents of the market were overpowered by the smoke and solvent and molten steel of the blacksmith's stalls.

At the entrance to a massive tent Cass stepped aside, letting Miri walk past him inside. The interior was hot and dusty and filled with the clank of metal being formed beyond the stall. Miri let her eyes adjust to the dim light as she stared past the folded brim of her bonnet to a wall of metal ornaments and shields. Long tables were situated in rows, each scattered with an assortment of cuffs and knives. Horseshoes rested in a bucket on the trodden earth, and farm tools and construction material sat on a table of their own.

A woman wearing a thick leather apron came forward, wiping her hands on a threadbare rag. "What'll do for you?"

"I need a sword," Miri said.

Cass's hand slipped deftly beneath Miri's cloak to rest on her back, and he smiled down at her like she was the best mare in the stable. "My wife would like a sword of her own, something light and thin, I think, for I trust she'll take to it brilliantly." At Miri's attempt at an apologetic glance, he added, "And sharp. For good measure."

The blacksmith laughed, but the sound was drowned out by the hammering of metal beyond the tent walls. "Aye," she said when the clatter died down. "Sharp."

She gestured for them to follow, and Cass let Miri go ahead of him. His fingers brushed the back of her arm as they slid free of her cloak.

She would try to remember the girl Bean had no idea about metalwork and weaponry, aside from the skill with her knives—those of a trader and a woodsman. They walked past a bench layered with ax heads and chisels as the woman slipped through the side of the tent. Outside again but away from the crowd, the woman led them to a cart built of thick, scarred lumber. She tossed back a massive sheet of leather to reveal half a dozen mallets and three well-made swords.

"We've not much in the way of options inside, but these are

maybe more what you're after." She lifted the shortest of the three and flipped it down to hand to Miri by the grip. "Ned's got a bit of a knack for this sort of steel. Shame he can't sell it outside of town."

Miri's gaze shot up, but Cass cleared his throat before her words escaped. "Restrictions?" he asked.

The woman nodded, her hands coming to her hips. Her fingers were black with dust. "New rules every year." She gave Cass a crooked smile. "Fancy seeing 'em try to enforce that at Blackstone."

So the rules were not coming from Pirn. It was new laws from Stormskeep or maybe the entire lot of those kings. Miri's fingers tightened around the braided leather grip of her sword.

"Fits you well, then." The woman's head tilted as she appraised Miri's slender form. "I reckon you could wield it for practice. But you've got no real reach with a weapon that size." She hummed. "Come back to me when you've got this one mastered, and we'll fit you with something with a bit more heft to it."

"How much?" Cass's tone was clipped but all for show. Miri knew how heavy the man's coin purse was. He was Cass the trader, well versed in bargaining and dicker.

Miri stepped back a pace to fall into stance. She raised the sword and spun, testing its balance and trying a few basic moves.

The woman laughed. "She's lost the deal for you before you've even started, boy. Look at her. You can't take that blade from such a pretty bride."

Miri did not have to turn around to see Cass's expression. She could imagine it full well by then.

"Seventy," he said. "It's a fair price for us both."

The woman scoffed. "Good steel's near impossible to come by these days, and you well know it. Look at those blades on your hip."

Cass had not displayed his best knives in the open, but that did not seem to matter one bit.

Miri turned back to face them, weighing the sword in both her hands. "I'll need a sheath and a strap as well. Throw those in, and I can convince my husband it was worth his while."

The woman cackled and patted Cass on the shoulder so hard he nearly stumbled.

Though Cass stared at Miri, she only said, "No sense in dally, my precious helpmeet. We've two more stops at least. I've a need for scarves and sweet-smelling soap, remember?"

Cass blinked at Miri then drew in a long-suffering breath and handed the woman her coins.

※

CASS CARRIED Miri's sword as they traversed the market beneath a midmorning sun. The sense of chaos and riot of smells had intensified, in no small part because of the preparation of the midday meals. Meat roasted on large iron spits, and vegetables were being cooked into pottage or roasted in metal baskets over the fire. Miri sidestepped a cluster of rowdy men to slip into a tent with candles and oil. Cass followed her, his constant scrutiny on the crowd.

A young girl approached Miri, her copper hair in a crown of braids. "Can I interest you in some oils, miss?"

"Yes," Miri said. "Indeed."

The girl's sharp green eyes took Miri in, and her freckled cheeks plumped when she smiled. "I'll wager you're a mint-and-lavender sort."

"You'll wager nothing at all!" The voice came from an older woman crouched beneath a table, stacking glass bottles into a crate. She had the same copper hair, only two shades lighter.

The girl rolled her eyes. "And for him," she said, gesturing at Cass as if she'd not been reprimanded at all, "sandalwood and sage."

Miri chuckled. "Aye, boys are a stinky lot. Maybe something stronger."

The girl nodded sagely. "I've just the thing." She gestured for Miri to follow, but it was only two steps to her table of wares. She offered up vials for appraisal, and Miri smelled rose water, lily, cloves, and lemon while Cass perused the deadlier stock on the shelves behind them.

She needed something in a powder and two kinds of oil. As the girl chattered about heated salves and the medicinal benefits of saffron and iris, Miri closed her eyes to take the various scents in. The musky, soil aroma of patchouli in one vial was replaced by another, its scent woody and something like lemongrass or citronella. Miri's cheeks heated when she realized what it reminded her of—it smelled like Cass. She opened her eyes, placing the stopper back in the vial.

The girl's smile warmed. "Oh, you like that one. That's vetiver. Excellent for repelling lice." She took the vial from Miri and set it aside in a pile of possible purchases. "You'll need some almond oil for base, and we've got fresh cinnamon bark just in from Smithsport. It was delivered today."

The word cut through Miri's distraction, driving a sudden spike of fear through her veins. She'd no idea why, because truly, goods from Smithsport were exported to every city in the realm. She suddenly felt Cass beside her. His presence was a calming reminder she was not alone and that nearly no one knew who she truly was. She pressed away the voice that said the count of those people was fewer and fewer every day and that she might never be that person again.

"Have you found what you need, my lady?" Cass's voice was gentle, his entire manner attentive and nothing like that of a thief. Miri hoped he didn't haggle with the merchants, at least, to make up for the offense of pocketing poisons when the girl's attention had been turned away.

Miri nodded, and the woman approached from her bottle-sorting task, her sleeves rolled up, presumably to keep the oils from the cloth. Miri smiled automatically in greeting, but her eyes caught on the edge of a dark mark on the woman's skin.

Miri felt her face go slack, and the woman jerked her arm away to brusquely unroll the sleeve to its place.

"This is a lovely shop," Cass said smoothly, as if he'd not noticed the exchange. "We've been traveling the forests for ages, and I've not seen a single variety of hyssop and purslane to be had among other tradesmen."

The woman nodded hastily and adjusted her apron then her hair. "Yes, of course. Get most of our stock from a farm outside of Blackstone. They've a hot house to be envious of, I'm sure."

The girl added, "We grow all the common herbs ourselves. And Momma says that soon, we'll have enough saved to build a hot house of our own."

The woman's eyes seemed to dim. The promise she'd made was clearly empty.

"It's a pleasure to hear," Miri said softly.

The girl glanced at her mother, but the woman only patted her shoulder absently. "Wrap up the vials, blossom. I'm sure these two have other places to be."

Miri held the woman's gaze, wanting to make a promise of her own. The secret beneath the woman's sleeve that she was so clearly terrified of being found out would remain safely concealed—because the mark was one of loyalty to the Lion Queen.

CHAPTER 10

They made only a few more stops on their way out of the market: one for silks and scarves and one at a finery shop that sold utensils and metal jewelry. Miri was unsettled enough at the mention of Smithsport and the sight of the woman's mark, but when they neared the edge of the crowds, Cass stilled her with a sudden too-firm grip on her elbow. Her eyes shot to him then followed his gaze to the edge of the throng. Against the backdrop of serene cottage-style houses on cobblestone streets, three massive figures in the kingsmen colors of dark brown and red stood in a row. Between them, a slender man in sorcerer's robes eyed the crowd.

Miri's blood ran cold. Cass squeezed her elbow tighter, and she dropped her gaze to her feet. Gods, she wanted to run at just the sight of him so near. A second icy stab of fear jolted through her, lingering on the back of her neck. She wanted to swat at it like a horse would a fly. Seven hells, she needed out. A small sound escaped her before Cass jerked her toward him and dragged her away from the soldiers and back into the crowd. They moved as swiftly as possible without drawing notice, and Miri's hands trembled against the satchel of wrapped vials.

She wanted to look back and to see if they would follow. She wanted to bend over in the street and be sick onto the stone.

"Bean," Cass said, tugging her into his side. "Keep moving. Nearly there."

They ducked into a narrow alley between two buildings, their boots sloshing in a mud puddle.

Cass came to a stop and put his hands on Miri's arms as he made her face him. "Look at me, Bean. Right here."

She pushed against the dread, and whatever was swimming through her head seemed to clear, if just a bit.

"Two more streets, and we're back at the manor. Safe." He winced at whatever he saw in her eyes. "Can you make it?"

Miri considered that for a moment. The task of walking only two short blocks felt impossible for a reason she couldn't quite identify. She should want to get away, but she couldn't find her will to run. Cass was watching her and waiting. She managed a nod.

They moved with purpose, and before she had a chance to crawl from her skin or retch in the street, Miri was safely inside the walls of the benefactor's manor. She could finally breathe.

"Are you well, miss?" one of the kitchen staff asked.

Cass brought Miri nearer still. "A bit under the weather, I'm afraid. Can you—" He pressed his lips together, as if considering what might help. "Do you mind sending up an early dinner?"

"Of course," the woman said. "Poor dearie. We'll have whatever it is sussed out with some hot tea."

Cass said his thanks and led Miri wordlessly to their room, where he deposited her onto the narrow bed. She curled her legs to her chest to lean against the wall as he paced the room, none too subtly peering out the window on his route. He carefully unloaded the murder supplies he'd pilfered from the market.

A light knock sounded at the door, and Cass retrieved the tray of food. He deposited it onto the table in the front room and brought Miri a mug of steaming tea. The cup was laden with lemon and honey and several floating herbs. She breathed in the scent of it, wrapping her fingers cautiously around the mug. Her hands had seemed to stop their trembling, but she did not quite trust them.

Finally, he sat down beside her. "Tell me about your plans again, Miri. Tell me what happens in two days' time."

She nodded, understanding that he wanted her to discuss something she'd thought of a thousand times—not the new terror that had so unsettled them both. "I've been in the castle before, many times, when King Casper was no more than a lord. He's too secure in his safety now that the Lion Queen is gone, and the lot of those lords turned kings have aimed more for palaces than fortresses. Pleasure over protection." She swallowed against the lump in her throat, not mentioning the precautions Edwin had taken in the tower at Stormskeep. "As the years wear on, their confidence only grows. They're selfish. Vain. Creatures of habit. And I know the secret faults of every single one."

Cass nodded. "How do you know, Miri? How do you know Casper?"

"I befriended a serving girl while my mother met with the lord. She was tall for her age and had wide brown eyes and cropped hair. My attentions gave her leave to escape her chores, and she took me on a tour of the castle. We didn't marvel at the art and sculptures the lord had amassed or the grand rooms meant to impress. The girl and I stole down to the basement cells to see the prisoners—which wasn't allowed, by my mother's own laws. We felt our way blindly through secret passages, held our hands over the steaming cauldrons of the castle laundry, and dipped our fingers into the dyes."

Cass took the mug from Miri and set it onto the window's ledge before facing her more fully. "Tell me about the stables."

She stared into his eyes, felt the safety of telling him, and remembered that she'd told him the same only the night before. "The stables border the forest, but there is an old guard house nearby where deliveries used to be allowed through. The wall between the stables and the guard house is solid block, but the repairs were not kept up when the woods grew thick."

"And what's there, behind the trees?"

"A chink in Casper's armor." Cass's mouth turned up a bit at the corner, and Miri went on, her voice low. "A split in the wall from roots formed beneath the earth, ignored because the opening is so small. No one would get in because of the tree, but even then, it would only permit someone very small."

"Like a child."

Miri nodded. "Like a serving girl who sometimes might want to sneak into town."

"Or a woman."

"Yes," she said. "But who's afraid of those?"

Cass did smile then, if just a little.

Miri said, "And it wouldn't even matter, since the only access through the wall is to the stables. It's not as if a queen's army could chop down a tree and cross the courtyard to reach Casper in the safety of his rooms without notice. Why bother even inspecting beneath the roots for cavities large enough to burrow through?"

Cass watched her, and Miri realized her chest had loosened, as if she was once again herself. He took her fingers—still warm from the mug—into his hands. "How often have you been near a sorcerer?"

He wasn't comforting her. He wanted her trapped—held there should she decide to run away. She shook her head. "Not since... *before*."

"Never?"

"Any time they came—even word of a single kingsman—Nan hid me away. The entire time in Smithsport, and before—Cass, not since I was a girl and my mother was—"

"I need you to tell me, Miri. I need to know what happened."

There it was, the thing that hurt her and would cause her to run. She tried to jerk her fingers from Cass's grip, but he held fast.

"You know why I need you to tell me."

He was her guard. He was meant to protect her.

At her expression, Cass sighed and let go of her hands. "I know you felt it. We both know something is there. You're stepping into a dangerous task in two days, and you refuse to give me the tools to help you should you need it. Gods dammit, Miri, I don't want you to die."

Her arms drew tight around herself at his words, but Miri did not run away. *Want*, he'd said. Not duty and honor but *want*.

He seemed to realize what he'd said as well. He stood, pushing a hand through his hair, and resumed pacing the room.

"When I was a boy," he said, "my mother used to tell me a story about a changeling. It was a child stolen from its crib, secreted away by magical beings—fae creatures of the forest." He stopped his pacing, his gaze coming back to hers. "In that child's place, they left one of their own whom they'd deemed unworthy or at least worth the trade." He shook his head. "Can you imagine, Miri? Can you imagine what this was like for the rest of us?"

For me, he meant to say. For the boy Cass who'd been taken from a family who loved him so much that they felt his life was better served at the hand of the queen. But Cass was not the changeling. That distinction had gone to a poor serving girl who'd been murdered in the skirmish only moments before.

The kingsmen had been coming. They'd already taken Lettie captive—Miri had heard her screams. They were coming for Miri next, her mother had said. It was time to put the plan into place.

Cass's brothers of the queensguard had stripped Miri's thin frame down to her shift. They'd dressed the dead girl in the clothes of a princess and lain her body by the queen's to let them both burn.

Later, the kingsmen had thought it was Miri, and every day for a solid year, Miri had wished that it was. She'd longed to have been laid beside her mother and turned to ash so that even the sorcerers could no longer tell it was her.

Miri had been jealous of a dead girl—a servant and child who would never again draw breath. Cinders.

It had worked, of course. All thought the second princess was burned, not carried away in drapery, half-naked and bleeding and covered in ash. They'd shoved her into a box on a boat, and she'd ridden in that hell down the Maidensgrace River alone and nearly dead. The feeling of being choked, the feel of the icy sea as the box had been dumped over, and the way the salt water burned her aching lungs were with her still. She'd wanted to die there, wanted so much for it to only end. That was when her hand remembered the pendant. Her childhood fingers took tighter hold of the only thing she had left—on a thin chain pressed to her flesh as she was choked to death by fire, sea, and loss.

Then Thom's men had pulled her from the water. They'd cracked the box open so that she felt the shattering and splintering of the wood. Those men had cradled a broken, blistered shred of a thing and carried her to the place she would soon call home.

When the blisters had healed, Nan had shaved Miri's head. The hair had been half burnt away, melted in the sorcerer's fire. Nan had forced a bonnet lined with salve over Miri's raw and ragged scalp. Miri had hated that bonnet. She'd hated everything. She hated it still.

※

CASS STARED at Miri's hand where it rested at her hem. She felt for her mother's pendant at the memory, checking to be certain it was still there. It was. She was no longer choking. She was no longer a battered child who'd escaped with nothing but minor burns and a broken heart.

She might not be a princess of Stormskeep while those kings

held their rule, but Miri was still a daughter of the Lion Queen. She would get Lettie back, and those kings would pay for what they'd done. Miri would have revenge in their name.

Her gaze was steady on Cass, his shoulders sagging beneath the weight of his duty. His lean muscled form was clad in tradesman's rags, though he belonged in the uniform of a guard.

"They took her blood," Miri told him. "The sorcerers used it against her. It was the only way they could have won."

Cass pressed his lips together, which meant he was concerned about the extent to which Miri could be affected and how much of her own blood the sorcerers might have.

"I can handle it. If I'm no closer than I was today, I can do it. I can kill the kings. And they don't realize that I'm alive. None of them knows."

His mouth turned down, but he didn't remind her of the risk she was taking or what could happen the moment those sorcerers realized she still drew breath.

"I will do everything I can for Lettie." Miri let him see the truth in her gaze. She would not back down. "I've no other choice."

CHAPTER 11

Miri woke two days later with a flock of sparrows fighting in her chest. By the time she and Cass had dressed and packed the horses, Miri was convinced the fluttering would burst free and spill out of her with her very being. But Cass had forced Miri to eat and—because she was stubborn and refused to back down from her plan—take a shot of brandy from a flask he'd been given at the Silverton Inn.

The brandy had burned all the way down, and if it hadn't settled her nerves, it had at least given her something to focus on besides imagined scenarios of being caught. They rode through the town, casually greeting passersby and talking of a trip north to Blackstone and whether the snow had yet melted from the mountains of Ravenskeep. They did not talk of the stables or of their plan to kill a king. Cass had made Miri detail that plan so often that she wanted to shout that she'd no idea what the words even meant anymore.

Then, when they'd negotiated through the thick forest to the old, broken wall, the words had come back to her again. "And what will you do?" she whispered to Cass.

He shook his head with a rueful grin. Cass would likely be

standing as if relieving himself on the wall surrounding the castle, should anyone find him in the thick of the trees.

He put a hand on her shoulder, squeezed it once, then turned to survey the woods. Miri drew a settling breath, repeating the steps in her head. *Burrow through beneath the roots, find the crack in the wall, shift the block I was shown as a girl, and slide into the stables in a crawl.*

"Don't break the glass," Cass warned again.

Miri snorted. The place beneath the roots had grown to a tangled snarl, damp and rank, and she hoped the worst thing in the darkness with her was the salve in that vial. She took shallow breaths, stretching her body in ways it was not meant to stretch, and resisted the urge to grunt when her knuckles scraped against stone and a tree root jammed against her ribs.

She felt blindly for the loose block, carefully slid it across the others, then stopped to listen for footsteps or voices on the other side. Satisfied she was alone, she crawled through the too-narrow space to the packed earth and dusty manure of the disused corridor behind the old stable stalls.

Miri looked behind her but could not see that she'd left much disturbance or any way of being tracked. She listened longer to the goings on outside, the muffled nicker of far-off horses, and the birds in the trees outside the wall. Everything was safe, secure, and going as planned. She crept down the corridor, momentarily disoriented by the passing of years. She had to backtrack twice, but the stable was not so changed that she was entirely unprepared. The kings were about habit, routine, and ritual. They didn't deviate without due cause.

She found the corridor to the room she needed, one where the king kept his riding gear. Listening, she waited then unlatched the ancient metal and carefully moved the door on its weary hinges.

Miri inched into the room, letting her eyes adjust to the dimness. Shelves as old as she was held carved leather bridles, shining bits, and the formal riding gear of the king of Pirn. A shock ran through her at the recognition and the feeling of being so near something so personal to that king—one of the men who'd killed her mother and held her sister captive and sat boldly upon a stolen throne.

Gritting her teeth against her anger, she peered through the space to be certain she would not be detected. Satisfied she was alone, she stepped forward, the mantra of her plan repeating in her mind again. *Find his gloves and his mantle then carefully remove the vial.*

A bout of laughter sounded outside the room, coming from the entrance that had been more recently put into use. Miri nearly fumbled the sweat-slicked glass. She held painfully still as a muffled voice called down the corridor, then she wiped her palm on the material covering her thigh. Her hand came back slicked with mud from beneath the root mass, and she bit back a curse, trying again with the material that made up the inside of her shirt.

They were not Miri's clothes. Her pendant waited in her spare garments with Cass, outside the wall.

Miri took the narrow stick of wood from her pocket and dipped it into the poisoned salve. She carefully spread it over the fingers of the right glove. Not wanting to harm whoever might dress the king, she avoided the wide cuffs as best she could. Then she dropped the piece of wood into the vial and returned the stopper.

In the castle at Stormskeep was a great carved map attached to the wall. It had fallen in the attack, the scores that divided the realm splitting the wood into broken chunks, separating the kingdoms from the whole. The image of that shattered carving, the realm split to pieces, had been burned into Miri's memory as they fled. She was setting that splintered block back into place.

Miri gently set the gloves in their proper position. As she stared at the very implement that would commence her years-old plan, she whispered, "The Lion has come for you. It is time to pay your due."

CHAPTER 12

Miri had killed a king—not at the moment, of course, but within the week. Again and again, she reminded herself that she had time as her trembling hands worked to lace up her boots. She and Cass need not run. They had time.

Her fingers slipped on the button of her vest, and she cursed.

Cass came around the horses and took hold of her arms. "Breathe, Miri. It's done." He did not wait for her to nod, only made quick work of the rest of the buttons and buckles that adorned her belt and vest. He secured the mantle of her thin cloak before he looked at her again. "Ready?"

She could only manage a trembling nod.

"Right," he said. "Up you go." He grabbed Miri's arm and helped her astride before climbing onto his own horse with a swiftness that belied his apparent lack of concern.

Cass gave her one more quick glance before he kicked up his horse, and they rode through the thick woods at an unsteady pace. They came out of the forest near the church, and their pace finally settled. They rode from Pirn as if heading north, but the moment they'd traversed enough land not to be seen, they turned west. Late morning became midday and early afternoon.

The summer sun bore down on the clearings between each patch of trees, and the spicy scent of yarrow was stirred into the still air by the flowers crushed beneath their horses' hooves. Two flies nagged at Miri's ear, and two more hovered near Wolf's.

Then it was evening, and Miri drew the cloak tighter around her shoulders and held her reins closer to hand. At nightfall, Cass finally stopped beneath a copse of close trees. He strung a rope between two of those trees and tied loose slipknots to keep the animals near. He did not start a fire or leave to hunt.

Cass settled a blanket onto the ground and handed Miri a piece of dried meat and a hunk of dark bread. Both felt like pulp in her mouth, and she chewed absently as she stared past the horses into the dark. She should clean the dirt from beneath her fingernails. Miri's maids had hated it when her play had left her caked in mud. They had fussed away at her with brushes and tools, scraping all of it clean.

She was a princess. It wasn't proper.

Miri didn't realize she was crying until Cass's arm came around her and he pulled her to him. Her chest rose and fell in racking sobs. Cass didn't speak, only held her tighter, and when she finally settled, he moved his palm in soothing circles over her back.

He shifted to lean against a tree, drawing Miri with him so that her arm and cloak made a pillow against his leg. Long after she'd settled, warm so near him, Cass began a story in a low, steady tone. It was a story of Miri's mother and how he'd been hurt and humiliated by failing a minor task, and she had set him to rights. The Lion Queen had been kind, her wit as sharp as a blade.

Miri understood why he was telling her. Cass was bloodsworn, the highest of the queensguard and closest to the queen. He knew as well as anyone that she had been a good ruler and did not deserve her fate, even if he didn't agree with Miri's plans.

When Miri finally spoke, her voice was a raw whisper. "I'm not sorry he's dead, only that I was the one who had to do it."

Even the words felt like a betrayal, as if speaking them aloud was a vow broken. There should be no guilt or regret in Miri's heart, only honor. She should have had done with it and been strong enough not to blubber like a fool on Cass's shoulder. She should have the heart of a lion. She should be worthy of her blood.

Cass brushed the hair away from Miri's face, his finger grazing her cheek as he tucked the lock behind her ear the way Nan had done when Miri was a child. "I'll not judge you for taking a life. Not with the things I've done."

He was of the guard and could understand what drove her and what she was going through. But that did not mean he approved. She was, after all, putting both his life and his vow to protect Miri on the line in order to carry out her plot.

"Casper was cruel to Lettie," Miri said. "He'd use carefully constructed words to trap her and maneuver her into situations in which she looked the fool in front of everyone, no matter what she did. Like she was incapable. Unworthy." Gods, she'd been just a child. *What sort of man could find pleasure in besting a girl?* He'd made Lettie feel those things, like she would never have been good enough to be queen.

Miri wondered if her sister would be glad of what she'd done.

"Casper will get what he deserves."

Cass's tone was low, but Miri thought she heard something beneath. She wondered, not for the first time, what other things Casper had done when the queen's attentions were elsewhere.

When a person found pleasure in cruelty, it was rare that they found boundaries in how far they were willing to take it. The poison she'd left him was quick but not painless. The grim thought that he would not suffer enough swam to the surface, and she wondered at what point her desire to fulfill her duty might morph into something cruel—when the lion might become a monster.

IT HAD BEEN CUNNING to plan the first killings with enough leeway for escape, but their luck would only hold out so long. Miri waited on pins and needles to hear word—desperate with dread that it hadn't worked or, worse, that it had and she was a murderer. Cass did his best to attempt entertainment, but Miri's mood left little room for conversation, and they had very far to ride. In a few days, they would pass near Stormhold, named—like Stormskeep—for the first queen of the realm. Miri couldn't recall the first time she'd seen the gate, but she'd been in awe without exception since. A massive structure stretched so high that one could barely make out the guards at the top, and carved into the stone of the archway was a relief of the Storm Queen herself.

The queen wore armor and a helm, and her thick braid was curled over her shoulder in a style Lettie had emulated. Legend had it that the first queen had abolished magic and broken the chaos of the realm by conquering the men who practiced dark arts. She had created order, and within it, only the sorcerers who held fealty to the queen were allowed to have that knowledge passed to them. It had been such for every queen since.

Her realm had stood for years beyond counting, and as children, Miri and Lettie had thought the Storm Queen a god. But queens were only mortals. Queens could be killed.

"There's an inn not far from Stormhold. We should rest here for the evening and start again tomorrow."

Miri nodded her assent, ready to crawl off her horse and straighten her legs. That morning, Cass had found a soft patch of earth far from their trail to dig a hole and bury the vial. So when he started a fire well before dark, she did not ask what he meant to do.

He burned her clothes, the simple garments that had been provided in Pirn. They held evidence of the mud and earth from beneath the tree. The evidence was gone, but the king was not yet dead.

Miri settled onto the ground to stare up at a cloudless sky, wondering how many kings might fall by her hand and how soon she and Lettie might die. A shadow fell over her a moment before Cass came into view. He stared down at her, outlined by endless blue, a well-made blade in his grip. "Exercise," he reminded her.

She stifled a groan as she rolled to her side but took Cass's proffered hand. "I'm a bit rusty. Nan wouldn't let me spar with anyone good."

Cass chuckled. "Thom and Nan were two of the best swordsmen in Smithsport."

She crossed her arms. "Are you saying they let me win?"

He handed her the sword. "I wouldn't dare."

Miri's progress was slow—it truly had been a while since she'd practiced. The movement felt good, though, and the more she worked, the more she fell into the familiar routines of thrusts and cuts. It wasn't long before she felt comfortable, and Cass increased his speed.

Miri dodged and parried and was soon sweating, her moves just a little too slow. She felt nearly up to his challenge, but he was a guard. Cass never had to dedicate time to sewing and gowns—he'd used all of his time and energy to train with weapons and hone his instincts. But Miri had been taught something of tactics herself, and she was not above using them in a fight. She stepped into his swing, bringing her blade up to block, and spun into Cass as he reset, twisting her leg deftly into the back of his knee. He was only off balance, but Miri had drawn her dagger and held the pommel at his ribs.

Cass gave her a look.

"Oh," she said sweetly, "did you let me win?"

He inclined his head, his eyes lingering on her face as he extracted his body from hers. "I would never."

Miri smiled despite herself and realized it was the first time she had since Pirn and the sorcerers in the market.

Cass slid his sword into its sheath. "Dinner," he said. "Then stories."

Miri's smile would not return, but she managed a nod.

Cass was trying to draw the details from her, but Miri was not yet able to let them go. What had happened the day her mother had been murdered had simultaneously been seared into her memory, unable to leave her alone, and was unbearable to look at directly, like the sun, impossible desires, wishes that could never come true, or truths that would never be less real.

"Did you know that Henry was a childhood friend of my grandfather?" Cass poked at the fire with a broken tree limb, settling the logs before he started heating the pot.

Miri shook her head.

He went on, though he did not stop in his task to look at her. "They grew up south of Ravensgate, one the son of a well-to-do lord and the other the son of a river captain."

"Seems an unlikely pair." Miri sat on the ground behind where he worked, curling her legs beneath her before stretching them out again. She was still restless and would be glad when news finally came—when it was over.

"Aye. But it seems the lord enjoyed a bit of gambling, so when he found himself down at the docks, Henry's father would leave the boy outside the establishment—not fit for a young man of stature—to fend for himself."

Cass glanced over his shoulder at Miri's soft laugh.

"And your grandfather was a captain's son?"

"Yes. They immediately fell in together, peering through windows at seedy goings-on and joining in street games with somewhat lower stakes. It wasn't long before they were fellows, and young Henry had inherited an estate." Cass situated the pot over the fire and moved back to sit beside Miri. His elbow rested over his knee, his attention, by all appearances, in the distance.

Cass was good, Miri realized. Maybe he hadn't been spent his time training entirely in weapons and duty. Maybe he'd learned something of extracting information and making his prey fall into comfort.

"Henry offered to use his connections, but apparently, my

grandfather refused the help. He wanted to make it on his own." Cass gave Miri a look that implied he did not altogether believe Henry had not done his part, but he didn't say so outright. "So by the time my father was born, the two families were closer in social stature. Eventually, my father and his brothers were sent to the same tutors as had attended Henry, despite my family being lesser in the eyes of some."

"A ship captain is no less a man than a lord. I've known enough lords to see how little they actually accomplish."

Cass chuckled at Miri's assessment. "In matters of toil or money, that's certainly true. But not in social status. Not the power they hold."

"Power is an illusion. Any man can gain or lose it by a toss of the dice." The words came automatically, and she could tell by the way Cass averted his gaze that he remembered too. It was something her mother had said. Miri had not understood when she was a child that the words, though spoken lightly, could be taken as a threat, which was especially effective when coming from a queen.

"Soon after, preparation began for the coronation of the young Lion Queen and, with it, openings for Henry and my grandfather in the royal guard."

Miri leaned forward. "But the guard doesn't marry until they retire. How could your grandfather have had a son so young?"

"His arm was broken in a training accident."

Cass's tone made it clear that there was more to the story. Miri hoped it was not that it had been broken because of a social standing before entering the guard.

"So he retired early." He gave Miri a crooked grin. "And immediately started having sons."

"Only sons?" Miri plucked at a piece of grass, unable to take her eyes from Cass too long.

"As far as he was concerned, every one would pick up a blade."

"Sounds like he was looking for redress."

Cass shrugged a shoulder. "Maybe so. But my father was soon a member of the queensguard."

"And his son a bloodsworn." The words came thickly off Miri's tongue. She cleared her throat. "Unexpected that you would end up at a port after all he'd done to escape it."

"Yes," Cass said. "Unexpected."

Miri had been with Cass for weeks, and she'd never thought to ask what he was leaving behind. Henry had raised Cass as a father and had taken Cass into the guard when he was young and spent each day training him in their ways. Cass had likely had little choice, but there was no denying how he'd felt as a boy. Miri had seen them together, how hard Cass had trained, and how badly he'd wanted to impress.

She wondered who else Cass had lost and who else he had watched die. But the idea, like her memory, was too hard to look at for long. Cass's brothers of the guard had died in their attempts to save the queen and Miri. Their blood was on her hands. And from that, Miri could not look away.

CHAPTER 13

After dinner, Cass sat quietly spinning an unadorned short-handled knife in his hand. Miri had a full stomach and was drowsy but could not seem to draw her eyes away from the dance of the blade as the flicker of firelight caught on it. How many hours he must have done so, likely in the streets of Stormskeep while on his watch, mindlessly twirling a dagger, as if it were not an implement capable of inflicting death.

The light brushed his knuckle, and she reached over to still his hand and traced a finger across a faint mark.

"Not from a dagger," he said. "I slipped from a balustrade I'd climbed on a dare."

Miri snorted. "I hope you won something for the trouble."

"Only repute."

She smiled, shifting to rest her head on an elbow with a yawn. "I'm surprised you're not covered in scars by now."

Cass ran his finger across a faint line on Miri's temple. His touch was gentle enough that she shivered. "And what of you, Princess? How did you come by this scar?"

Miri pressed her lips together, fighting her desire to run from the memory. "My sister and I got into a tussle over a silver brush." Miri could remember the heft of it, the delicate carved roses that vined up the handle, and the molded silver lion that stood out in relief. The lion's long and sharp claws had wrapped around the edges of the paddle. "She took hold of it, trying to wrest it away while she screamed." Miri wanted to shake her head but only nestled closer into the warmth of her arm. "I was so stubborn. The more she fought, the less I gave. I saw it in her eyes, that look, and I knew I'd taken it too far. She let go with a shove, swift enough that I wasn't able to regain my balance from our tug of war, and it cracked my scalp just as I turned my head."

Miri had fallen on her rear and stared up at her sister through the blood that streamed from her temple. Lettie had not been sorry.

She sighed. "Momma found us and ordered every single mirror out of our rooms. Apparently, one of the lords had been taunting Lettie, telling her that the younger Lion outpaced her in beauty as well as wit. I hadn't known." Miri wasn't sure it would have mattered—she couldn't say she would have let up if she'd known.

Miri's mother had been furious that the lord's taunting had worked and appalled that Lettie had drawn her own sister's blood. The queen had taken Miri aside to tend her wound. Her assurances were as soft as her touch. "Beauty is everywhere in you, my child. It can never be erased with something as simple as the slice of a blade or a layer of mud. Remember that, my little bean. Remember that your heart is that of a lion."

Their mother hadn't understood Lettie's fears the way Miri had. The queen didn't know that Lettie was afraid she might never earn a true name like the Storm Queen or like the Lion Queen herself had, barely two years past her coronation.

Lettie had been afraid she would only be known as the Lion Queen's daughter, as a princess who'd had a great and powerful mother, one who had not truly earned the throne. What had happened instead was far worse than any of them could have imagined.

Cass's gaze weighed on Miri. His silence said something she didn't particularly like and that dug into the comfort she'd managed like an ill-placed burr. She shook it off, only offering a final "We were just girls. Children," before she drew her cloak over her shoulder.

Miri recalled something she'd heard from Henry the very next day. "Scars are only proof that a person has experience in battle and that they've earned a victory and survived to fight again."

Miri didn't know if that was true. Sometimes scars were earned by battles lost.

※

THE NEWS of the king's death arrived at the inn near Stormhold well before Miri and Cass. They heard the chatter of men from the trail, travelers standing idle with the locals for news they deemed too important to wait for a decent setting. It only grew louder as they neared the inn. Horse-drawn carts were stopped in the road as a young boy in short trousers retold the tale. By the time they reached the stable, Miri had heard it again and again.

"The king has been killed. Fallen from his horse. His neck broken so that he couldn't even speak. Blood bubbled from his lips, no words. A terrible accident."

The whispers followed. "The man was such a fool for his riding. Never skilled but a braggart, constantly on that he took his stallion out to hunt every week. A second cousin had a boy who was a groom there, said they'd pushed him onto the beast every single time. Trotted him through the courtyard and into the woods on parade. His knights would shoot a fox for him and lay it in the weeds the morning of. Fool of a thing. It's a wonder he lasted this long at all."

Miri met Cass's gaze, but when he was approached by the stable hand, Cass only shook his head sadly, as if dismayed by the unfortunate news. "No, of course we've not heard. We've been traveling for weeks. Yes, traders from Kirkwall. On our way home to replenish our stock."

She was grateful he'd gone along with her plan. A time to implement the spread of rumors would come but not yet. Too soon, and the kings might raise their guard—before their suspicions had been triggered by Miri's actions. She had one more kill, maybe two, then things would get exponentially harder—one more before the risks became higher still.

"My lady."

Cass offered his hand, but Miri didn't flinch. She took it gratefully and let him settle her onto the ground. She had two feet, and she could use them to get to the inn—she hoped, anyway.

"Terrible news," the stable hand said. "And no son to bear his throne."

Miri's teeth pressed together so hard that she feared they might crack.

"We've ridden such a long way," Cass said. "Please excuse the lady. I fear we both need a hot meal and a long rest."

The stable hand smiled. "To be sure. You've come to the right place, I tell you. Mags has on a beast of a stew. Sure to be a busy one tonight. Even a bard or two, I'll wager."

Cass took Miri by the elbow to lead her away from the stables, through the milling travelers, and into the inn. The exterior was large and unadorned, made of wattle and daub despite being so near the town at Stormhold. It was an older establishment, and though Stormhold was rich in trade, the inn was far enough out to see less traffic. No one would bother trading there when it was only a day's ride to the central trading spot of Stormhold, situated between two rivers with the port to its south and the wealthy kingdom of Stormskeep to its north.

They walked into the inn to find it lit by a dozen hammered-iron chandeliers and wall sconces and smelling strongly of the promised stew. Few patrons waited at the tables, but the staff was busy milling about in what was undoubtedly preparation for what would have been a previously unexpected crowd. One of the servers glanced up at Cass, and something like recognition flashed in her eyes. It was gone a moment later.

"Is it too early for dinner?" Cass asked.

"No, to be sure." She smiled. "Have yourselves a sit down, and I'll be back in a wink with plenty for you both."

Cass settled onto a bench across from Miri, giving her a look that asked how she was. She managed a nod, but if she were being honest, she didn't feel like a criminal about to be caught. She felt almost relieved. The waiting was over. The first king was dead. It was an accident, they'd said. Everyone thought him a fool.

"He'll be replaced by one of his advisers, a cousin, I'm told..." The words echoed from across the massive room, a space filled with rough-hewn lumber, pottery, and trenchers on every table.

The rumors were true—those of succession, at least. King Casper had no heir. His fool of a cousin would be no threat, should the true queen be raised again to her throne—should Miri make it to Lettie in time.

"Ale for the lady," Cass said. "Cider for me."

The server, younger than the first, smirked at Cass's order, which did not bode well for the quality of his choice. He thanked her, anyway, and when she returned a moment later with two mugs, the older woman followed after. She was the aforementioned Mags, Miri guessed.

The woman settled their stew onto the table, her gaze lingering on Cass's placid face before she straightened to place a hand on her hip. "Will you be having a room then?"

"If we're lucky." Cass gave her a grin, but it was not the lopsided one that surfaced when he really meant it.

"Aye," she said. "You do look like the lucky sort."

Miri bit her lip at the color that crossed Cass's cheeks. She was feeling more than a little unbalanced, but she picked up the ale anyway and drank heavily.

The woman nodded. "I'll set you up with a room and bring back another helping. You both look like you could use some fattening up for the trail."

Cass thanked her then took a draw from his mug. He choked loudly and set the cup on the table, his eyes watering. Miri slid her ale toward him, and he took it with a grateful look once he was able to draw a solid breath. "Gods," he muttered. "Remind me never to try that again."

Miri chuckled, but it was only half-hearted. She knew Cass would not sleep easily with so many about at the inn. He would stay awake and listen from his spot on the floor. He would be close enough to protect Miri but always kept an ear to the crowd.

The stew was warm and salty with large chunks of vegetables and a hearty portion of meat. Miri hadn't realized how hungry she was and was quickly feeling settled and steadier by the warmth and the food. By the end of the second bowl, they'd finished three glasses of ale, and Miri was comfortable enough to entertain sleeping on the bench right there in the dining room.

"Another ale, I think," she said lazily before Cass slid the mug to his side of the table.

"That'll do," he said.

Miri quirked a brow at him when she realized he wasn't drinking it, only moving it away from her. She wondered a bit vaguely how long that had been going on. Surely, he'd helped her drain the previous mugs.

The room had filled with an early-supper crowd, and over the chatter of scuttlebutt and jest, Miri could hear the patter of rain. It would be dark and wet and maybe warmer in the stable near a dozing horse. She could certainly picture herself sleeping out there as well.

Laughter erupted from across the room, deep bellows from broad-chested men and the cackling crows of the serving women. It had been something the bard had said, she thought, but Miri's gaze caught on the fire in the massive stone hearth. There, it would be warm. There, she could sleep.

"Well enough," Cass said. "Time we retire."

"No, I'm fine. Very well, in fact," Miri answered. There was no need to rush on her part. Cass the queensguard could listen all he wanted.

Cass frowned, stood, and came around to bow toward Miri. "My lady."

Miri snorted a laugh but stood to meet him. "Good sir." She put her elbow out and let Cass lead her toward the stairs.

As they crossed in front of the door, a large man came in, shaking rain from his hat and rolling his shoulders like a dog shedding water. He had brass rings braided into his beard and boots fit for the sea. He was from Smithsport, then. Cass leaned into Miri, his face nearly brushing her neck as he swept her toward the stairs. They were only a young couple, traders newly wed, not the harbormaster's spy from Smithsport and the daughter of a dead queen.

They climbed the narrow stair toward their room, and Miri glanced at the space below. Not a single man seemed disheartened. Not a tear was shed in Casper's name. It was nothing like the loss of her mother but still the same.

"You've had too much to drink," Cass said. The door had only just shut behind them, closing them into the room. A small window looked out into the darkness, and rain pattered against the thick and bumpy glass.

"Pshaw." Miri flopped onto the bed, boots and all. "I would never."

Cass paced the room once, which didn't take long, given the space, then was back at the door, listening to the goings-on outside. A woman gave a low and sultry laugh. Then came the muffled sound of a door closing down the hall.

Miri's head spun. She'd definitely had too much to drink. She should probably unlace her boots, but it didn't seem entirely worth the effort. Cass poured water from a carafe into a short cup and offered it to her. She waved it away.

He paced in front of the door. After a long while leaning beside the entrance, Cass finally moved toward the bed to unroll his cloak and settle it over the plank floor. He lay on it, his back flat and eyes closed. Miri's gaze turned from him to stare at the ceiling, a very low affair that was heavily spotted with evidence of leaks and patches. Minutes passed to the steady sound of their breathing and the rain outside.

Miri had killed a king.

Her fingers found the lump of metal beneath her layers of clothes. The small trinket was all that was left of her mother. Eyes to the ceiling, Miri whispered, "Do you think it will work—that we'll actually get away with it?"

Cass let the silence stretch before he answered. "No," he said, voice tinged with sadness. "I think you'll die."

Miri sighed. She had imagined the killing of each king as long as she could remember and had felt the hate in her heart and the pressure of her vow. She'd dreamed of the day she might meet Lettie again and what she would say and how they would cry. But Miri had never thought past that moment or devised a plan on how to escape the kingsmen and the sorcerers and restore Lettie to her throne. It didn't seem conceivable, because it was too much to hope.

Cass did not argue with her again or tell her it was not too late to stop. He understood. She could not give up or let them win, even though he thought she was going to die.

Miri closed her eyes to whisper into the darkness, "I think I will too."

CHAPTER 14

The ride to Kirkwall had taken two full weeks. The rain had been relentless, and Cass had managed to find inns only four of those nights. Miri was soaked through and should have been in foul spirits, but she had never been more eager to carry out her murderous plot. The map on the wall was being pieced back together. She was one step closer to Lettie and to being free.

The sky had cleared to a hazy gray, and the air had finally stilled as they approached the top of a ridge looking down toward Kirkwall. Miri groaned at the sight of smoke rising over the bordering wall. She could imagine the smell of roasting meat. The idea of warmth and a dry bed conquered any guilt over manners.

Cass shook his head and pushed back the hood of his cloak, which had long since been sodden with what felt like endless rain. "It's market day," he said. "Well timed, if I do say so myself."

"Finally, a bit of luck," Miri agreed. She gave him a playful glance. "I suppose Mags was right about you after all."

He returned her glance sidelong, not quite as playful. "Yes. Lucky."

Miri's cheeks stung when she broke into a grin. "Let's get to it, then. I'm ready to be off with the lot of this sodden linen and wool."

Cass kicked up Milo as they came over the ridge. The ground gently sloped and was covered in soft, short meadow grass dotted with wild summer flowers. The horses nickered at travelers in the distance, and Miri gave a small tug on Wolf's reins to bring him back on task. The animals were tired of the trail as well, and sloppy ground made the work of stepping through forests and mucky trails more laborious.

The land eventually leveled off. The grass trodden by traffic funneled into muddy, wagon-tracked patches before reaching the packed roads that led to the wall. They followed a horse-drawn cart toward the gate, which was open for market day and posted with several guards. The guards were not dressed in the standard wardrobe of kingsmen but appeared to be hired hands. One had a pike, another had a sword, and two more were armed with apparently no more than their knives and wits.

But no one would have reason to attack the town of Kirkwall. Besides, the king was safe within his castle at the center of it all. That, Miri thought, was where the kingsmen waited. She couldn't know for certain whether the castle housed a sorcerer, but her hope was that he still resided in the church tower, away from the king and Miri's ploy.

The gate guards were quite distracted by the cart, which appeared to be well stocked with pottery jugs that smelled heavily of wine, but Miri kept her head down as they passed through the gateway in the massive stone walls.

Miri didn't believe King Simon had any real concerns regarding his soul, but his people—the people who lived in Kirkwall and had once been ruled by the Lion Queen—did not abide by magic and the dark arts. They'd been prone to wearing charms and warding hexes, the last time Miri had visited with her mother, but when times were hard, sometimes faith was difficult to uphold. And Kirkwall had suffered mightily at the hands of its king.

Regardless, the town had been given a sorcerer, and by rule of local law and to protect from uprising, Simon had installed that sorcerer in the proposed safety of the tower. The tower was a massive stone affair, its base carved with signs of the maiden and reportedly mounded with offerings—to the maiden, not the sorcerer.

Miri had considered, long ago, letting rumors stoke the people of Kirkwall to incite a riot against their king. But she had learned of uprisings in her studies as a child and knew that more would be killed by such tactics than if she did so alone.

"There," Cass said, gesturing toward a path away from the market. "Lodgings will likely be full after the rain and during market, but it'll be our best place to ask."

She nodded, leading Wolf over the winding stone paths and away from the smell of food. The crowd became thinner the farther they rode. Most were on foot or hauling handcarts toward the market square. When they finally reached the lodge, stacked tall and towering above them, Cass glanced at the street before stepping down from his horse and handing her the reins.

His gaze was severe. "Should I be too long, please don't wait." He gave her a smile, in case anyone heard, but Miri understood it was a warning. Apparently, Kirkwall was not as friendly or filled with benefactors who were loyal to the rightful queen.

Miri held tight to the reins, her hand turned so that the gold band on her finger was hidden, and kept her expression bland as she glanced down the street. Kirkwall was dirtier than she remembered, the buildings in desperate need of repair. She was not certain whether Cass was worried about thieves or kingsmen, but the idea of abandoning him to save herself seemed strangely unsuitable. They'd been riding together for weeks—four, had she kept count properly—and in that time, he had somehow seemed to become part of her plot. He wasn't. Cass did not approve of her mission or what it risked. But he was there nonetheless, and she didn't imagine she would be brave enough without him.

Determination had never been her problem, after all. It was the fear that broke her.

The fear that gripped her most was that Lettie was so near—no more than ten days' ride north of their stay in Stormhold. But Miri couldn't get to her sister. Too many kings, too many sorcerers, and too many walls were in her way.

In two months' time, at the end of summer, Miri's sister would be dead. Lettie would never make it through her name day and would never wear the crown of the one true queen.

"Bean," Cass said from beside her.

Miri startled, hand twitching toward her knife. He stared up at her, making no move to rein her in. "Of course," she said, with regard to nothing at all.

His mouth turned down on one side. "There are rooms at a smaller inn down the way. We'll get settled then walk into town before nightfall."

"Of course," Miri said again. *Of course.*

༄

IF THE MARKET at Pirn had been a lord's feast of imported spices, hearty meats, and well-dressed guests, the market at Kirkwall was pottage and sour ale at a back-alley inn. The town was gated and closed off to many traders, so goods were more focused on staple foods, practical cloths, and locally made household necessities. Fortunately, Cass had gathered what Miri needed from the herbalist at Pirn, and thus far, they had not been robbed of those goods. The way Cass stayed near both Miri and his blade, she did not have confidence in the unlikeliness of just such a thing, in which case they would have to choose between fighting for their possessions and being taken into custody for stabbing said thieves.

The idea made Miri a bit sick, because her plans did not have room for too many corrections or for too much to go wrong.

"In and out," Cass told her. "Get what you need, and we'll return to the inn."

Miri nodded, picking up her step to stay with him, not that he'd let go of her. "Clothes," Miri reminded him. "Everything else can wait."

They dodged through a crowd of women trading scarves, keeping tight to the storefronts and stalls and away from the milling men in the center of the streets and the small children with quick little hands. The children were thinner than Miri remembered, and there seemed to be far more scavenging and lurking about.

The smell of fresh bread caught her attention, and when Cass noticed, he passed the woman peddling the baked goods a small coin. In return, she gave him two hard rolls and a toothless grin. A pair of elderly men sat leaning against a building, their eyes covered with black strips of cloth. Miri slowed, her gaze caught on the sand-covered stones beneath them. A mark had been drawn in that sand, the outline of the symbol Miri had seen on the arm of the woman in Pirn.

Gods, she didn't understand how so many still held fealty for a queen who would never return. *After so many years...*

The thought made Miri's stomach go sour, because she was the one speeding through a market in Kirkwall, prepared to kill its king. *For a queen who could never come back.*

A small child darted toward Miri, and she held up a hand, warding him off with a severely pointed finger. Behind her, as swift as a whip, another darted a hand toward her satchel. Miri snatched his wrist, and the boy drew back for a kick, but one quick move, and Miri had him pinned in front of her body between her and the other child. "Boys," she said in a tone that brooked no reply. "I've no quarrel with you." She gave the wrist in her grip a bit more twist. "Yet."

"Yes, m'lady," the boy in her hold squeaked. "Apologies. Truly, we meant no harm."

Cass watched as the first boy blinked up at Miri then turned to run, the soles of his worn boots flashing with impressive speed. Miri let go of the second boy and barked a call at him before he darted away. He turned, still moving but apparently clever enough not to leave his back to her, eyes wide and arms out while he decided which way to go.

She tossed him the roll. "Don't try it again."

His eyes, as green as the sea, shifted between Miri and the bread in his grip before he turned tail to run.

Miri stared after him. "Not even a thank you."

Cass gave Miri a look then awarded a longer one to the few watching from the crowd. It would not have been an unusual scene, but she wasn't meant to draw attention to herself. "My lady," Cass said sternly, taking her by the elbow as he handed her his roll.

"Of course," she said. *Of course.*

They neared a stall selling textiles. Silk and linen were on display as a young woman sat near the street, knitting. Miri felt Cass's grip tighten on her hand and let her gaze roam the street to find the source of his tension. Kingsmen dressed in black cloaks, their signature dark-brown uniforms trimmed in red and adorned with the emblem of the king's guard, roamed the street. Miri tried to look away and not see the bear emblazoned on the chest plates of their armor.

She could feel the sudden remembered pain in her wrist from her mother grabbing it so long ago. Her hand was slick with blood, and she held her too tight to pull away. *You're hurting me,* Miri had wanted to scream. But Miri couldn't say a word.

"Bean," Cass whispered through clenched teeth, suddenly in front of her. His face blocked out all else.

She nodded mutely, swallowing against the memory, the fear, and the feel of a blood-slicked hand. She pulled her fingers from Cass's. "We'll shop for candles first."

Cass watched her for several moments, likely wondering if she was losing her mind. But when she only faced him steadily, he drew her with him into the stall selling tallow and lanterns, touching her gently at the elbow instead of gripping her sweating palm.

It wasn't long before the kingsmen moved on, and in their wake swelled the murmuring of the crowd. The kingsmen were less well liked than the kings of the realm, which was more than a shade of distaste. It did little good toward her cause, though, because the kings and their sorcerers held all the power. Miri complimented the stall owner on her wares, and Cass bought a candle that was entirely unscented and unadorned. She smirked up at him, her humor returned since the pain of the memory had passed, but he seemed to have no idea that his purchase had been an uninspired choice.

As they walked the street toward the clothing stalls, Miri leaned closer to him. "What is your favorite scent, Cass?"

He glanced at her sidelong. "That is a strange question."

"Not the sea, then? The stink of fish and soured ale?" Miri didn't suppose she minded those smells at all, if truth be told, because she was a little bit homesick for Smithsport and more than a lot for Nan and Thom.

He shrugged, glancing down the street. "I don't know. I'm partial to sweet orange, I suppose."

Miri skipped a step to catch his pace. "Oh, I love sweet orange. Nan used to make it special for me."

A flash of color tinted Cass's cheeks, and Miri felt something strange pool in her gut. She pressed her lips together, feeling as if she'd said something wrong.

But she hadn't. The scent had been rare, imported from across the sea. Nan had only made sweet orange soaps for Miri alone.

Cass didn't glance back at her as he turned into the tent that sold clothes in the local style. The material would be similar to that in the king's castle. It was of lesser quality, but she wouldn't need an exact match. No one looked too hard at servers and maids.

She brushed aside the awkwardness she'd felt the moment before, concentrating on finding the garments that would serve her best. There was little to choose from in the color she needed, but a pair of dark pants, two tunics, and an embroidered jacket would give her the material she needed to craft her ruse. When Cass paid, he gave Miri a glance that said they needed to get back to the inn.

The sun was falling low on the horizon, casting the market in a rosy glow. The scent of dinner and mead mixed with the less pleasant aroma of so many bodies and streets damp from weeks of rain, and they wove swiftly through the crowd to find their escape. Miri held tight to her satchel, glancing behind them for would-be thieves, and ran straight into Cass. She stumbled, pressing a hand to his back as she caught herself.

He stared onward, his face pale. Miri followed his gaze.

In the distance, among a milling crowd, stood a tall figure in a plain black cloak. It was a moment before Miri realized where she recognized the face from. She'd only seen it for a moment, in the heat of an attack by the kingsman, with sorcerers near and the forest closer still. *Terric.*

No wonder Cass looked like he had seen a ghost. But Terric was not dead. Cass turned his gaze away from his brother-in-arms.

"Go to him," Miri said. "I can fend for myself."

"No." Cass shook his head once and grabbed Miri by the elbow. "Not here." He rushed her again, and she meant to protest, but Cass shot her a warning glance. His voice was low. "If he needs to get me a message, he will."

The message, Miri thought, was clear. Terric was alive. Cass was not alone. Miri's fool decision had not cost another man his life.

CHAPTER 15

Miri and Cass returned to the small inn just as dusk settled on the streets of Kirkwall. They were greeted by the innkeepers, a middle-aged couple with dark curls and bright-green eyes. The man picked up the last remaining evidence of a card game while his wife spread a cloth over the table. "In the spare of time, you are," she said. "Dinner is coming out, and all guests must be at the table or doomed to go without."

Miri bit her words back while Cass inclined his head politely. "How fortunate," he said. "What can we do to help you?"

The woman hissed at him and waved a hand, ordering both him and Miri to sit and be served. Another two men, young traders, by the looks of them, and a second couple who had been playing cards were ordered to sit as well. Miri settled onto the bench across from the other travelers, and Cass slid his sword and her satchel under the bench beneath them before he took a seat beside her.

"Ah, look at you," the woman across from Miri said. She had long dark hair tied up in braids and long dark fingers that gestured toward the band on Miri's hand. "Newly wed and on the trail together." She gazed longingly at the burly man beside her. "Remember those days, my love?"

The man snorted and took a chug of what was likely not his first mug of ale. "Remember them? Lass, I'm still living them."

She chuckled and gave a swift elbow to his arm, with a bit more force than pure affection would call for, Miri thought. The woman's sharp gaze cut to Cass. "And what of you, young man? Still in the flush of newfound love?"

Cass stared back at her for a moment, his lapse only broken by the innkeeper's wife slipping a mug of cider in front of him.

"Leave the man be, Ginger."

Cass seemed to ease a bit, his chest falling as he reached for the mug, but the woman added, "Clearly, he is. Can't take his eyes off her long enough to even take in a drink."

Laughter erupted around the table. Cass good-naturedly raised his glass to the crowd as Miri was served her own mug of cider. The innkeepers brought out large platters of vegetables, a meat pie, and salted herring covered in a suspiciously colored brown sauce. Miri exchanged a glance with Cass, which only incited the teasing to start again.

She pressed her eyes closed for a moment then took a sip of her cider. It had a bite to it but was not unpleasant, and Miri let the warmth fill her chest and settle in her bones. Terric was alive. She'd found clothes that would work well enough. The second king would soon be dead, and another piece of the kingdom would be returned to its place on the map of the realm. And they could leave that cursed inn.

The innkeeper and his wife settled at the table beside Cass, and the eight of them began the evening meal. It was loud and close but, like the bite of the cider, not altogether unpleasant after weeks in the woods and the rain. She and Cass had settled into quiet routines on the trail and grown used to each other's moods and manners, and it had helped fill the void that leaving her second home with Nan and Thom had carved in her heart.

Thom had trusted Cass and chosen him above the others to send at Miri's side.

As the chatter and meal carried on, Miri fell into a comfortable silence, letting the sounds fade to the background of her thoughts. She'd gone over her plans countless times, and memories of her past held nothing but heartache, so she let her mind wander over the past few weeks and let herself linger on the markets and forests and all that she had seen since she'd left Smithsport and her strange captivity. As a child, she'd seen too much, then she'd been trapped in the house and barns at Thom and Nan's and unable to live at all. It was so peculiar to be free of both situations yet free of nothing at all.

Miri realized quite suddenly that her hand had slipped into Cass's beneath the table. She glanced at him, intensely aware of the contact despite that he'd done the same a dozen times in the market. But that had been to drag her along behind him and keep her safely near. What Miri had done, as unintentional as it was, had been a gesture of comfort, a familiarity she should not be sharing with anyone, let alone her mother's guard—particularly not her mother's guard. Cass didn't look at her, only sat as if listening to the others. His grip was soft within hers. His other hand rested on the mug of cider, which he'd barely touched, the same as his meal.

Gods, he had thought Terric, his brother-in-arms and one of few remaining queensguard, was dead. Miri should have pulled her hand away that very instant, but she couldn't seem to make herself.

"Send him to the seven hells, I say. Kingdom's never been worse off. All he does is sit there in his castle, rubbing oils over his pasty skin while his own people starve."

Miri's attention snapped to the bull-necked man across the table at his mention of the king.

The woman beside him gave him a sharp pinch. "Enough with your fool mouth, Hugh. Talk of treason will make you no friends."

"Aye. And what'll they do? Pike my head at the gate?"

The woman narrowed her gaze on him. "That's exactly what they'll do, and you know it. Kingsmen were out just today, fishing the markets for the same sort of talk. They'd love nothin' more than to make an example out of the likes of you."

He looked at her, expression crestfallen. "What d'you mean, 'the likes of me'?"

She rolled her eyes. "Oh, a pike won't bother you with fear, but a simple word'll send you running." She shook her head, gaze landing on Miri. "I'll tell you what, girl. No matter how big they come, they're all just little boys."

The innkeeper and his wife snorted in laughter, but the two younger men only reached for more food, evidently unconcerned with keeping company in the talk of treason.

Cass drew his hand from Miri's. "I'm afraid my lady and I should retire for the evening. Good company is rare, but we've a long journey ahead of us on the morrow."

Ginger smiled up at him. "We'll be off tomorrow as well. Fancy that. Perhaps we'll see you on the road. Heading north?"

Cass took Miri's elbow as she stood, ostensibly distracted by the task. "Yes, Ironwood, should the grace of the maiden allow it."

The stocky man gestured with his mug. "Ironwood is where we head as well, lad. Let us ride together!" Ale sloshed over the rim of his mug and splattered onto the empty platter before him.

Ginger waved him down. "Look at them, Hugh. They don't have need for the likes of us impeding on their newly wedded bliss."

"There you are with 'the likes of us' again. What exactly are you getting at, woman?"

Cass tightened his grip on Miri's elbow, and she managed to look embarrassed—or at least she hoped the mortification she felt at the idea of travel mates came across as such. She could not be sure she'd pulled it off, because Hugh and Ginger had taken to bantering over *the likes* of Hugh.

Cass grabbed the satchel and the sword he'd stowed beneath the bench and said good evening before talk of traveling together could carry further. But as Miri and Cass made their way to their room, she could hear Ginger reminiscing about the days she and Hugh had been newly met and the things they'd done alone in the woods.

"Seven hells," Cass muttered as he closed the door to their small room behind them.

Miri only nodded, because between the kingsmen, the shock of seeing Terric, and the closeness of the inn, she felt very much like she was dropping through several levels of hell. She sighed and sat heavily onto the bed to unlace her boots. It was going to be an entirely new level of hell figuring out how to escape for the morning's murdering without those two on their heels.

Cass tossed the satchel onto the bed beside Miri and took a seat on the stool as he lit a lantern and a second candle, and she suddenly recalled that she still had work to do.

Miri rubbed a hand over her face. "I don't suppose you've trained in sewing?"

※

CASS HAD NOT TRAINED in sewing, but he was excellent with a knife. By midnight, they'd managed to make a workable costume that fit well beneath her cloak. Before dawn, Miri had tied her long hair into a knot at the base of her neck and covered her head with a scarf. Cass wedged her small sword against the door, and they escaped out the narrow window of their room. Miri had left her mother's locket in the straw mattress inside that room, as much as it pained her, because she needed to be able to leave her current wardrobe behind. They traveled swiftly across the rooftop to a rickety ladder that took them to the street. Dark alleys, still damp with runoff from too much rain, led them through a maze of the city until they could blend with the slew of servants and laborers headed toward the center of the city and the castle grounds.

It felt like an endless journey, but the sky was just lighting red when the castle walls came into view. Miri drew a steadying breath then glanced at Cass. His eyes were already on her, his brow set and his mouth a determined line. She inclined her head, and he responded with a sharp nod.

Miri slipped into the crowd. She walked amid a cluster of black-garbed women whose robes were clean but faded with age. They were not the servants who worked within the castle. Those resided inside its walls. But the group would certainly serve as Miri's way in.

Long shadows were cast across the cobblestones that led to the castle walls, and Miri slipped from among one group to another, carrying baskets and hauling goods until she reached the gates where supplies entered. She loosed the ties of her cloak and let it fall to the ground among the shadows as she hung tight to the stone wall and away from the king's guards who watched the gate. A sudden commotion came from the opposite direction, a cart overturned and a horse's cutting scream.

Miri darted through the gate with several other women, keeping her stride as even as she could manage against the desire to run. She did not look behind her or even raise her face. She was a servant, a maid, no one of consequence to the watching guard.

She knew she was being ridiculous. Not a single kingsman would be alert to her there. No one could reach the king from that part of the castle. A lone woman could not possibly be a threat to them. They would be watching for men of the queensguard, for loyalists, but not for a maid. Miri drew another breath.

"Simon is far from the vainest," Miri could remember one of the ladies saying when she'd only been a child. Simon was not then a king, only a lord, yet to be etched on Miri's list as one of seven murderous kings. Vainest or not, Simon had been, apparently, quite concerned about his virility. And that information had not come from a single source alone.

Miri's mother had held no compunction with regard to explaining the faults of men to her daughters. Her acquaintances had relayed information quite the same. But neither was the source of the particular information that Miri planned to use. That had come from Lettie's giggling ladies-in-waiting. Miri would not normally risk her neck over rumors spread by girls, but her time in Smithsport had proven valuable for information as well. Thom had taken note of any shipments destined for the kings, so that he might be aware of the kingsmen's movements ahead of time to keep Miri hidden away.

She felt a pang of loss at the idea of him and the month she'd been apart from Nan and Thom both. Then she felt a strange sort of emotion when she realized Thom's information on the deliveries had likely come through Cass. There were perks to being the harbormaster's spy, after all.

Miri snuck through the castle corridors, her head bowed in the posture of a maid, one hand wrapped about the scratchy rope of a bucket handle, the other holding a dirty rag. She had studied each of the castles in hand-scratched maps she'd made when devising her plans, alone in her room at Nan's, a single candle lighting her work. But actually being there was different. It was real. The hard lines she'd drawn as walls had sometimes been slightly wrong, and the short, sharp hatch work of doors faded with ink, always open, were sometimes blocked by man or construct or wrong by a few lengths. She knew the layout, though, and which direction would get her where she needed to be. No one paid her mind, just as she'd expected, and the corridors were filled with the early-morning busywork that the upkeep of the castle required.

Eventually, the sweat on her palms dried, and her racing heart gave way to a steadier beat. She found the rooms where the king's ointments and potions were stocked.

Two guards moved through the doorway, and Miri dropped

to her knees, sloshing water over the rim of the wooden bucket and onto the stone-tiled floor. They did not even glance at her, but she kept her head low, her knuckles white at the pressure with which she brushed the floor.

It was a long while before the patterns of movement through the room became apparent and longer still before she managed to pick the lock. Once inside, though, she worked quickly, and she found each vial of the black glass shipped from a sandy isle far away, the tonic Lettie's maids had tittered so brutally on about. They had not been wrong. Thom's notes had not been wrong. Simon was stocked with more of those vials than a man needed water.

The lock was what saved her, because Miri knew the tonic had been tested the day it arrived. The shipments could not be tampered with without being discovered by the king's taster, but the mixture was too valuable to the king and taken too often to test every one, every time.

As Miri stared at the overly full shelf, she knew Lettie's maids had not been exaggerating. The worse Simon began to feel, the more he would take. It would work.

Miri wiped her palms on the fabric of her makeshift uniform then shook them out to release the tension that made her fingers tremble. She had never liked the idea of poisons, but weapons would draw attention that she wasn't ready to attract. She carefully unstoppered each vial and tilted a single drop into each of the tall, narrow containers, thanking the gods that they'd been sealed with wax. The oil inside was not particularly costly or particularly rare. It was only that Simon believed the single place to source it was from a sole island across the unnamed sea and his witch-worker of a supplier the only one who could trade those locals for it. Simon was a fool, just like the others.

With her work done, Miri turned, her empty containers of poison tucked into her inner layer of clothes. She dipped her hands into the bucket, carefully washing each clean, and meticulously brushed beneath each nail. She dried her hands on the outer clothes, pressed her ear to the door, and listened for the pattern of footsteps so she might make her escape.

When the room outside was quiet, Miri came cautiously through the door, closed it behind her, and set the bucket on the stone floor as if she meant to work. Two more guards came past and found Miri on her knees, scrubbing the floor with the single determination of someone who had nothing else in the world. The moment they were gone again, she went back to the lock and worked the mechanisms back into place.

She did not hear the approach of the kingsman, only felt his sword on her shoulder and heard his whispered words.

"Trying to pick a lock, girl?"

CHAPTER 16

Cass stood in the shadow of Kirkwall Castle, completely helpless to aid Miri in any way. She'd been right, but that did not make it any easier to let her go alone.

He'd been watching her for years. He knew her skill with a blade, the way she could land a solid kick, and exactly how clever she was with maneuvering through tight spaces and around heavily laid rules. But the past weeks on the trail, he'd seen another side of Miri—hesitation, doubt, and the distant look that came over her when she remembered what she'd lost.

Miri was too good to be a killer. Her heart was perilously kind. He'd watched her stop to hand the last of their supplies over to the sick and the poor and noticed how she'd seen their suffering for what it was. Miri's gaze had not skirted that pain but took it in with steady determination and well more than her share of evident guilt.

She thought it her fault, all of it, that it was somehow her responsibility to repair the damage done by seven kings who had done their level best to put themselves before the realm and had murdered its one true queen.

That was why Miri held Cass's concern—because that heart

could be her downfall. Not because of anything else, he was certain.

Cass jumped when a hand rested on his shoulder, and he spun before the man had a chance to move fully away. Terric's grin was slow, maybe the only slow thing about him, and it said all that he did not speak aloud. *Nearly got you,* Cass could almost hear.

In fact, he had. Cass knew better than to let himself get distracted. It was the very reason the men of the queensguard were not meant to court until their service had ended.

Terric's brow drew together. "Gods, brother, what's with the face?"

Cass shook his head, utterly disturbed that the thought of courting had even risen. He stepped forward, grabbing the hand of his brother-in-arms, and tugged him closer with a relieved sigh. "Thank the maiden you're well."

Terric slapped his free hand hard on Cass's shoulder and held him tight in his grip. "You're never alone." His voice was low, his words a vow, and Cass thought he'd never heard anything more welcome. Terric used the grip to pull Cass even nearer. "Does this seem like a good idea?"

Cass frowned. "It was obviously not mine. She's got a will of iron."

Terric chuckled. "She is her mother's daughter. I'll give you that."

Cass glanced toward the street. He kept his voice low as they let go of their grip and he asked, "How goes the strategy?"

"Support is steady. As you've likely seen here, conditions have become worse for most. Those who remember *before* will rise. But we build back support as we speak."

The words were purposefully vague, but Cass understood. Nearly all who'd lived through the Lion Queen's reign would relish the chance to have prosperity back. They would follow the true queen the moment they were given the chance. But the queensguard had been unable to act before. The sorcerers had ensured as much.

Timing would be critical. Miri had been hidden for years because the sorcerers would have come for her the moment they found out she was alive. Or they would have used Lettie to draw her out. And Cass knew Miri. She would be caught in that trap all too easily. It was the fault of honor and duty and those who upheld all they believed was right. If, while in search of support, the queensguard let Miri get found out or let slip to the wrong person that a second daughter of the queen lived, they would only hasten the death of both daughters. The last of the true bloodline would be lost.

They had tried before and failed. The queensguard was betting all on their last chance. They believed in Miri—not because she'd actually managed to kill a king—though she had—but because they'd had faith in her all along and in the plans in place to restore her line. They were queensguard. Their duty was to protect her. And she would need them now more than ever.

"Should she make it out," Terric said, "you'll have friends in Ironwood Forest."

Cass looked his brother-in-arms straight in the eyes, letting Terric see the promise in his gaze and how much his brother's vow meant. "I hope to see you again," Cass said. "By the grace of the maiden."

"By the will of the gods," Terric said.

As he turned to go, the clang of a massive steeple bell rang through the streets, shuddering against Cass's bones. When Terric's gaze snapped to Cass, he'd gone as pale as snow at the sound. The bells echoed into the peal of half a dozen more, the alarm spreading in a series of bells across the castle grounds.

The princess had been found. The kingsmen were on alert.

※

CASS RAN through the street with Terric hard on his heels. He was not certain which way Miri might have gone when she found trouble and could only follow the sound of the bells. If they rang still, then surely that meant she was not in their hands and had a chance of escape.

His heart beat so strongly that he wanted to clutch at his chest, but the fear only pushed him harder. His booted feet crossed the cobblestone of the path that led to the gate, and Cass watched with dread as the kingsmen slammed it shut. The metal landed with a hollow clang, the sharp ringing of the bells still echoing off the stone.

At their approach, the kingsmen took note of Cass and Terric, their speed among the chaos drawing attention they didn't need. Cass moved his hand away from his sword belt, forcing his racing pulse to slow. He needed to think. They'd laid plans for so many outcomes, but from outside the gate, he could not know where Miri truly was, only where the kingsmen were.

Two smaller bells rang in quick succession on the north side of the castle, followed by the muffled shouts of running men. Cass let his gaze meet Terric's, and they each gave a nod without acknowledgment that it might be the last time they saw one another. Then Terric was gone, and Cass was on the move, each intent on foiling the kingsmen where they could.

Calls of "What's happened?" echoed quietly among the black-garbed laborers. Their voices were no more than whispers to avoid notice from the kingsmen.

Cass made his way toward the sound of the bells, hooking the edge of a basket to spill fruit so that it rolled over the stones. He kept moving, as if he'd been entirely unaware of the commotion behind him as several black-clad figures moved to pick up the mess. His palm itched for a sword hilt, the feel of his dagger handle, or for any sort of action. But that was not his duty yet.

He slipped closer to the wall, passing two half-helmed kingsmen close in conversation, their words clipped. He heard "Stabbed him in the thigh," then "Broke his jaw." Miri had been smart. She'd left her assailant so that he couldn't chase her. And no doubt the jaw had not been an accident, either, not when the man's words would have her found out faster. But something else must have gone wrong, because Miri had not killed him. She'd not left him unable to sound the alarm. Maybe more guards had turned up, or worse, someone who might be able to identify her in detail or might have recognized her for who she truly was.

Cass swerved near two more kingsmen as they ran past and heard "Covered in blood. Short. Female. A maid."

There it was. They thought her still dressed in black. It would give her the chance to escape, if she could.

Cass moved faster, toward the sound of the bells, and felt his hope drop to the pit of his stomach at the sight of a mass of horses approaching at speed. It was a dozen kingsmen, swords drawn, and between them, as if the demon needed protection, a sorcerer dressed in the long black robes for which they were known. The robes hid their bodies, scarred from the drawing of blood. They had been paid for by the deaths of Cass's brothers and were rich fabric trimmed with gold.

As the horses neared, the gates opened wide, and Cass spotted the familiar figure of Terric, swift on his feet and somehow already dressed in kingsman garb, as he edged toward the entrance. Gods, he meant to slip inside. Cass drew one long breath before he could change his mind then pulled the sword from his belt, shouted an obscenity about the king's men, and waved the blade toward the sky.

The kingsmen only gave him the briefest glance, but that was all Cass would need. The group on horseback didn't give chase, but three on foot certainly did. Cass turned to run, leaped toward an alley he hoped was not a dead end, and prayed his brother-in-arms had made it inside.

CHAPTER 17

Cass would much rather have dispatched the three kingsmen and hidden their bodies in a dark, unfindable place instead of evade them. But Miri had, as near as he could tell, only stabbed a single kingsman before she ran away. The castle guard was on alert, but there was no reason for them to think it was anything other than a rogue attack. It was just a single maid who'd had it out with a guard. If he killed any more, they would know the truth, and Miri's plans would all be spoiled.

He leapt to a perch on a rooftop, high enough to see over the castle wall. Below him, in the courtyard, stood two dozen black-clad figures around the man in the sorcerer's robe. The kingsmen were some of the best-trained men in the lands. Coin was scarce, and though most didn't favor the kings, the guard was a place of status that paid well enough to gather skilled men. But that did not mean the men of Kirkwall were as capable as those at Stormskeep. They housed a single sorcerer and an ineffectual king and lacked the stores to hold much sway among the six other lords who'd taken the realm. Kirkwall was the least powerful. Stormskeep had surpassed it not due to its own king but because of the port. And Blackstone was constantly on the edge of rebellion.

If Miri couldn't execute her plans at Kirkwall, she would succeed nowhere else in the realm, particularly not if they realized who she was.

As servants were rounded up in the courtyard, Cass scanned the street, searching for a figure moving swiftly away. He searched for the color of her hair, the set of her shoulders, and the way she moved, that familiar surety in her step, the way she held her head high with her gaze straight.

Cass drew a sharp breath at the sight of her long, loose brown tresses, those he'd held in his hands. She'd peeled the outer layer of her clothing away to reveal the soft linen in brown and green, but she held something wadded in her arm, balled just right so that it helped cover what might have been a stain. He hoped it was not her blood.

She strode down the street, along the castle wall where, on the other side, stood the sorcerer and so many kingsmen. Cass felt sick at the nearness of that sorcerer and the memory of Miri's face only weeks before, when they'd crossed paths with one in Pirn. He edged closer, searching for any sign of distress, but Miri only crossed behind a row of carts, making her way toward the opposite side of the street.

He crept backward, shuffling carefully over poorly kept thatch and onto another rooftop, then scurried down to run after her again. He realized, too late, that she meant to go back to the inn.

Kingsmen trailed after her, three silver half helms glinting in the late-day sun, and Cass let slip a whispered curse.

His feet moved swiftly over stone, following as the kingsmen drew their swords. The far one gestured to his side, in the same area where Miri's wadded bundle poorly concealed a stain of blood. They would know it was her.

They would be able to identify her the moment she was brought back to the other guard. Or worse, they would not question her at all. They'd no idea she was a princess and thought her a lowly maid.

Cass leaned against a building, glancing down at his hand as if distracted, and cut a sharp whistle. The kingsmen's glares were swift, but Miri had turned too. She had looked backward and saw them advancing.

Cass wanted to face the soldiers and incite them instead to give chase to him. But he knew they would not. They'd seen the blood on Miri's side. It was only by the grace of the maiden that they'd not already called an alarm.

She was only a maid. They thought they could take her. But Myrina of Stormskeep was no maid. She hadn't run at his warning call. Instead, she'd turned and moved back toward the soldiers in their momentary distraction. A scarf was suddenly over her face, a blade in her hand.

Cass moved, too, but the kingsmen had drawn up on her. They hadn't realized they'd walked into a trap.

Don't kill them, Cass wanted to call, but he held his tongue and instead drove the hilt of his sword down hard on the base of a kingsman's neck. He staggered forward, and Cass followed, shoving the man to the ground.

Miri crouched low, her dagger hand ready. The guard muttered a curse and reached for her, as if to knock the weapon away. Miri's other hand slammed into his chin, knocking his head back, and she reset and followed with a solid blow to the nose.

Cass hit the back of the third guard's knee an instant before his forearm was pressed against the kingsman's neck. There was a short, grunting shuffle as the first two rose and were batted down again. Miri produced a rope from somewhere and tossed it to Cass. He looped it around one guard's wrists as she swung a brutal kick into the side of another's head. She yanked off her belt, threw it at Cass, and shoved a sword away from the third guard with her foot.

Cass made quick work of the second's wrists as Miri pulled a vial from her waist.

He caught her gaze and gave her a look.

"It's not permanent."

That was all she said before she pressed a soaked cloth over their noses. Cass's eyes watered against the fumes, but he dragged the bodies behind a wall of crates. Gods, they'd been in an open alley, in plain view. It was beyond foolish.

Miri tossed the cloak into a bin at the opposite wall of the alley then checked the end of the street. No one had seemed to notice. Or possibly a hundred kingsmen were on their way.

They moved a few crates to block the pile of men, then Miri glanced at Cass. *What do we do?* her look seemed to say.

"We get through the outer gates. Now."

※

"WE HAVE TO GO," Cass hissed. He'd argued against going back to the inn, but Miri had threatened him with blood. She was impossible and unbearable, and he would not stand for watching her be killed. "The moment they realize their rogue maid is not inside the castle walls—" It would be too late. They would all be done for.

Miri jerked her shift from inside the mattress, glaring up at him. "I know. They'll close the main gate."

He glared at the garment in her fisted hand, remembering all the times she'd reached for her hem. "You have to tell me, Miri. If you're caught, if you end up dead—" He bit down the words but didn't look away. "There is a sorcerer within these city walls. If we lose you, nothing will stop the remaining queensguard from moving on the kings." They would attempt a rescue of Lettie and give everything in a final attempt.

He could see Miri understood. She knew it meant they would all die.

"I need to know," he said quietly. "I need you to tell me."

Miri's hands shook. They did not have time for this and needed to escape. The kingsmen had seen Cass. They would be searching for a maid Miri's size and possibly a man of Cass's.

He realized his hands were on Miri's, and he drew back, glaring at the straw mattress.

She shifted nearer and said, her words no more than a whisper, "Why can you not even look at me?" There was hurt in her tone and concern that she'd somehow done everything wrong.

But Cass's answer slipped angrily free before he could rein it in. "Because I like looking at you." Expression hard, he forced himself to face her. "And that's something I shouldn't."

Miri did not move. Her entire being had gone terribly still. Her voice was all air when she asked, "Shouldn't *do* or shouldn't *like?*"

Cass's fingers curled into fists. "Either." He snapped the fists open. "Both." He turned, moving to peer out the window. He hated that he'd said it and that he'd had to move away.

Behind him, Miri said, "I like looking at you too."

Cass felt his shoulders drop. *Of all the things she might have said.* "That only makes it worse."

Miri moved closer. "I've never told. Not anyone."

When Cass turned, her gaze was cast down. He let it stay there and only stood before her, inches separating them as Miri breathed her confession.

"Mother had been reading, and I had fallen asleep. She'd left me there, though I should have been in my rooms, like Lettie. When I woke, Henry was already covered in blood. He was saying something, grabbing at her. His hands were so tight. I remember his knuckles going white, snowdrop pale in the midst of all that rose-red blood. I didn't even listen. I couldn't even hear. I only stared."

Miri's arms wrapped around her middle, and Cass could almost feel the heat of Henry's warning.

"The doors crashed open, and men ran in. They were dressed like the guard, but they were not bloodsworn. They didn't—" She shook her head. "I didn't recognize a single one. Henry had his sword out. I'd not even seen him draw it. It must have been in his hand already, I thought, but his hands had been on my mother. She was standing, too, then, a dagger in each fist. The silver ones with the lion paws that wrapped around the cross guard. Her favorites. The men rushed her and Henry. And those daggers sank through the men's chests. They didn't... no one said a single word. Just stabbed. Fought. Fell."

Miri was silent for a moment, as if remembering and reliving the nightmare she'd faced as a child. He remembered, too, his own nightmare of the wet sounds of blade entering flesh, the muffled grunts, and heavy bodies as the king's men and queensguard fell.

"'Kill her,'" Miri said abruptly, her gaze finally raising to Cass's. "That was what the head of those guards said when he finally spoke. He pointed at me and said, 'Kill her,' to his men." Miri swallowed. "And my mother went very still. Her daggers came to her side, and she adjusted her grip. My limbs were frozen. It was like I couldn't act. All I could do was watch. She stepped forward one pace, Henry at her side. She meant to rush the head of that guard. I could feel it. She was going to stab him for what he'd said. Because of me."

Cass didn't speak. He did not argue with the idea she'd had as a child. He let Miri go on and let her get it out. It was too late for anything else.

"The men smelled like smoke. The room tasted like wet ash. I didn't understand what was happening. I didn't help at all. Henry's sword swung, but Momma stumbled back. I can still hear the clatter of her daggers on the tile floor. I can still smell... well, I didn't know it then, but it was burning flesh and treated wood. It was the other levels the sorcerer had set aflame." Miri drew a breath, her eyes closing to the memories. "I stared down at her. My mother was sprawled half across the floor and half over the chaise where she'd read. Where I had slept. Blood as dark as pitch ran from her nose. As Henry fought the last of the men, I fell to my knees before her, palms pressing her shoulder and chest. 'Momma,' I said. That was all. She didn't let me finish. She seized in pain, her eyes going wide, then she came back, found my face, and took hold of my hand. Her locket was pressed to my palm. She wrapped my fingers around it until I held it firm, then she grabbed my wrist."

"'Henry,' she whispered, but her words were followed with blood. So much of it. So dark. I knew what color it should be. It was red on her daggers. Red on her hands." Miri's fingers trembled, and she wrapped them into her ribs harder, tight enough that Cass could see the strain. "'You know what to do,' she told Henry, but I didn't look. I knew what Henry would do. What he always did when she gave him an order. He would nod and do as she asked. I heard Lettie then, her screams tearing through the halls like the roar of a lion."

They had not been Lettie's screams, but Cass didn't interrupt. Lettie had already been taken captive. The sorcerers had gone after her first. The true heir was held as ransom, should their plans go awry. She was last true queen and the kings' only recourse to hold sway over the sorcerers.

Miri swallowed again, pale and looking more than a little sick. "Her hands were wrapped so tight around my wrists. Her knuckles were white, and I could only think of Henry's. How they'd just been the same. How even he had shown fear." Miri shook her head. "I'd never seen them scared. Either of them. And there, on my wrists, were my mother's bone-white hands. Covered in blood. Just like Henry's." Miri pressed her lips together. "She was holding so tight that I wanted to pull away. I tried to fight her, Cass. As she lay there dying, I fought to get away."

A wave of emotion washed over her face, but Miri soldiered on. "'Henry will take you now, my little bean. He'll get you to safety.' She held me tighter, though. She wouldn't let me escape.

I wanted to scream that she was hurting me. I wanted to scream like Lettie. To roar and kick and fight. But all I could do was let her hold me there. She jerked me closer, forcing me to look into her eyes. They were so black. So huge and dark, and her nose spilled blood like tar."

"'You will come back, Myrina of Stormskeep. You will earn your name. I command your vow that you will end the traitor for good. Only a true Lion will hold the throne.'" A tear tracked down Miri's cheek, but she didn't wipe it away. She didn't even seem aware it was there. "'Swear to me, Myrina. Swear you will do this, by our own blood.'"

Miri's voice cracked, and Cass wasn't certain whether it was her emotion or an echo of the command of a dying queen.

Cass knew what happened next. The plans had already been in place. He'd gotten the information he needed and understood how the sorcerers' work was done. But Miri went on. "She coughed, dark blood spattering on the bright red of the other. She was drowning. Choking on her own blood as it boiled within her. 'Vow,' she ordered. And I did. I nodded, just to get away. Just to make her let go." Miri shook her head in disgust, at herself, it seemed, and the helpless child she'd been. "She died. Right there in front of me. And all I'd wanted to do was run. When I realized she was gone, when her eyes went blank and her muscles no longer taut, I screamed. After all the things I could have said and didn't, my voice came back. Henry grabbed me. He jerked my mother's dead hands from my wrists, shoved a cloth in my mouth, wrapped his arms about my ribs, and tore me away from her. He ran, and my body flailed, fighting and kicking as he went."

"The girl had already burnt." Miri's tone had changed, somehow steady and still. It had gone someplace that felt darker. "They must have brought her up from another level. Henry stood me on my feet and stripped me down to my shift, right there in the corridor. I watched as they put my gown on the body. I'm not sure I understood what I was seeing, if I was seeing anything at all. I certainly hadn't understood that they were going to burn my mother. But of course, they had to because of her blood. My hands were tight in fists, my arms rigid. My mouth tasted of blood. Henry didn't bother dressing me, only wrapped a drape around me and tossed me over his shoulder. He ran through the secret passageways—through tunnels that should have been safe."

They had not been safe. That much, Cass knew. Henry had been killed in their escape. The sorcerers had known secrets that had belonged only to bloodsworn.

Miri seemed to become aware of Cass and recall she was speaking of a man he knew and had been like a father. "He didn't make it out," Miri said. "Two other guards took hold of me, tossed me into a crate, and carted me to the river."

There, she stopped and looked as if she might truly retch. Cass had learned the story of her arrival and how many close calls she'd shaved through in the hands of his brothers. She'd arrived at the mouth of the river with two dead men steering the boat. Their corpses lay sprawled over the floor of the small vessel, no more than a rowboat, one draped bleeding over her crate. She'd been trapped by the weight of him, unable to remove the lid. The vessel slammed into a piling, pressed on the current, and had overturned into the sea. Miri's crate began to sink to the bottom, and Thom's men had barely saved her in time. She'd been dragged from the smashed coffin choking on water and blood, blistered from sorcerer's fire and battered and bruised.

They had rushed her to Nan. No one had thought she would live.

She had escaped Stormskeep to the screams of everyone she loved. It had probably felt like no escape at all. She'd refused to speak for a very long time, but the girl that was Miri did not die. Cass understood that it had not been lack of want. It had been the vow.

He also understood that the Lion Queen had known who her

betrayer was. As the blood had boiled from within her, she would have known. She had not asked Miri for the vow for no reason. She had understood that the sorcerers had not done it on their own. Someone else had let them in. Someone had given the sorcerers the Lion Queen's blood.

CHAPTER 18

Cass should have never told Miri how he felt. It was a weakness, one that would have had him thrown out of the guard. He was bloodsworn to the queen—a queen who was dead at the sorcerers' hands.

He pressed his heels into his horse's flanks as they rode through the forest, kicking the beast faster between a break in the trees. They'd barely escaped Kirkwall with their lives, and until he had Miri safely inside the boundaries of Ironwood, he would not count her out of harm's way.

Miri's confession regarding her mother made his duty infinitely more complicated, and he wished he'd had time to leave a message for Terric. Someone on the inside, close enough to have taken her blood, had betrayed their queen. He couldn't imagine how the queensguard would manage the sorcerers if they held a queen's blood—not that they'd been able to conquer them yet—or how to discover who had betrayed the queen. Blood magic was not a subject Cass had studied. No one aside from the sorcerers had been allowed knowledge of the dark arts, by order of the oldest laws.

He could only hope they didn't have Miri's blood and that it was merely the presence of the queen's inside of her—the connection of mother and daughter—or the nearness of Miri's exposure to that dark magic while soaked in her mother's blood that had caused her reaction to the sorcerer's presence in Pirn. She had nearly frozen, her eyes had gone misty and far away, and only distance from the sorcerer had made her recover.

If Miri could not function in proximity to a sorcerer, she would not have a single chance of setting foot near their home at Stormskeep. There, sorcerers were everywhere. Like the hungry wolves of Blackstone's forests.

For Miri's part, she'd been quiet, barely a word spoken since the flood of memories she'd shared at the inn. Cass understood why she'd held it so near. He understood, too, that what drove her was not bloodlust or the need for revenge. It was the vow—a promise made.

Miri was no fool. She knew the lives she risked outside of even her own. The sorcerers were beholden to the kings because magic required blood—life. Had the sacrifices been made on the streets, they would have been called murders, but under the protection of the crown, the killings were deemed necessity in their duty to the throne and to law.

Their relationship to the queen was governed by much older laws, bindings that protected the realm. The Lion Queen had been more than sparing in her use of the sorcerers, and because of it, they had turned on her. They had yearned to be set free, and with the lords who desired the throne, they found their way. That left the queensguard figuring out which of those kings held the blood of the Lion Queen, which had control of the sorcerers in a way the others did not.

Blood was power, and by the way Miri reacted to the sorcerers, they clearly held at least some power over her. He had to find out who was the betrayer. He had to be sure. The Lion Queen's blood had to be recovered and destroyed.

Cass was no betting man, but should he be forced to guess, it would be Nicholas, the self-named king of Stormskeep, who held the key. He, above all others, seemed to be at the helm of the treachery. And in Miri's plans, Nicholas would be the last to die, which meant she suspected him too. But Nicholas was locked in a tower, surrounded by magic and kingsmen.

"Cass." Miri's voice was a low hiss, her fingers tight on the reins.

He broke out of his ruminations to take in her expression of evident concern. She nodded toward the ground, where the tracks of three horses, two carrying a burden, marked the soft earth. They were fresh.

The horses slowed as Cass considered which route to take. They could risk meeting strangers in the wood or risk the less passable ground.

"We'll head west," he suggested. "Just off the trail that borders the ravine."

Miri nodded, but when she began to turn her horse, both she and Cass stopped cold. A shout came from the distance, and as they watched, above the trees rose a pillar of smoke. Kingsmen.

Cass met Miri's hard gaze. "It's too damp. They'll see our tracks," he said. "Follow the trail, and we'll split off over rock or water as soon as we can."

Miri kicked her horse into a run without further instruction or a single response. She knew what would happen if they were caught and how lucky she truly was that they had escaped at all.

They rode at speed through the thickening trees, keeping their horses over the previous hoofprints to confuse the trail. They would need to find a clean escape. The kingsmen were far from poor at tracking, especially when they'd been given to hunting down sympathizers at every turn. The sun was falling low in the sky, and if they could only cross onto rocky ground before nightfall, they might have a chance.

"Ho!" A voice called from the trees, just before a burly man in a short cloak stepped into their path.

Miri shifted her shoulders, but whether she meant to go for her dagger or ride the man down, Cass couldn't say. But she drew up short, her face flashing in some indiscernible emotion as she glanced back at Cass.

"It's you!" The man's arms went wide, and he gave a deep and barking laugh. "Well met, young friends." It was Hugh, the trader from the inn.

Miri slowed her horse to a broken stop as Cass drew up beside her. "Well met." She'd managed to sound as if the greeting was light and friendly, as if she and Cass had been on a playful run. But her gaze flicked to the trees, searching.

Hugh noticed. "Just out for a hunt," he said, gesturing with a thumb over his shoulder. "Ginger's got me gathering roots while she tends to the horses. Boss of a woman, she is." His arms came to his waist as he smiled. "But don't I love her."

Hugh leaned to glance beyond Miri and Cass then straightened. "So do tell me, lad, how, at a pace like that, we've managed to get ahead of you."

Miri's gaze hit Cass, and Hugh chuckled, apparently mistaking the exchange. "Oh, but I do forget." He waved a hand. "Forgive me, lass. I mean no insult. Ginger is always riding me for speaking the wrong thing." He stepped closer, as if they'd moved to friendly conversation, though Miri and Cass had barely said a word. "Come, join us for supper. Let me make it up to you."

Miri cleared her throat. "We appreciate that, Hugh, but we—"

"No," Hugh said, "I know you're newly wed and require your privacy, but Ginger will skin me alive if she finds out I came across you and let you go." He nodded. "Absolutely. I insist."

Miri glanced again at Cass, who had bitten down at least three responses. The kingsmen were looking for a group of two: a man and a maid. They would not be as obvious a target in a group, but they would be risking Ginger and Hugh, should it come to a fight. Miri seemed to recognize the reasoning in his answering gaze. Her eyes seemed to remind Cass that the fires behind them could happen to anyone in the woods, not just those who aided criminals.

"We don't want to trouble you," Miri said quietly, but the words were a concession. She'd decided to give in to Hugh and face the kingsmen should they come.

※

Hugh led Cass and Miri to their camp and an enthusiastic welcome from Ginger. She took the horses and shooed the guests off to a small stream nearby to wash for dinner.

"I'll throw on extra fish. It's no trouble at all," she promised at Miri's protestations, and soon enough, Cass and Miri were knelt beside the water, a shallow trickle that had swelled to something usable with the aid of the recent rains.

"We can leave now on foot," Cass offered.

Miri frowned at him. "The more we run, the more others will suffer in our place."

"Others will suffer regardless."

Cass's tone was hard, and he regretted it the moment he saw the recognition on Miri's face. She'd been sheltered from much of the goings on in the kingdom by Nan and Thom. The news she did receive had been carefully filtered of details like torture for sport. Miri had seen enough of the kingsmen to know the truth of the matter, and she'd been raised by a woman who laid bare the faults of men, but she'd not realized the scope of the kingsmen's exploits and the freedom they'd been given by their lords.

"So we should run?"

Miri's words were soft, her fingers hidden in the folds of her cloak. Cass shook his head. "It wouldn't matter. We bring no more risk to Hugh and Ginger than they are risking alone." In fact, the four together held better odds, as the kingsmen preferred to cull the weak from the herd and catch stragglers alone and unaware. "Besides," Cass said, "Hugh's already spoken highly of treason."

Miri smiled, but the tension didn't leave her eyes. "There is quite a difference between talk over drinks and facing down an armed man." Miri's gaze lingered on Cass, and he forced himself to look away.

It was plain that neither had forgotten their earlier words. Every time they looked at one another, it held the reminder that they should not, and it was only made worse because they'd owned to knowing it was wrong. But Miri had also given him trust. She'd shared the details of her mother's murder, finally, and the secret those details held was far worse than he suspected. There was little left to hide from or to protect. One king was dead, and the second would soon follow. By the end of summer, it would be the rest, or it would be Miri and Cass. If it was the latter, the hopes of the remaining queensguard would die with them.

Miri rinsed her hands in the stream and shook the cool water free before patting her palms on her cloak. She stood, spinning the gold band on her finger while she waited, and Cass hastily splashed water over his face and arms.

They returned to the campsite to find Hugh and Ginger setting up a second tent. Hugh smiled, too broad for any good to come of it, and Ginger elbowed him hard in the ribs.

"Privacy," she said proudly. "I told Hugh we'd not be having you feeling uncomfortable at our expense, and we had an old one in the pack we've been planning to trade at Stormhold. I am nothing if not a good host." Ginger brushed her palms together, as if the matter were entirely settled, and pointed Miri and Cass toward the fire.

Cass wondered if the couple had heard the bells at Kirkwall. Surely, they'd not been far enough away by then to be out of earshot. But if they'd been troubled by the idea of kingsmen on the hunt, they did not appear concerned enough to forgo a fire and risk drawing them in.

Miri settled onto the small rug on the ground, leaving room for Cass at her side. Had he thought their constant nearness could be no more difficult than being alone with Miri had, he was wrong. It seemed Hugh and Ginger would be forcing them even closer than before, newly wed as they were. Cass and Miri would eat with the couple, at least, and spend a single night at most. Then by dawn, they would ride from the trail and into the deeper forest.

Cass had sworn a vow. He would uphold it, even if it cost him everything.

CHAPTER 19

Miri woke in the hours before dawn to the warm darkness of a small, tattered tent. She'd laughed with Hugh and Ginger, eaten far too much salted fish, and had a bit of a headache from the smoke of a damp wood fire. She was tangled inside two thin blankets, unsure where one ended and the other began. Once Ginger had forced both Miri and Cass inside, her pretend husband had quietly situated himself lying opposite her and facing the fabric of the tent. Miri had removed her boots in the night, and as she lay very still, she felt the warmth of Cass's palm against her bare ankle as he slept. He would be mortified, and she couldn't make up her mind whether to attempt sliding her foot away and risk waking him or to leave it there and risk enjoying it. She had never had a man's hand on her ankle. It was very unlike holding his hand.

She'd just decided to slip it away when she heard the sound of approaching hoofbeats. Cass's hand tightened on her flesh, the pad of his thumb pressing into the back of her leg. There was a moment of stillness as they listened, then Cass's hand slid from her skin before a rustle of fabric and the sound of steel indicated he'd readied his sword. It was more of a knife-fight situation, by her judgment, but only because she had every intention of forcing the kingsmen down from their horses. Because she was sure it was kingsmen who were coming. No one else would ride up on a camp in the night.

Miri didn't bother with her boots. She would rather be caught barefooted than half-laced into either one.

The sound of the galloping horses drew nearer, then the tent was ripped from the ground. The night was dark, but the tent had been darker, and Miri's eyes adjusted quickly. A shadowed form towered over them. It was the outline of a man on a giant beast. The man's half helm glinted in the moonlight, and Miri had the realization at the sight of the emblem that she very much felt as if she were being pinned by the threat of a wild bear.

Cass was on his feet, his sword low and his movements disoriented.

"Drop it," the kingsman said.

Cass tossed the short sword to the ground, and Miri's mouth tightened as she fought a smile when she saw that it had been hers. The sword had never been his intended weapon at all—he'd held it only as a distraction. Miri stumbled to her feet, untangling her limbs from the warmth of her blankets.

Across the camp rose a shout and a grumble as Hugh shared words with another kingsman. Three sat on horseback near the fire, and two more waited near the trees.

"Aye," Hugh muttered, stomping closer to Miri and Cass. "I heard ye the first time. We're going."

The kingsmen had them corralled in their group of four. Miri had a dagger in the sheath at her hip, and two more waited beneath the blankets at her feet.

"What do you want with us?" Hugh growled. Ginger gave him a swift elbow to the ribs, and he flinched. "Woman, they dragged us out of our beds before dawn. It's my right to ask why."

"Search them," the kingsman ordered.

Another dropped from his horse and stuck a torch into the

embers of the campfire. As it flared to life, each had their first glimpses of the others. The torch passed in front of Ginger. Her skin was too dark and her limbs too long for her to be the maid. Hugh's broad, muscled torso was only covered by a thin shirt, and they were clearly not the pair they were after.

The guard slowed on Cass, but Miri could see the kingsman was not one of the three they'd fought in the alley—should those men have even awoken yet. But on her, small and thin, the kingsman held his light. "Down to your shift."

Ginger gasped, and Hugh threw his arm out as if to prevent her from acting as Cass stepped between Miri and the torch.

"I don't know what you're about," Cass said coolly, "but perhaps you should reconsider."

The kingsman gave him a solid backhand to the jaw. Cass didn't fall but made to stagger back, and Miri's dagger was out of her sheath and in his hand behind his hip.

"She is my wife," Cass said.

"She is on king's land. She belongs first to the king." The voice came from one of the kingsmen on horseback. He said the words as if they had been said countless times before. "Off with it," he ordered Miri.

Miri had no idea what precisely they were looking for, but she was certain her ribs and legs were heavily bruised. She did not step from behind Cass.

"What are you after beneath her clothes?" Hugh's voice sounded like a warning, and Miri suddenly regretted accepting hospitality from a man itching to call out treason.

"A criminal."

The kingsman's tone brooked no argument, but that didn't deter Hugh. "You'll nay find one here. We've been traveling together since Smithsport, up to see my cousin in Ironwood and trade for goods."

Miri felt her mouth go dry and saw the stillness in Cass's shoulders. Hugh was lying for them—or possibly to spite the kingsmen.

"Asking a woman in the woods to disrobe." Ginger *ts*ked.

The kingsman's gaze snapped to hers. "Do you question an order of the king?"

The stillness spread through the clearing then as each of them understood the threat.

The kingsman with the torch pressed it toward Cass, forcing him to either step back or act against the man. Cass pressed back toward Miri, but she stepped to the side. She would not watch a single one of her group die on her account.

The torch came closer. "Do we have sympathizers among us?" the kingsman purred.

Miri could feel the interest in his tone and his desire to fight. She could taste a thousand more satisfying responses, but all that came was a cold "The queen is dead."

The kingsman with the torch did not let his gaze stray, but Miri's words were for the nearest on horseback. He was the head of their little gang, and he would be the one she went for first. If they killed five kingsmen, she wasn't certain how far they would get. As she stood facing the torchlight, she wasn't certain she cared.

Cass's hand shifted on the dagger, as if he knew she was about to cross a line. The kings would discover their missing men. Miri's time in the shadows was nearly up.

The nearest on horseback stared at Miri, his patience evidently up. He reached for his sword, a deadly-looking thing with a bear-carved pommel, but a sudden sharp call came from the trees. It was followed by shouting, and the kingsmen waiting near the trees drew their animals to face the oncoming threat.

But it was not a threat. From the trees came another kingsman, tall and thin. "The girl," the newcomer shouted. His hand shifted in an odd gesture, one Miri had seen before. "She's been found. King's orders to bring her in."

Miri's gaze returned to the kingsman on horseback. He was watching her face. Miri supposed it was fortunate he'd not been watching Cass instead. She waited for the kingsman to say, "Take her," and it all to be over. He seemed to be considering just such a thing. But he had received an order. The king's word took precedence.

"Go," the kingsman ordered his men, giving Miri a final look that made her feel as if there were nothing final about it at all.

The torch was tossed carelessly at Miri's feet, and as a blanket caught fire, Cass kicked the stick away and stomped the flame. The kingsmen disappeared into the trees.

"We should move." Hugh was suddenly between Cass and Miri, his voice low, tone severe. "They'll be back."

Ginger shifted closer. "They found her. Whoever they were looking for."

Hugh's dark eyes were on the trees. "They don't need reason to kill or take captive. Not when sorcerers pay for blood."

They would be back. Because Miri was still free and the girl had not been found. Her gaze met Cass's. The kingsmen would be back, because the newcomer who'd drawn them off had been Terric. Not a kingsman at all.

※

GINGER RUSHED THROUGH THE CAMP, rolling their gear in a hasty mess as Hugh tied it to the horses. Miri laced her boots where she had stood, her hands trembling, and Cass knelt beside her, placing her dagger onto the ground at her side.

"Keep it close," he warned. "We need to get into the forests of Ironwood." Before the kingsmen were back on their trail, he meant. Terric had given Cass a warning. Miri didn't know what it meant.

"Dawn," he said, answering the unspoken question.

It was how long they had. Every moment would count.

Cass moved to gather her sword then shoved their blankets into a pack. He was tossing Miri astride Wolf before she had a chance to so much as think, but it was not a situation to ponder. It was a time to run.

CHAPTER 20

They rode hard through the darkness, their legs and the horses damp with dew as the sun rose and the light of dawn peered through the trees in a hazy orange glow. Summer heat was soon upon them, drying the damp and forcing the buzzing gnats and biting flies into the shadow of the trees. Then Miri and Cass were also within those shadows, their trails disappearing through thick brush and over patches of rock. They'd made it, for the time being, and relief swelled with exhaustion to steal the tension from Miri's limbs.

Hugh and Ginger had been quiet, either anxious about meeting the kingsmen again or sensing the tension in Miri and Cass. But by late afternoon, Hugh drew his horse to a stop, suggesting that a break and some food would do them all well. He did not build a fire.

As Miri stretched her legs, Ginger approached with a proffered waterskin. "Are you well, Bean?" Miri glanced up at the woman, and Ginger explained, "I can see that you're strong. That doesn't mean we all didn't have a fright."

"Yes," Miri said. "I appreciate the concern, but I am well."

Ginger squinted at her for a moment before apparently

deciding Miri spoke the truth. She gestured for Miri to hold out her hands then poured water over Miri's palms. As Miri rinsed her hands, Ginger splashed her own face with the cool water then shook her head briskly with a noise of relief. "It isn't safe on the trail these days, but I cannot say it's any safer inside the kingdoms. Not when even behind the walls, you run into the king's dogs searching for blood."

Hugh and Cass stood with the horses out of earshot.

Miri asked, "Have you run into many?"

Ginger's hand settled solidly above the curve of her hip. "Seven stopped us the last trip, just me and Hugh alone. Didn't think we'd get out of that mess, I'll tell you, but apparently, I'm not young enough to sell for blood." She glanced over her shoulder. "Likely clear Hugh would put up a fight too. The kingsmen are damnable, but they're not fools." Her eyes came back to Miri, her lashes long and dark beneath a sharp brow. "I know you are newly married and relish being alone, but it's not the time to be traveling without company, as young and pretty as you are."

Miri smiled at her. Ginger could not have been much older than Miri and was more than merely pretty. But Ginger didn't know that Cass and Miri were capable of handling a few kingsmen, should it come to it. "I'm glad to have you both," Miri said, hoping it was not a mistake and that they didn't end up killed for being in a princess's company.

"The queen may be dead," Ginger said, "but the kings are fools if they think they'll ever eradicate her supporters."

Miri startled at the words, until she remembered she'd spoken them to the guards the night before. Ginger didn't know who Miri was, only that she'd said the words to save her life. The kingsmen had forced her.

"Come now, let's get some food in you," Ginger offered.

It was more than a week's ride from Kirkwall to Ironwood, but Hugh and Ginger had traveled enough to know the best routes. They'd stopped at another inn near the city, and everyone inside treated the traders like friends. The couple didn't have a cart or a wagon and didn't carry obvious stock, but Miri soon discovered they traded in small trinkets and jewels. It was not something they spoke of, likely to avoid being robbed, but she saw an exchange with the innkeeper and heard a discussion between Hugh and Cass. It seemed they traded jewels fit for lords.

Cass had been distant, allowing Miri to ride beside Ginger and not holding Miri's gaze longer than was necessary for his duty as her guard or at least appropriate for a pretend husband. But every evening, they sat shoulder to shoulder at dinner, arms brushing as they ate and listened to stories from Hugh. And after, when the fire burned low and the moon was the only light, Cass crawled into the tent beside Miri, closed away from the light and the night bugs, and they lay together in the stillness of the night with a closeness neither could deny. Miri had begun to look forward to it, even though she knew it was wrong. Cass was honoring his duty, the same as her, and neither should be taking comfort in the other or allowing the unspoken accord to carry on. They were walking a dangerous line, and Miri had the most difficult task she could face at risk with every turn.

She rolled over in the dim morning light of that tent, less than a day's ride from the next king and Ironwood. Cass was already awake, watching her. He had stopped lying at her feet after the kingsmen had attacked, and his hazel eyes were level with hers. He was painfully handsome, particularly when mussed from sleep. She reached up to brush a dark eyelash from his cheek, and her fingers came away slowly from his skin. It was another action that felt dangerous—and entirely too right.

"Tell me about Edwin." Cass's voice was no more than a whisper, his expression serene despite his words.

Miri swallowed. It was time to prepare for the next king, whether she was ready or not. "He collects snakes. He keeps the poisonous ones caged but likes to bring them out to intimidate guests. He is well trained with a spear. I've seen him strike a man from across a courtyard without even pausing to aim. He laughs too loudly at things that aren't funny. His smile is too sharp." She drew a slow breath. "His rooms are at the top of a small keep. A woman will be sleeping beside him, but she's not his queen."

Edwin's mistress had been sneaking into the tower through secret passages since Miri was a child, but the woman had since grown brave. Rumor told that she walked the halls as if she were more powerful than the queen. And if she had Edwin's ear, such could be exactly the case.

"What waits in his rooms?" Cass asked.

He'd heard the explanation before, but Miri repeated it dutifully. "A low stone tub surrounded by the king's favorite incense and oils." It would be as simple as poisoning Casper. She would just place the poison in the oil and leave then let time and habit run their course. But it would be more dangerous as well, because it was not a remote stable. It was the king's own rooms, and she would need to get in while he slept.

"And how will you escape?"

Miri's gaze snapped to Cass's, and it was only then that she realized she'd been distracted by her thoughts for too long. He was constantly having to draw her back. She wondered if she'd spent too much time alone. "I'll walk from his rooms as one of the ladies. The guards will pay me no mind, not at the hour before dawn when the ladies make their journey to the chapel."

"If you are not able?"

Miri frowned. "It will work." The plan for Edwin was one of her least favorites because there were no backup escape routes. The keep was secure and only had two ways out: down a tall flight of stairs or through a tower window to crash to the stone below. She would not be able to return through the passageways from which she had come, because climbing into a tower was one thing. Climbing out from a height was something else.

Cass watched the emotions play over Miri's face, and she let out a long sigh. "It will work," she said again. Miri had set to rights one piece of the map of her realm, and the second would come in a month's time. Edwin made three, less than half the kingdoms when summer was already more than half gone. "It has to."

CHAPTER 21

Miri and the others came through the borders of Ironwood all at once. There was no other way for it to be done. Thick forests surrounded the town, and only a few routes were used heavily enough to keep the roads and trails from becoming swallowed by growth. Massive stone structures rose in a sprawling assemblage, their tiled roofs baking in the late-day sun. The group had made it well before nightfall through the muggy heat beneath the trees, and Miri had never been so eager for a bath.

"There we are," Hugh said, gesturing toward the west side of the town. Cass's gaze moved to him, and Hugh chuckled. "Oh no. Don't you go telling me you've other plans. You'll come to our home and sup with us, at least for tonight. Let us thank you for the company in the only way we can."

Cass opened his mouth to reply, but Ginger made a gesture that cut him off. "No," she snapped. "We'll not hear otherwise. I'm terrible at farewells, and I'll need a moment before I can manage to send off the likes of you."

Hugh gave her a look.

"For the maiden's sake." Her eyes rolled toward the heavens. "It's not an insult. Don't make me explain it again." Ginger shook her head and kicked up her horse, smacking Wolf on the rear as she rode past. "Come on, Bean. Let's get you into clean clothes and bake something sweet now that we're finally off the trail."

Cass drew a resigned breath and pressed his heels into Milo's flanks to ride beside Miri. They traversed the cobbled streets through a town that was better fed than some of the others, for Ironwood was self-sustained with access to ample water and wildlife, the ease of shipping goods down the Maidensgrace, and a king who relished splendor and rewarding his people when they showed their loyalty. Edwin had treasuries aplenty before he'd joined the other lords in their plot. He hadn't allied with the others for money or power. He was in it for the standing, to be the central figure, the most important in his kingdom. It had worked. Edwin was king.

They rode past cottages and small buildings, heading through the winding streets toward the manors and shops. A man was selling ribs, and a woman near him hawked bread. The soil was rich in Ironwood, and many houses had small gardens for vegetables and herbs. They didn't have room for pasture, so meat was supplied by rabbit, fowl, and wild game. Miri had been educated in the current workings of the kingdoms by Nan and Thom, but she remembered those kingdoms from when she was a child. Even where they seemed to prosper, Miri could see signs of the toll the kings had taken on the people and the land.

"Here we are," Ginger called over her shoulder, smiling broadly at an impressive two-story home between a cottage and the yard of a small manor.

Hugh whistled, and a figure moved behind the shutters in the neighboring cottage. A freckled girl with long braids sprang through the doorway a moment later, eagerly meeting the group in the street.

"Hugh!" she said.

He gave the girl a smile. "Aye, it's us. How are the goings-on?"

She stared up at him solemnly. "I've watered the plants and

tended the animals. The laundry is fresh, and I'll have perishables brought over before the sun sets."

"Good girl," Hugh said. "What about Izzy?"

The girl scowled and held up a long-fingered hand. "The beast scratched me. I've never met a creature who enjoyed so much sin."

Hugh snorted a laugh, pointedly not acknowledging the disgruntled sound that rumbled out of his wife. "Cannot argue with you there, my girl. Now, how about we settle for your work with an extra copper for the scratch, and you take these horses to the stable for grain and a decent brushing?"

"Deal." She glanced only briefly at Ginger before she leaned in to whisper, "And next time, let Harry mind the cat."

At her comment, Hugh laughed full out, stepping down from his horse as he patted the girl on top of her head. "Thank you, Sarah. For your work and the utter joy of your honest soul."

Miri and Cass dismounted as well and slid their packs over their shoulders after the horses were tied in wait for their turn with Sarah. Ginger led them into the house, stopping in the center of the front room to swoop up a large tabby cat missing half an ear.

"There's my girl," Ginger murmured, but the cat only stared at Miri over the woman's shoulder with a look that promised blood.

Cass gave Miri a grin then took their packs as he followed Hugh through the house. "You'll sleep here," Hugh said, leading Cass to what was apparently a spare room off the kitchens.

Ginger set the cat back onto the floor, and the creature let out a low warbling growl. "Now," Ginger said, "I'll start the bath water while you get out of those filthy clothes. I'll send them with Sarah when she's done with the horses, and she'll have them fresh bright and early for you." Ginger's expression fell. "I'll be sorry to see you go, Bean. But I'm happy to have been graced by your presence while I could. Maiden's blessings on you both."

Miri hadn't come to like goodbyes any better but let herself relax into the bittersweet feeling of cooking alongside Ginger and eating to the sound of the couple's banter and Hugh's hearty laugh as a game of backgammon was overtaken by stories from his youth.

When Hugh and Ginger retired to their upstairs rooms and Miri and Cass finally made their way to the small bedroom, Cass's fingers brushed against Miri's in the narrow hallway. Her eyes caught his as she turned through the doorway, and an inescapable urge rose through her. Cass seemed to recognize it, and something in his gaze told Miri he was feeling it too.

He moved toward her as her steps slowed, bringing her backward into the room, and Miri could only think of how it would feel when he touched her, when his warm, soft lips pressed to hers, and when his hands, always gentle, tightened around her in something that wasn't comfort or protection. It was something that felt as reckless and urgent as she did.

A screeching yowl came as Miri stumbled over the cat. The creature danced underfoot before sinking its claws into Miri's skin. Miri hissed a curse, and Cass grabbed her arm to steady her as she hopped on one foot and the hateful feline shot through the door.

"Isabella," Ginger scolded from upstairs.

Cass stared down at Miri as she leaned to rub the tender leg. Her feet were bare beneath a borrowed homespun gown. She sighed and straightened, acknowledging whatever foolishness that had come over them. Miri was of queen's blood. Cass was bloodsworn. They both had duties to fulfill. Cass's was to protect her. Miri's was to kill a king. In the morning, by the grace of the gods, each would see it done.

※

MIRI RUBBED salve over the angry scratch on her leg, and she and Cass said their farewells to Ginger and Hugh with a promise to visit, should they ever return. Their packs had been filled with supplies, and their clothes had been laundered and scented with violets. Their first stop had been the seamstress, where Miri procured a lady's dress. Their next was the stately manor where they would linger until nightfall while their horses hid in the stables. Their cover stories were secured in case Miri was noticed.

"We have friends in Ironwood," Cass had said. He meant friends loyal to the dead queen.

Miri dressed in a richly furnished bedroom while Cass waited in the parlor. She would not allow a maid to help, should something go wrong and Miri be caught. She was already risking more lives than she cared to think about for long.

Miri tied her corset, wondering if Lettie had been able to track time where they kept her. It was impossible to know if Lettie was even aware her name day was approaching. It was possible Lettie felt as if centuries had passed, as if there were no torture greater than waiting for her death.

She also wondered if Nicholas visited her sister's cell to taunt the rightful heir. It was unlikely. Nicholas might have named himself king of Stormskeep, but that didn't mean the man had changed. He didn't relish attention like the other lords. He quite enjoyed his secrets. Lord Nicholas had been able to hold his tongue. King Nicholas was doubtless even better at the task.

His son, however, had a tongue like a snake. He was a whispering, slithering reptile of a thing. Lettie had made sheep's eyes at Augustus every time they were forced into his company. Miri had never understood it or been able to see why Lettie needed so badly the approval of those lords and their sniveling sons. And now she was prisoner to the very lord she'd wanted so much to impress.

Of all the kings of the realm, Miri hated Nicholas the most. But he was not the king she would kill next.

A soft knock came at the door, and the rhythm of it tugged Miri's scowl into something softer. It consisted of the three short raps Thom had always used. "Do you need... assistance?"

Miri let out a resigned laugh. "Apparently. Please come in. I'm decent enough."

Cass came slowly through the door, his eyes meeting Miri's before he closed the door again behind him.

She shrugged. "I've gotten as far as I can, but the laces will need tightening in the back."

He gestured for her to spin as she muttered that she should have chosen a better gown, and Cass was suddenly behind her, his clever fingers on the laces and his breath on the back of her neck. Miri swallowed.

He tugged each row tighter then paused. "I've never—I don't know how tight these should be."

Miri looked down at her chest, where it swelled perilously from the bodice. "Tighter, I'm afraid." She raised her arms, testing to be certain she would be free to climb and move. "But not much."

The bodice was black cambric, embroidered with delicate vines. The skirt was black as well, traditional in style and entirely ordinary. She appeared to be a lady of no real stature who would serve at the beck of Edwin's queen. A lady on her way to mass warranted no attention.

Miri turned to face her guard.

Cass dutifully did not look at her chest. "Do you have your blades?"

She nodded. "Three. Two within easy reach."

"And the vial?"

Miri carefully patted the small pouch hidden beneath folds of material at her waist.

"And your courage?"

She smiled. "I'm unable to leave it, though I might like to."

Cass's gaze stayed on her a moment too long. "Then we should go."

CHAPTER 22

As they stood in the shadows of the chapel, the only light was the flicker of far-off torches and lanterns. Miri looked up the tall tower of the castle. Its stone was tinted blue by a scant bit of moon through the clouds. She would part with Cass, climb that tower, and kill the next king.

Miri turned to her guard in the darkness. His eyes were on her face as she drew the cloak from around her shoulders. She handed it to him wordlessly, unable to say goodbye.

"We'll need to dye your hair soon. It's getting lighter. On our way to Ravensgate."

It was a promise that she would make it and they would escape with their lives. She nodded. "On our way to Ravensgate."

Miri hoped it was true.

She said no more as she slid into the shadows, her slippered feet silent on the path. It would not be a maze to find Edwin's rooms. There was only one way: up. She entered through the postern gate, her hands carefully positioned in front of her waist, fingers clasped together. She kept her gaze on the smooth stones beneath her, moving with purpose through the quiet corridors. The whispered swish of her skirts echoed through the hall, barely audible as she turned toward an inner castle wall.

Kingsmen were posted at a wide arch across the small courtyard, their shoulders straight but their eyes on the darkness before them, not behind—not where Miri was.

She unclasped her dusty hands, grateful for the lack of rain or dew and that the stone was dry as she wrapped strips of cloth tightly around her palms. Miri wasn't certain she would have managed the wait if weather had impeded her plans. She tied her skirts back as well as possible and gripped a wood beam then a carved corbel. Her feet slipped into the narrow cracks of stone as she pushed herself up. The construction curved outward, so if Miri fell, it would be to the flat stone covering the earth, not the rough pieces she was crawling over. It was why she'd had to dress as a lady and why there would be no return using the same route. After her task was complete, she would have to descend the tower while the ladies made their way to the chapel under the cover of early morning, but her disguise was not foolproof. She couldn't pass for a lady in the light of day, not when all eyes were upon them as they returned to the queen's rooms, so the way up had to be in the dark of night, through the second-level window.

Miri's fingers slid from the gritty stone, and she slipped. Her elbow slammed against the side of a support before she caught herself, black dress pressed against the shadows as she waited to discover if the guards had heard. When her breath returned, she raised a hand toward the carvings beneath an oriel window and drew herself up and over the ledge. Her arms trembled with the strain, and she wanted nothing more than to collapse on the floor inside.

A hideous tearing sound came as Miri's skirt caught on the edge of a carving, and she was suddenly jerked to a stop—stuck between the frame of the window and the ledge outside. Her eyes snapped to the space above her, her heart skipping with fear that someone might have heard, but she couldn't let go to free the material. She was caught, every measure she tried to shift stolen by a determined snag. She felt without warning more hopeless than when the guard at Kirkwall had touched her with his sword. She couldn't go backward, or she would fall. She was trapped, snared by a foe she could not fight or stab. Gods, she felt hot tears welling in her eyes.

It was not how she would die. Miri gritted her teeth and drew herself forward with all of the strength in her arms. The material ripped loudly, but with a finality that let her fall over the ledge inside. She panted, fingers trembling as she jerked the frayed threads free, then with more horror, she checked her pouch to be certain she'd not lost her vial. It was there, so she scurried into a nearby alcove to sort the torn bits of her dress into reasonable order. She pulled the fabric from her palms, unsurprised her fingers were tipped in scratches and blood. She would not have to climb any farther—not that she could have with the sheer flat walls of the upper levels. She'd only needed to bypass the lower level and reach the second floor so that she could gain access to the spiral stairs that led toward the lady's rooms, which had secret passages.

It was quick work when the castle slept, but Miri had to skirt several guards on her way. The king's mistress's sitting room was empty. Most of her ladies were asleep in their beds after so many years of going unneeded. A scattered few lay sleeping on the cushions before the windows of her bedchamber, where the cool night air brushed against a dozen sheer silks hanging from bedposts and over chairbacks. Miri crept through the room toward the massive stone fireplace, which was bare of wood. She pulled a candle, which had cracked during her climbing, from the pouch at her waist and lit it from a taper that had been left burning near the bed. She stepped through, careful of soot, and behind the hidden panel to be engulfed in the damp, stale air of the passageway.

The space was narrow, sandwiched between two walls, and left her no choice of which direction to go. She held a hand before the flame of her tilted candle, making her way as quickly as the air would allow. When she finally reached the end of the passage, she dampened her fingers and pinched the flame, waiting for the scent to dissipate as she prayed she'd been right about which corridor led to the king.

Miri listened for a painfully extended length of time, alone in the darkness and yearning for fresh, open air. She heard nothing, could see nothing, and felt no sense of movement beyond the wall. Holding her breath, she reached for the panel, pushing down the fear that the king had since blocked the way. There could be any number of furnishings on the other side, but her only other option had been climbing through the tube that evacuated his garderobe, and no one had attempted that since the uprisings following the Lion Queen's murder. It had not ended well for the men who'd tried.

The panel came free of its frame with a wooden *pop*, and Miri held very still for another torturous moment. When she heard no movement from inside the room, she slid the panel aside, only to find more darkness. She reached tentatively forward, feeling the heavy woven back of a tapestry. Miri moved to her knees to peer below it and saw the bottom of a wide, open space. Its floors were covered in finely woven rugs, and its ornate fireplace was bare of wood. There was another passage on the far wall behind the massive wardrobe, Miri had been told, but that one led to a tower that held two sorcerers, something Miri hoped she would never face again.

She shook off the cold thought, crawling from the passageway to avoid shifting the massive tapestry from its place. Moonlight streamed through high windows. The air near her was still, but it rustled the sheers across the room. Her gaze roamed the far space as she searched for any dangers, trying to discern shapes that might be sleeping men. Miri eased forward on her knees, jolting and nearly screaming when she came face to face with the tangled mass of a hulking snake. She froze as it stared at her, its dark eyes unmoving and its head low. One more move, and the creature would have struck. Miri winced, silently begging the creature to let her go as she backed slowly toward the wall she'd only just emerged from. When she'd given it enough space, the snake slithered from its spot, crossing the floor at an angle and speed that made Miri's stomach turn.

She leaned back, giving herself a moment to catch her breath, then settled on putting the panel back into place. She'd made it to the king's rooms, clearly, and should she find the bath and complete her task, she did not want to have to come back to hide her trail.

After smoothing the tapestry with a scratched and filthy hand, she followed the wall through the room, avoiding baskets and structures that might be hiding more snakes. She stuck to the shadows, her eyes catching on a low, wide bed draped in heavy fabric. The curtains were drawn closed. She stared at it for several moments, feeling the thundering of her heart. Behind the curtains slept a king—a lord in wolf's clothing who'd murdered to name himself king.

Miri swallowed back bile. She was a murderer too. Vengeance might have been her duty, but it did not feel entirely clean. She forced her eyes off the drapes surrounding Edwin's bed and crept through the door to the next room.

Edwin was known for his rituals, foremost his private bath. He'd had the stone tub built when he'd only been a lord, but as king, it had been said that the servants heated and hauled his water twice a day. His oils were imported from across the sea, blends that he chose not as the king of Kirkwall—for their supposed healing properties—but because Edwin was pleased by their scents. The windowed room was sparse with furnishings, its central feature and only real purpose the tub. Miri crossed slowly to the circle of smooth stone, impressed by the detailed carvings despite herself. Rows of candles and incense lined one rim, and the other was worn with use. There, Edwin would sit, his arms spread wide, eyes closed as his tensions eased in the heated, fragrant water. There, Edwin would die.

He would lose his ability to control his muscles, slip beneath the surface, and drown, in darkness and alone, the way Miri nearly had as a child. She took a steadying breath, kneeling onto the stone to choose a vial. One was dark-blue glass, its liquid half gone, and appeared as if it could be his favorite. Another beside it was nearly gone. She considered which of the six to use, but it was all a gamble. She needed his death to wait until they'd taken care of the next king, but Edwin had to be gone before the end of summer and the festival of moons.

Miri pulled the poison from the pouch at her waist and cautiously opened the stopper. She dripped the liquid into the oil then returned each to their original positions. She had never imagined she would be a poisoner. Miri was a princess, daughter of the Lion Queen. Her fate was to wield a sword in battle, secure her sister's rule as head of the guard, protect their blood and their name, and shore their legacy. It didn't feel as if she was holding to her duty, but Miri knew there was no one else who could save Lettie. It was Miri's sacrifice to make.

She had done it. Pressing her palms to the stone, she prepared to push herself to standing—and was seized by the knot of hair at the back of her neck. A blade pricked the flesh beneath her jaw, and Miri felt the line of blood run from the wound even as her head was wrenched backward. Her fingers curled against the stone, but the blade was already at her throat. Trying to toss the man forward into the pool would only get her throat cut.

Miri stared up at her attacker. His skin was tinted pale by the light of the moon, and she recognized the narrow face and bright eyes of the king of Ironwood.

※

INSTEAD OF FEELING COWED by a man who was king, Miri felt rage at a man who had killed her mother. His eyes were not on hers but the swell of her chest. She was arched toward him, trapped by his grasp and his blade, and Miri watched as his gaze followed the line of blood that ran from the wound beneath her jaw and into her dress.

A lady's dress, Miri remembered. She was a maid to the queen.

"She tries to murder me?" Edwin hissed into Miri's ear. "In my own castle?"

Miri drew a careful breath, focusing on the stone beneath her palms and her knees. She could press him back, rise suddenly into him and knock the blade away—as long as she managed before he stabbed her. Edwin had always been quick. But he thought her a lady-in-waiting to the queen, not a threat or a fighter.

Edwin pressed the blade harder to Miri's skin, angling the point right where a bit of pressure would be deadly. He would watch her bleed out slowly and likely gather the queen to make her watch. If Miri had to guess, she thought he was probably considering how to best punish his wife at that very moment.

"You've punished her enough," Miri whispered. She only meant to buy herself time and throw Edwin's attention for a heartbeat while she made her move, but Edwin jerked her closer, the blade going deeper into her skin. Gods, she was done for. She whimpered, and it was not part of the act. "She's had to watch you make a fool of her all this time as you parade a lowborn through these halls."

Miri knew the insult would hit him hard, but she did not expect the rage with which he would attack. Edwin slammed her face toward the stone. Miri's arms barely protected her from a solid ledge capable of fracturing her nose. He twisted her, coming down hard with a knee into her ribs, and held her in place with his weight as he pressed the knife to her stomach. Slower, he'd decided, then. He would let her guts spill over the floor and into his precious tub.

His golden eyes burned into hers, finally staring at the woman he plainly intended to kill. Miri's fingers were already under the folds of her dress, her palm wrapping tight around the handle of a dagger. The moment his weight shifted, she would have to stab him and run.

But his weight didn't shift. His dark brows drew together, and his gaze roamed over Miri's features—not the blood or the disdain for a simple maid. It was different. It was the line of her face, the press of her mouth, and both of Miri's honey-brown eyes. Edwin's knee pressed harder into Miri's frame, his blade pricking her skin through her dress as his free hand latched onto her jaw. He gripped hard, turning her head in the moonlight, and examined her. His weight was too much to draw her trapped dagger free, and Miri's chest heaved beneath the burden of him and a corset that felt far too tight.

She saw the moment recognition came—the moment Edwin, self-named king of Ironwood, recalled the second daughter of the Lion Queen.

Miri gave him a feral grin. "Murderer."

Edwin drew a breath, but Miri couldn't know whether he was merely startled or intended to call for the guards. She'd already slid a foot from her slippers and pressed her bare sole hard against the stone, and she shoved him back so that she could free her arm. It drove his blade at her stomach closer, but the corset and the movement had twisted it from what otherwise might have been a deadly blow. He'd stopped her momentum, though, his grip on her jaw sliding in blood, but his entire body spun over her to pin her back down. Edwin was no fool. He'd noticed Miri's prowess as a child. He'd said as much, in front of crowds of watching lords. "That girl is deadly. I pity any man who draws her ire."

Miri was a girl no longer. She wasn't a fragile thing, half his size. She was a lion, raging for vengeance and desperate to survive. The struggle rolled them into the carved stove edging the tub, and Miri freed an arm to slam it into the inside of Edwin's elbow, making him loosen his grip and crash his knuckles against the stone. His blade clattered free, and he raised a fist to strike her, but she twisted beneath him, all claws and knees and teeth. Her daggers were trapped beneath her skirts and his legs. Edwin's hand, slick with Miri's blood, went for her neck again. She let him try then landed a solid strike to his throat with the base of her hand. He choked out a cough but did not let up, his long limbs trapping her.

She struck him in the side as he raised his fist again, and when his blow landed, it glanced off her blood-slicked jaw. Her ears rang, and her pulse hammered, and Miri twisted beneath him once more. She finally thought she might have him off balance, but his hands were knotted in her braids and her dress, and he hauled her toward the edge of the tub. To drown her or smash her head, she wasn't sure, but he'd moved, and her hand was on the second dagger at her hip before he'd made it two steps.

Miri slid the knife across the back of his knee, the only decent spot she could reach in their struggle, and Edwin hissed and lowered automatically. The thin material of his nightclothes gave him no protection from her steel. As the blood blossomed over the material, Miri grabbed Edwin's wrist where he held her hair and pulled herself upward with one hand as her dagger drove home between his ribs. He bit down a cry, jerking her head with him as their bodies crashed to the floor, and Miri pulled the blade free, her eyes on Edwin's as she ran it into his neck.

The king's blood was everywhere, a warm pool that ran over the stone too fast and too red. Edwin couldn't draw air to call for help, but the light had not gone out of his eyes. She had to pry his fingers from her hair, then she stumbled back from him and the blood. She tripped on his legs and landed hard on her bottom, and through the tingling of her limbs and the pounding of her heart, Miri felt the first stings of pain.

Miri had been nicked in at least three places by his blade and punched half a dozen more. She pushed the hair from her face and felt the sticky mess that was matted on her cheek and in her hair. She suddenly stood, staring at the blood that coated the floor. It was her blood.

Miri remembered the sorcerers, who were only a few towers away, and her hands began to tremble again, her entire body nearly shuddering in panic. She grabbed a bucket from near the tub and upended it so that tepid water splashed over her bare foot and the blood on the floor that was hers. Then she took a full bottle of oil—one that had not been poisoned—and doused it over the mess. She hoped it worked.

Miri stared down at herself, a monster in lady's clothes, and wanted to weep. At a gasp from across the room, Miri glanced up, the bottle in her fingers smashing to the floor when she saw Edwin's mistress. The woman stared at Miri then the king, her slender hands going to the flesh at her naked throat.

"No," Miri whispered, holding a bloody finger to her lips. "I don't want to kill you. Please do not make me."

There was a moment of silence. Then the woman screamed.

✦

MIRI BURST into the corridor outside the king's rooms, and her dagger found the thigh of one kingsman as the second ran toward the screams through another pair of doors. Shouts rang through the hallway, and her footsteps staggered, one bare, the other in a damp and bloody slipper. Both were beneath a mass of torn skirts. She'd lost a dagger, her palms were slick with sweat, and her body shook with exhaustion and fear. She would never make it out alive or even down the stairs. But she had to try anyway.

When she glanced over her shoulder, she saw the second guard coming from the king's room.

"She's killed the king!"

His shout echoed off the stone, and Miri stumbled to a graceless stop at the top of the stairs.

More than a dozen guards were climbing the tower, fully armed and by all appearances eager to kill.

"There!" one shouted, and all eyes came to hers. Miri cursed and ran back toward the king's rooms and back toward her death. She couldn't escape it.

Her choices were the tower to the sorcerers or the passage in the darkness, but she could not face the sorcerers, not with the way her body reacted to their magic, and she didn't have time to kill the mistress and the other guard with a dozen more on her heels. Miri turned into the solar, running as fast as she'd ever run. She only paused to topple a cage of vipers. As they spilled over the floor, she picked up a statue and smashed it through the window of a carved case. Something bigger waited inside, a dark and dangerous thing, but Miri didn't waste time watching to see if it moved. She crossed the final distance and leaped onto the ledge of a high window into the strange glow of coming light.

The castle was awakening. She should be walking silently through its halls and down that long flight of stairs as if she were a lady on her way to the chapel, not perched on the edge of a tower, staring down a sheer stone wall to her death below.

"Maiden save me," Miri whispered.

The clamor of kingsmen and weaponry was behind her, and there was only one way out. She grabbed a long silk drapery and threw herself out the window. A spear rushed through the air beside her, shaving Miri's shoulder as she swung wide and slammed into the wall. The drapery came loose of its mooring, and Miri slid lower along the wall, her arms scraping rock. She kicked against the building and held her breath, letting go of the fabric to drop to the narrow roof of a garderobe below. It was slanted, and she managed to land, but her feet slipped over the stone, skidding as she tried to gain purchase. She could not, and as she careened downward, her body slammed into a support that knocked her wider from any decent path. She fell.

Princess Myrina of Stormskeep, daughter of the Lion Queen, was going to die on the stones of a stolen castle, covered in the blood of a bastard king.

CHAPTER 23

Cass watched a dark figure fly from the king's tower window. He had moved nearer the moment the first scream had sounded then watched without breath, as it had been followed by the shouting of men. Something had gone wrong, but he hadn't expected the woman to fling herself out the window on nothing but a thin strip of fabric. She landed hard on the roof of a garderobe then slipped. Her descent was slowed by various corbels and lintels before her body disappeared onto the rampart.

Cass ran, though he feared her already dead. Arrows were launched through the air toward the rampart, and Cass's frantic heart picked up pace. Terric had said the queen had friends in Ironwood. Cass hadn't realized they would be willing to fight.

Alarm bells rang through the air before Cass reached the castle walls, but his boots were swift in their flight. It was only nearly dawn, but inside those walls must have been sixty kingsmen at the ready, two sorcerers, and gods knew what else. He rushed toward the wall, hearing the shouts and running men atop the parapet. Fighting and the sounds of swords clashing led Cass toward the castle gate. The portcullis had not yet dropped, and if he went through, he would likely never escape. But that did not slow his pace. He rushed forward, assured in his fate, and was knocked solidly from his feet by a heavy black mass.

The breath rushed out of him with a huff as the body that had landed on him groaned. Cass struggled to right himself and saw a dark figure gesture at him through the hole above. The man turned and clashed swords with another, and Cass jerked to stare at the form over him.

It was Miri, covered in blood, her eyes closed, and her head lolling to the side. They'd shoved her through a bleeding murder hole. He shifted her body, carefully rolling her to her back, but she was still warm, still limber, and thank the gods, she still breathed. Her eyes fluttered open for a moment, but she immediately winced in pain. He'd seen enough—the honey brown of her eyes had been swallowed by darkness. She was not the Miri he knew. The sorcerers were too near, and her body was too injured to run.

Cass hauled her into his arms and ran from the gates just as the portcullis's chains began to rattle.

He bolted from the castle with kingsmen coming from every direction in the half light. There were other figures, too—men and women who stood in watch, those who would have heard the bells and come from curiosity, and those who held weapons and wore fighting gear. The last ones would be loyal to the dead queen and willing to risk life and limb in any fight with the king's men.

Cass ran forward, turning down the first alleyway that came in an attempt to get Miri someplace safe. But the manor was too near the castle, and the grounds would already be swarming with kingsmen. He had no place to hide her, no place that was safe. Terric and the others were fighting kingsmen, dying in the name of the queen. He glanced down at Miri and felt a stab of fear run through him.

Clumps of blood covered the side of her head. A chunk of torn hair was pasted to it in a tangled mess over her cheek. Blood caked her chest and soaked the bodice of her dress. Cass swallowed whatever was rising in his throat, pressing on with very little in the way of breath. He had no idea how far he'd carried her or how much farther he could go. Wary faces peered through windows. All of Ironwood had been awoken by the bells and the chaos behind him. It would only take one to do them in, one loyal to the king to call out to the guards.

Cass raised his head to the sky, breathing in through his nose and praying for strength. There was only one place to take her to give him a chance to keep Miri alive and scrape out of the mess. He shifted her in his arms and walked on with the last bit of strength he had left.

*

Cass burst through the door into Ginger and Hugh's kitchen. They stared blankly up at him for a moment as they sat at their table with mugs of morning tea. Cass's arms trembled beneath the weight of Miri's form, and his legs were ready to give out, but he was prepared to grip his dagger if need be. He hoped he didn't have to.

Ginger shoved to her feet, hand going to her mouth as her eyes trailed over Miri. Hugh's chair slid back with a noisy growl, but neither approached. They stared at Cass.

"I need your help," he said. "It will put your lives in danger." He did not say the rest—that he would be forced to kill them if they didn't agree. He would kill them to protect the daughter of the Lion Queen. The idea made him half sick. He hoped he had chosen well and wasn't wrong about them.

Ginger moved forward without even glancing at Hugh, her hands outstretched to take Miri from Cass.

"Understand..." Cass said before she reached them. "Understand that she... she has killed the king."

Ginger stopped, blinking up at Cass, but Hugh still hadn't moved. Housing someone who'd murdered a king meant not simply death. It would be torture, disgrace, dishonor, and punishment to anyone they knew.

"The bells," Ginger said. Her eyes fell to Miri. "Is it true?"

Cass realized that she was not merely asking about the killing of the king. Ginger had, somehow, suspected Miri was more than simply the trader girl Bean.

"Myrina," he said, voice broken by an emotion he was too exhausted to name.

Ginger swayed and moved forward a step to keep from falling to her knees. "Myrina," she whispered, her eyes going damp at the sight of the poor, broken princess. "Hugh, leave if you need to, but I will stay."

Hugh crossed his arms. "I'll not leave a daughter of the queen. What do you take me for, woman?"

"Then bar the door." To Cass, Ginger ordered, "Take her to the bed. I'll bring water and supplies."

Cass collapsed into a chair beside the narrow mattress where he'd lain Miri, his arms so shaky and limp that he wasn't certain he would be able to draw a sword.

Hugh was suddenly beside him, flask in hand. "Drink it," he said.

Cass took one quick draw, coughed, and wiped an arm over his brow.

Hugh grimaced at the blood that covered Cass's arms and face. "I've got the shutters drawn, and no one expects us to be about today, since we've just returned from the road. I cannot promise they'll not send scouts, searching the houses for sign of the girl." He gave Cass an appraising look. "Did you carry her all the way from the castle?"

Cass nodded but said nothing else. Hugh was right. They needed out of Ironwood before the queen ordered Edwin's murderer found. But it was not the kingsmen who worried him. It was the sorcerers—Miri was covered in blood.

"Do you have a plan?" Hugh asked.

Cass stared up at him. "I have... I had friends." He didn't know if they were still alive.

Hugh nodded. "Aye. I'll help you find them. If not, we'll get you free."

Cass's aching hands curled into fists as feeling began to return to them. He'd just asked Hugh and Ginger to give up everything—their home and life and everyone they knew.

"Out!" Ginger ordered Hugh. "This wretched corset is coming off, and you've no business in the presence of a half-dressed princess."

Hugh frowned at her but turned and did as she ordered.

Cass started to get up, but Ginger shoved her supplies into his arms. "Not you. You're helping."

🙚

CASS STARED as Ginger wiped the blood from Miri's wounds. They'd cut the dress from her body. Half the gown had already been torn to shreds and was thick with blood. But it had not all been hers. She lay beneath two thin blankets in nothing but her underclothes, the thin shirt, which—inside of her hem—held the trinket Miri's mother had given her. It was the last possession of the dead queen, the only thing left aside from two daughters, who were captive to their fates.

"It's not deep," Ginger murmured of the cut beneath Miri's neck, "but she's lost a good deal of blood." She held a hand out to Cass. "I'm ready for the needle. I'll stitch this one up, check her over once more, then heat another batch of water so you can clean up yourself." As Cass handed Ginger the supplies, she glanced back at him. "Do you have fresh clothes?"

He shook his head. All of their possessions, the horses and supplies, were at the manor near the castle.

"Light," Ginger said.

The sunlight from the window was not enough, so Cass leaned forward with the lantern.

Ginger added, "We'll get Sarah to find you something. She's a good girl. Smart."

Cass opened his mouth to protest, but he'd already put the girl in danger by her association with Ginger and Hugh.

"She'll come with us," Ginger said.

The thread tugged at Miri's skin, and Cass had to look away. He'd seen a thousand battle wounds and injuries, but none had unsettled him as much as watching Miri tumble from the side of the tower. Not even when the sorcerers had taken Stormskeep, but Cass had only been a child then. He hadn't realized what that day would cost him and everyone in the realm.

"The girl's mother too," Ginger said. "We'll take you north and, once we're in the mountains, head east. Hugh has family at Blackstone. We've an ample supply of jewels."

"You will be repaid," Cass promised.

Ginger cut him a sharp look. "Don't insult our generosity. This is our duty as much as it is yours."

Cass was bloodsworn to the queen. It was no one's duty more than his.

Ginger rolled her eyes heavenward before she returned her focus to her work. "Men are fools as often as they aren't."

Cass gave her no answer, because in that exasperated look, he saw and heard the fondness with which she complained of Hugh, and something else, something Cass did not want to tear open with Miri so fragile. Ginger had seen Cass and Miri close, acting as husband and wife. Ginger had known Miri was the daughter of the Lion Queen.

"Woman," Hugh said from the doorway, "I've heated the water myself. We foolish men have tasks of our own. The lad can't be your nursemaid all day."

Ginger snorted but kept at her work, her long fingers dark against Miri's too-pale skin.

Hugh gave Cass an expectant glower, and Cass reluctantly set the lantern near Ginger's work.

CHAPTER 24

Cass gripped his brother-in-arms with all the strength in his body. Terric had lived. He'd saved Miri and saved them all.

"Easy, brother," Terric said. "We aren't safe yet."

Cass drew back to look at him, grateful to the point of pain. The queensguard and those faithful to the dead queen had misled the kingsmen and fought on her behalf. They hadn't known the assassin was Myrina, princess and daughter of the Lion Queen. They had only known they had a chance to rise up, and they had taken it with eager courage.

"We need to leave by nightfall. Will she be ready?"

Hugh spoke from behind Cass. "Wife says she'll be fine. Beaten and sore to be sure but not badly injured."

Terric's gaze slid over Cass's shoulder. "She needs to be certain. This will be no easy trip."

"I know what's at stake," Hugh answered. He had, after all, risked his own neck. "And she knows her business around wounds. If she says it, I stake my life on it being the truth."

Terric nodded. "Then we leave tonight." He handed Cass a leather pouch. "Your horses will be ready, and we've managed to retrieve the things from your rooms. There is no evidence either of you was there."

The only risk would be hearsay, and there would be more than enough of that floating about after the murder of a king. Cass tugged at the collar of his new jacket. Sarah's estimation of his size was only a bit small. She'd brought Miri loose, soft, and layered gowns made of nothing that would irritate her wounds. Cass would ride with her, and Hugh and Ginger would be at their sides with a small party of loyal guards, while Terric and others misdirected the kingsmen.

Bells rang through the street outside their meeting place, and Cass startled at the sound.

Terric gave him a wry smile. "It's not an alarm." At Cass's expression, Terric explained, "It's a call to assemble. The queen's first order of business was to seek vengeance on the woman she's accused of being the source of the plot. The king's mistress is being hanged for treason."

"What of the sorcerers?" Cass asked.

"They have been busy examining the scene. Word is harder to find on the decisions of those..." Terric's gaze flicked to Hugh then back to Cass. "We've no idea what they're planning. I don't expect we will anytime soon."

"All the more reason to move right away." Hugh crossed his arms, glancing toward the window, where passersby headed toward the castle to watch a woman hang.

Terric took hold of Cass with a firm grip on his forearm. "I will see you again. By the grace of the maiden."

Cass locked his fingers over Terric's forearm and squeezed back. "By the will of the gods."

※

MIRI JOLTED awake with the feeling she'd fallen. But she was not plummeting helplessly from a tower window. She was in Cass's arms. His hair was cut short, and his neck was covered in a high-collared jacket embroidered with fine leaves. She breathed in relief then winced at the stab of pain in her ribs.

"You're safe," Cass whispered. "But we've got to move. Ginger is going to give you something for the pain."

Her mind was foggy, but Cass was warm and his tone reassuring. She wanted to fall back to sleep, but they wouldn't stop jostling her. She felt a warm palm slide beneath her neck, tilting her head upward. Her jaw ached, and her throat was dry.

"Here, my Myrina," someone said softly. "Drink this."

Miri drank then felt her brow draw together before her heartbeat took to racing in an unsteady gallop. Her eyes went wide, but she had to blink to clear her vision to see Cass's frown as he looked at the woman before them. *Ginger.* Ginger had called her Myrina.

"Bean," Ginger snapped, more to Cass than anyone else.

Then her fingers slid carefully over Miri's hair, and Miri felt herself pulling involuntarily away from consciousness.

She woke again near horses, twice more being jarred and jolted in the darkness, and though she couldn't quite draw it from her memory, each time Ginger fed her the sweet, oily drink, she felt as if she'd done it half a dozen times before.

It was daylight when she finally refused the concoction. Her tongue was thick, and her eyes matted with sleep. Her head felt as if she'd been trampled by horses, and her body throbbed in so many places that she couldn't sort where each injury was. "Water," she croaked.

A small hand offered her a waterskin, and Miri took it gratefully, unsure where she'd seen the girl before or why there was a girl at all. A warm body rested beneath her, and Miri realized it was Cass.

The girl held a finger to her lips in a gesture to stay quiet. A figure behind the girl—who was Sarah, Miri suddenly remembered—leaned closer, and Miri blinked to clear her vision.

Ginger whispered, "It's the first he's slept at all. Better to let him."

"Where…" Miri gulped. Her neck felt too big, stiff, and raw. She raised a hand to touch it and found a bandage at the base of her jaw.

Ginger waved her unspoken questions away. "The swelling will go down soon. You've taken quite a few hits, I'm afraid, and the jaw remains puffy and bruised, but the stitching went well. Shouldn't have too much trouble with it after a few days." She offered Miri a piece of bread, but Miri couldn't quite manage to shake her head to refuse. "We're nearly two days north of Ironwood, on our way to Ravensgate." The girl glanced up at her, and Ginger amended, "You're on your way to Ravensgate. We'll be headed to Blackstone, to be sure."

Miri tried not to remember what had happened and how the agonies in her body had been delivered, but she couldn't look away from the memories—falling from the garderobe roof, slamming into the stone wall, landing on the edge of the battlement and being tossed onto the rampart, the shouting kingsmen, the swords and arrows, men taking arms against their own and fighters who had not been their own at all, and the men who had shouted, "For the queen."

Miri's head ached, and her stomach felt sour and hollow.

She could see Edwin's eyes when he'd recognized her, the change in his expression, and the blood that had spilled from his wounds.

Miri retched onto the ground, covering her blankets as well, and the girl leapt back as Ginger moved to steady Miri.

"Easy," she cooed. "Best not to strain."

Miri coughed up the water she'd drunk, eyes running and arms shaking as they held her weight. Cass was suddenly behind her. His hands shored up her shoulders, and his words full of nothing but concern as the shivering started.

"It's fine," Ginger said. "To be expected. Hold her against you until the chill passes. Sarah and I will tend to the wash." Ginger patted Cass's hand over Miri's shoulder before gathering the blankets in a bundle and stepping over two more sleeping forms.

Sarah carefully laid another blanket over Miri's legs, and Cass drew her back to him, settling her into the warmth of his embrace. His arms were bare, and sweat beaded at his temple. It was summer, daylight, and Miri shook as if she'd been doused in cold water.

A large tabby cat strode onto Miri's blanket then turned in a circle before settling against her leg.

Cass's sigh brushed Miri's neck. "Beast has been doing that for days. You've apparently won her approval."

Miri coughed. "Perhaps she's waiting for my death."

Cass went very still behind her, and Miri regretted the words. She couldn't continue, though, because another round of shivering racked her frame. She pressed harder into Cass, drawing his arms tight around her. And soon, despite the horrors behind her eyelids, Miri fell once more to sleep.

❧

MIRI HAD LOST count of the days on their journey to Ravensgate, but she knew her plans were well behind schedule. At first, she couldn't bring herself to care, but Ginger had been right, and after the first week, Miri had felt more like herself. Her bruises were mottled in greens and purples, but the tenderness of each of her wounds had faded. She no longer needed tonics and wore only a small bandage coated in salve over the cut at her jaw.

The worst was not that she'd lost precious days but that in three attempts, she'd been caught twice. Miri was no fool. The attempts would only get harder as she reached kings who were more secure. It was too soon to tell what good she had done, but she'd heard the others talking about the men and women who had risen in their defense at Ironwood. Many had lost their lives, but many more had died at the hands of the kings and their sorcerers in the past. It was their last chance to set right the realm.

The king at Kirkwall would be partaking of his tonics even as they rode for the fourth king, and if she had planned properly, he would die in nearly a month. By the festival of moons, he would be either too ill or too dead to command his army. A few men of the queensguard Miri did not recognize rode with their party, and Cass had assured her that the way had grown rocky enough that their trail would be impossible to follow.

They no longer slept within the tent they'd been gifted by Hugh and Ginger, because Cass was queensguard, and until they reached the next kingdom, there was no need to continue the ruse. They were not husband and wife, and the other men of the queensguard were more than aware of the rules. The others, straight shouldered and firm jawed, were a stark reminder of how the guard was meant to behave. Their eyes had not lingered on Miri, and their tongues had never been loose. But Cass had stayed constantly near her, helping her onto her horse and with every task she attempted on her own. Miri had let him, not because she couldn't have managed to suffer through the tasks on her own, but because he had needed to do it. And she had wanted him near.

Late into the evening, the last before Hugh and Ginger made their way to Blackstone and left the group, Cass and Miri sat under the stars in companionable silence, though she was certain he also felt the weight of what was to come. Two of the queensguard waited on watch, and the other sleeping near the seamstress and her daughter, while Ginger and Hugh's conversation was a low hum inside what must have been a sweltering tent. Cass's dagger flashed in the moonlight as it made endless trips between his fingers. The cat sauntered nearer and lazily dropped beside Miri's leg.

Cass glanced at the beast with a smirk. Miri only shook her head.

Her neck was still tender, and when she stopped midmovement, Cass's gaze was on her.

"It's fine," she promised. "I'll be ready."

"It can wait."

Miri cut her eyes to his. "It cannot. I've already lost too much time." At his expression, she asked, "What?"

"You'll need to adjust your plot. The king at Ravensgate won't throw a public ball after he hears the details of Edwin's death."

She shifted, and the cat growled at being disturbed. "He will. He's too vain not to and too afraid to let on that he fears it." She did not argue further, because though she was confident of the whims of the lords they had been, Miri had made other mistakes. She could be wrong about the reactions of men who had since turned kings.

"It doesn't matter," she said to the darkness. "We've no time for anything else."

CHAPTER 25

Miri and Cass said their goodbyes to Ginger and Hugh and continued north toward Ravensgate for two more days. On the third day, the queensguard parted ways with them, not to abandon Miri and Cass but to watch from a distance in case they encountered trouble and needed help. *More help*, Miri amended, because thus far she'd needed saving more times than she could count.

"Missing the company of your cat?"

Cass's words startled Miri out of her rumination, and she forced the frown from her face. "Hardly. Wretched beast."

"Are you in pain?"

She gave him a look. "I've told you a thousand times that I'm well. I'm not lying to you." At his expression, she added, "I have no need to lie to you."

Cass gave a small grin at her reply, and Miri felt her cheeks color. He had a soft curve to his smile, just on one side. She'd forgotten the way it transformed his face and how used to it she'd been. Gods, she was the daughter of the Lion Queen, and he could play her emotions with just a twist of his lips.

She straightened her shoulders. "I mean I don't have to because I'm the daughter of a queen."

His grin broke free then. "Oh, I knew what you meant."

She refused to look at it and be tangled in his underhanded tactics. But her breath huffed out, because she'd already forgotten what she'd been ruminating about in the first place. "Charm will only get you so far," she said caustically.

His smile fell. "You think me charming?"

"You've made your point," she snapped. "I'm sufficiently distracted from dark thoughts."

When he fell silent, Miri assumed he was appeased with her assessment, but as she turned to glance toward the call of a bird, what she saw on his face was not satisfaction. She wagered that it was concern for whatever dark thoughts Miri had admitted had been going through her head. She was off her game and needed rest to gain back her focus. In a matter of days, she would be faced with another king.

"Tell me about Peter."

Miri sighed. It was as if he could read her mind. She slowed to ride beside him. "Lord Peter, king of Ravensgate, likes to host fancy parties." She closed her eyes, remembering. "He has long hair and a smooth face. He's handsome beyond reason and knows it too well. The ladies flock to him, but he's never married. There will be time for that when he is old and gray, he always said. But he will, he's promised, because to rob the world of his heirs would be too great a crime. So, he'll have many sons, and even, he supposes, daughters to inherit his beauty." Miri opened her eyes, shaking off the memory of Peter's laugh. He'd thought himself so clever and perfect. But he was nothing if he did not have an audience. "He craves company and withers without it, fancy dress, and all the airs."

"And how will you meet him?"

"The king holds a ball every season, open to the public—of a certain standing—so that they might experience his displays of wealth and pay him homage." Her fingers slid over Wolf's reins. "It's a costumed celebration, masks for all."

"Sounds effortless."

She shifted in her saddle, careful not to let Cass see. In truth, she was still sore in places but only after long days of riding through rough terrain. She was fairly certain she would be fine if she could only get some exercise and movement. "It will be the most difficult yet."

"How so?"

"There is a thin-shelled mollusk that is considered a delicacy by the people of Ravensgate. It's not rare on the mountain but is elsewhere in the kingdom, making it worth more than it might otherwise be."

Cass hummed his acknowledgment, and Miri went on.

"Shipping the prized mollusks is difficult because their shells crack so easily. But they can be found readily among the markets and even in the wild."

"What else can be readily found there?"

"Rock spiders. They're not known for aggression but, when pressured, deliver a lethal dose of venom." Miri normally tried very hard not to dwell on the portion of her plan that required transferring the spider into the shell before sealing it with wax. "The presence of either the discarded shell, a delicacy brought in for the ball, or a spider so common outside the castle walls will not bring suspicion. In fact, the spider's body will likely be easy to find, given that the bite will immediately sting. As the king's body shuts down, all will be witness to the cause. His flesh will color, his limbs will tremble, and like so many hunters and travelers who've fallen prey to the spider's bite, there will be no way to stop it or to ease the pain. The venom will spread. Peter will die."

"And what if it goes wrong?"

Miri gave Cass a shrug. "Then we enjoy the ball and an entirely free meal." She would have no need to leap from a window or to run.

MIRI MANAGED to obtain the snails and two spiders more easily than she anticipated. The mountain was alive with preparations for the gathering, and no request seemed too odd or too complicated when coin was flowing like the Maidensgrace. Cass had procured a room with a local family, high enough in stature that they would be welcomed to the king's tables but low enough not to draw undue attention. They'd managed two simple costumes with little-enough flair and masks that covered much of their faces. Miri's mask had been slightly more complicated, but she'd managed to find one that curved down to one side, covering her wound with feathers and silk.

She had not mentioned that Edwin had recognized her, but it was a constant niggling threat that any of the kings—any of Miri's past acquaintances—could identify her as a girl who was meant to be dead. She did not need to fear the sorcerers, though, because sorcerers did not attend balls. Blood magic was not a subject the kings wanted touted when the blood it was bought with had been stolen from local women and boys.

"We've only two days to waste, now that our tasks are done. What say you, dear Bean?"

Miri gave Cass a flat look. "We've no days to waste. Those were meant to be used obtaining supplies for the next stop."

Cass hummed something that sounded suspiciously noncommittal.

Miri settled onto the chaise and leaned over the arm to peer at him. He was sitting on the floor, sharpening one of her knives.

"You weren't eager to trade south of Ravensgate."

He did not look up at her.

"Where your family lives."

His hand did not slow at his task, but the rhythm of his movements changed. "Henry was my family. They aren't—I can never go back there again."

"I'm sorry," she told him. She was sorry that they would kill his family, that sorcerers would find and burn their homes and destroy everything Cass had ever known. If there was anything the sorcerers hated as much as the queen, it was those who were sworn to her by blood.

Cass's face, clean-shaven and a shade darker from their time in the sun, turned up to hers. He smelled of mint and steel. "The fault lies with neither of us."

Miri nodded, but guilt had already settled heavily in her gut. She had been there and watched and done nothing to stop her mother's death. But it wasn't just her mother. They'd killed her maids, her tutors, and everyone Miri held dear. They had taken Miri herself. "I'm not even a princess," Miri whispered. *Not anymore, not while the bastard King Nicholas sits on the throne at Stormskeep.*

Cass set the blade and stone onto the floor to turn toward her. He was so close that she could see the flecks in his hazel eyes. "You will always be. They cannot take that from you, just as they cannot take my vow."

She swallowed the words that wanted to rise.

He came nearer still and with his voice impossibly low, he said, "You are the daughter of the Lion Queen."

Beneath his words, she heard, *And I am bloodsworn.* Between them crackled an energy that was capable of stealing her resolve, but Miri didn't look away. Everything had been taken from her. The vow was all she had. She could be brave enough to fulfill her duty—the promise she had made to her mother— even aware of its cost, but she didn't know if she was brave enough to do it alone. She didn't *want* to face it alone. Miri had seen small flashes of Cass while on their journey and seen the scars across his back. He had been whipped, though he'd hidden it from her, probably because he should never have been in such a position. He should have been at her mother's side, not playing a whipping boy for the local lords. And Miri was asking him to risk so much more. "I'm afraid I'm very selfish."

Cass's gaze trailed over her face. "You are the most selfless woman I've ever known."

She pressed her lips together. It was something Henry would

have said about Miri's mother but never in the tone Cass had used. The queen had, without fail, put the realm above all else. Her final request, the vow she demanded of her second daughter, was not based on any self-serving motives. It was to save the kingdoms from harm. The Lion Queen knew something that Miri didn't. Miri had always understood that and felt it in her very soul. It was all that kept her going when kings' blood flowed over her hands.

※

MIRI AND CASS filled their wait for the ball with much-needed rest and planning, and she was grateful for the ability to stretch her limbs and soak in a warm bath. Her aching muscles had eased to the point that she thought she might soon not feel the dull pains at all. They'd taken to eating in their rooms because of Miri's fear of being recognized. Cleaned and coiffed and dressed in the clothes of a lady of stature, it was less likely that gazes would skirt her face. Bean had been the best of disguises, but a common trader or cleaning girl would not be welcome in the castle. It was also likely that her wound would be noticed, and even Cass had not known how many details of Edwin's attacker had been noted by the kingsmen. The night had been dark, and blood had been everywhere. Miri couldn't be certain that the location of her injury had even been obvious.

But she suspected it very much was. She'd relived the event a hundred times since, and at least one sinister detail could not be resolved. Edwin's mistress had already been standing in the doorway when Miri had killed the king. Miri couldn't say how long her witness had stood in watch, because she'd not heard her approach. It must have happened in the struggle, and she must have seen the blade to Miri's throat, and maiden save her, the woman's silence during the struggle was all that had kept Miri alive.

"What are you watching?" she asked Cass as he leaned

against the open window, his shoulder cushioned by a thick pillar of brocade drapes drawn against the wall.

He turned from the window, clearly intending to change the subject and distract her. Miri had caught on to his tells, and she would fall for no more of his clever games. She pinned him with a glare and stood to cross the room.

The sun was low in the afternoon sky, casting shadows from the tall buildings that lined the plaza below. The mountain had been bustling with guests in preparation for the ball, but the crowd that had gathered seemed rowdier than the others. They surrounded a platform in the center of the stone, their voices rising in gleeful jeers and eager shouting. Men and women dressed in finery had joined with the local merchants to watch a proceeding that sent a dark foreboding into the pit of Miri's stomach.

"Who is he?"

Cass shook his head. His constant presence beside Miri was something she'd grown to expect. "A lord, I think. It's too far to make out the shouting, but his coat is dark blue."

Miri's skin went cold. "A sympathizer?"

Cass didn't answer, not as she stood beside him in a room supplied by true sympathizers and as they were about to watch another man be tortured for loyalty to a dead queen.

The man was dragged onto the platform, his fine coat torn from his body to cheers from the watching horde.

"How many?" Miri whispered. She was not certain what she was asking: how many this year? How many since the last attempts at revolt? The sorcerers had burned thousands in Stormskeep uprisings alone. Miri had no idea how many had been slaughtered across the realm.

"Too many to count," Cass said.

Too many. Too many to die. Too many who would pay for a crime that was not theirs.

Miri didn't look away as they bound the man to the post. She didn't turn her gaze from the blood or block out the sound of his screams. Miri watched as one more was murdered at the hands of the bastard kings, and she renewed her vow of vengeance once more. Miri would reclaim whatever kingdoms she could. The kings of the realm would pay their due. The Lion had come to collect.

CHAPTER 26

Cass helped Miri into her gown. The thin undershirt she'd worried at relentlessly over the past months seemed to do nothing to mask the yellowing bruises that covered her skin. He'd watched as she powered her face where the marks would show, as she dusted her healing fingers, and covered every bit that wouldn't be concealed by her dress. She'd chosen one that buttoned high up her neck and had layers of silk and beads that he feared were too heavy for summer and were likely to restrict her movements. "I'll not be fighting," she'd promised, but there was not much else to be done. Bruises on a lady would draw attention, and any flesh that was bare would be looked upon in such a crowd.

"Tighter," Miri told him. "Near the waist."

Cass tugged the laces and straightened the fabric, and when she approved, he finished the last of the buttons up the line of her neck. Her hair, dark again after Ginger had dyed it on their trip, was pinned into loops at the crown of her head.

Miri stared down at herself. "Garish color."

"It will look perfect with mine."

She laughed. "A matched set, indeed." She turned as he tied the sash over her dress. "Best get into your own regalia."

"Yes," he said. "I'll be back in a wink."

Miri gave him a smile as he left the room, then Cass drew his new attire from their things. The pouch Terric had given him was tucked safely away, and he only had a few of the gems on his person. Coin was all well and good near the port, but in the north, help became more expensive. He laced on his pants and shirt then put on his tall boots, hating the way they felt. He hadn't worn a formal suit in some time, and so many layers felt stiff and constricting. Cass saved the jacket for last, grateful that at least the ball was held late into the evening, when the air would be cool, and fastened the buttons lining his sleeves.

"Do you need help?" Miri called from the adjoining room.

"Nearly done," Cass said. "Are you impatient?"

She stuck her head through the doorway to give him a look.

He laughed. She'd been a shaking mess not two hours before, when the spider had to be moved from its wooden cage into the delicate shell and sealed with wax. Miri had nearly lost her nerve and might have been convinced to call the entire thing off, but she'd done it and since had seemed surprisingly untroubled. The night's task would be easy, she'd kept saying.

Cass reached into the pocket of his traveling clothes then crossed to Miri, trying not to stare at the color she'd added to her lips. She pressed them together, as if self-conscious, and looked up at him with eyes that seemed golden beneath lids as black as soot. Cass pinned the brooch to her dress.

"Where did you find this?" Miri asked.

He straightened the pin to his liking. "An astute trader by the name of Hugh persuaded me to purchase it for my new wife." At Miri's laugh, he added, "He did not offer to refund my coin when he discovered the truth of our arrangement."

"Cunning."

Her smile speared his chest, but Cass did not look away. "Indeed."

"How do we look?" Miri asked. She spun past him, moved toward the side table, and had the looking glass in hand before he'd a moment to even decide how to answer. "Gods," she moaned. "I should have used this one to apply the makeup."

Cass chuckled. "We still have the masks."

Her eyes caught on the scar at her temple, the one from when she was a child, then fell to the strip of cloth covering her neck. She put the looking glass down, with its reflection toward the tabletop. Her gown was snug against her frame, flattering despite its cut, and Cass wished it were cool enough for cloaks and fur, something bulky to disguise her effortless grace and bearing of a princess. She glanced absently at his things on the table, her pale, powdered fingers brushing over a short lock of hair.

Cass froze, his heart in his throat.

Miri touched the lock carefully. It wasn't the pale lion's mane that it should truly have been but the color it had been so long ago when they'd first left Smithsport. Her wide eyes snapped to Cass.

"It's not..." His hands came forward of their own accord. "It wasn't intentional. I just—I found it caught in the cuff of my boot, and I didn't—" He shook his head. "I had no place to dispose of it. Nothing seemed right, then..." He had no excuse for why he'd not done away with it since.

She was quiet as she stared back at him, expression unreadable.

"Miri," he said. *Please,* he wanted to beg. *Say something.*

She swallowed, giving a small, single shake of her head, as if dislodging a thought. "Of course." *Of course.* She waved a hand as if the whole thing were nothing then picked up the masks. "Final touches," she told the room. "And we're off to the ball."

⁂

CASS HAD NEVER FELT MORE unsettled by Miri's silence. As they walked toward the palace, she said nothing at all. Kingsmen watched at every turn. The myriad of masked figures trailing the corridors and walkways was an evident nightmare to anyone whose duty was to guard. Cass adjusted the fine sword at his hip as he did his best to keep their pace and maintain a good distance from the flock of bodies, but soon they were corralled into lines with the other guests, and stringed instruments conducted their way past candelabras, lush flowers, and gratuitous decorations. The crowd became thicker, and Miri offered Cass her hand. He took it, sliding his other across her back to guide her through the celebration and into the great hall.

Long tables filled one half of the room, and the other was an open space for dancing, while milling patricians lined the walls. Voices rose to a vaulted ceiling that was grand and meant to impress. The food was lavish, revoltingly so, given the tax the king demanded of the citizens of the kingdom, and dark drapes hung above low windows that looked out over the mountain. It was breathtaking, even for him, because it had been so long since the harbormaster's spy had been anything else—more so because it was a sharp reminder of times before.

Miri's hand tightened in his, and he let his gaze travel to hers. His mask—a wolf that covered his face from brow to nose—had been the least vision restrictive, but he wanted to tear it free regardless and have back an unhindered view. She stared up at him, the dark around her eyes seeming to draw them farther into the shadows of her mask.

"Dancing first?" he offered.

She managed a partial nod beneath the bulk of her costume. The pouch at her waist held a delicate carton, inside of which waited a deadly spider. To place it in the king's chair, she would have to approach his table while he danced, land it perfectly into his seat, and appear to only be greeting his guests and sampling his food. "Easy," she'd said before. He wondered if she was still so convinced.

Cass led her to the floor, through couples that were a dazzling display of fabric and excess, and found a spot that was less stifling than the rest. He bowed low before her, his hand beneath hers, and Miri followed with a curtsy. Gods, he'd no idea how they'd gotten there, why a princess of Stormskeep was bending a knee to him. He straightened then inclined his head as they began their dance.

It was much later when the king finally graced the festivities, his dark hair loose and his mask only a sliver of jeweled material, and longer still when Miri finally took her chance. She'd pointedly avoided looking at the king since he'd been present, but as soon as he made his way from the high table, she sauntered toward it, where the king's chair waited, empty as he paraded for his guests. Myrina of Stormskeep had years of practice engaging with nobility, and it seemed the time as Bean had done nothing to diminish her skill. She was in her element, and her practiced ease distracted each of the men and ladies from the skilled maneuver she performed beneath their very noses. Beyond the king's table stood a row of kingsmen, their gazes on the crowd. Cass watched closely, but none so much as flinched.

She tipped her head, raising her glass in toast, and turned from the table to trail slowly from their notice as if she'd never been there at all.

Cass shifted toward the window, his chest finally easing to draw a full breath. Her arm brushed his as she joined him, her hand steady as she set the goblet onto the window's ledge, its rim dripping honey. She'd done it. She'd returned.

"Shall we go?" she asked.

He slid an arm across the small of her back, his gaze over her shoulder at the kingsmen blocking the door.

"What are they doing?" Miri asked once she'd followed his indication. Her brow was pinched, but the floor was still filled with dancing royals, and fine music still floated through the air.

"There will be a display soon," Cass said. "Whispers of a surprise."

"They don't want to ruin it," she said, though she did not sound entirely convinced. "Well enough. Let us dance again."

Cass smiled, certain his feet would be raw from his boots,

and spun Miri to face him before the window. "Then let us dance."

They relaxed into the music and the steps, sated with the knowledge that Miri's task was done, and buoyed by sweet ciders and wine. Cass could sense the tension drain from her as her moves returned to the easy grace he'd come to know so well. She'd done it. She'd killed two kings already, a third would be overtaken by illness in a month's time, and the fourth would soon meet his end.

Her smile came easily, her relief palpable, as if she finally believed she might be able to pull the entire thing off. The mountain breeze was cool on Cass's skin as it whispered through the tall windows and was scented of pine and moss and something sweet. Miri leaned her head back, mask to the ceiling, as if the breeze could somehow reach the skin of her neck beneath all that silk. She seemed to float around him, a whirl of rich fabrics, her fingers light in his.

Then the candelabras were unexpectedly snuffed, and the ballroom fell dim with a suddenness that elicited sharp gasps. Cass's hand slid to the sword at his hip, his other stilled in Miri's grip. In the darkness outside, a strange orange glow rose past the window, and the echoing gasps shifted into delighted intakes of breath.

Miri stepped closer to Cass, her movement causing him to turn and forcing his gaze from the line of kingsmen against the far wall. "Lanterns," she whispered. "In honor of the maiden."

Half a dozen more rose into view, followed by too many to count. Tinted paper, lifted by a small flame within that cast a glow into the night sky, dotting the view outside with color. Cass had known they'd been imported from Stormskeep, but it had been impossible to imagine how ethereal the scene would be.

Miri laughed, her breath brushing his skin. He found her watching him and was captured by the change in her mood.

"You've got honey on your lip," she said. Her hand rose as if automatically to his face, which was bare below the mask. His mouth was sweet with drink. Hers would be, too, and it was all he could think of when her finger brushed his lip. She froze, staring up at him, her lips parting in a whisper of breath. He wanted nothing more than to taste them, and gods help him, he'd somehow leaned nearer. Her gaze danced between his eyes, and Cass had the strangest sensation that she was convincing herself it wasn't real and she could break the rules behind that mask and her lips could touch him just like her hand.

Cass didn't want to pretend. His fingers itched to tug free the ribbon that held her mask. He wanted to see Miri when she kissed him. He wanted it to be real.

They both startled when a voice slithered between them. Cass's gaze snapped to the reveler. His thin jeweled mask was nothing of a disguise. A spear of ice pierced Cass's chest.

The king smiled indulgently. "A dance, my lady?" he repeated, proffering his hand.

Miri had gone still. Cass's fingers tightened in hers, and her throat bobbed. "I couldn't—I'm not fit for the honor, Your Majesty." She had known Peter when she was a child and he was only a lord. She'd forgotten to curtsy.

"Nonsense." Peter reached forward and snatched Miri's hand.

Her other hand went loose in Cass's. He held her still, willing her to not attack the man in a room that held a hundred kingsmen. Peter's smile curved into something sly. The men at his back wore no expressions at all. They were not Peter's friends or members of his court. They were kingsmen as well, decked in fancy dress. Keenly aware of the gentle breeze behind their backs, a drop to certain death their only escape, Cass pressed his thumb harder to Miri's wrist, wanting to signal that they were in far more trouble than seemed and that she should hold her tongue.

But Peter's words slid liquidly over the warning, shattering any hope they might have had left. "In fact," he purred, "why don't you come to sit in my chair?"

Miri did not jerk from the king but instead feigned surprise. "I could not," she started, but Peter drew her closer.

"My dear, I insist." His voice was low and friendly, as if he were playing a game of seduction with a lady of his court. He gestured to the men behind him. "You see, my men saw you admiring it earlier, and I do so hate to disappoint. Especially at a party." He pulled Miri to his side, squeezing her too tight and out of Cass's reach. Cass shifted his hand to his side, nearer his sword in case he had a chance to draw it, but felt the presence of at least two more kingsmen behind him.

The king glanced up at Cass, and a soft laugh escaped as his gaze took in Cass's understanding that he was well trapped. Peter wet his lips as he ran a finger up Miri's arm. Her body was pressed to him in a grip he might use on a lover. Miri craned her neck away from the man as his finger trailed higher, but she couldn't truly escape his grasp. The king's fingers came across her shoulder and up the high collar of her gown, and he leaned in, as if he meant to brush a soft kiss to her jaw. "It is so lovely for you to have come," Peter murmured against her ear. "When I heard the news, I expected to have to wait."

Miri's chest rose in a shallow breath, but she didn't speak.

Peter did not seem to mind. He brushed his nose against her hair, keeping his eyes on Cass. The moment he moved, blood would be spilled. The threat was clear. "Talk had already reached us, of course, of the assassination of Edwin." He chuckled. "As if we would believe the fool was taken down by a plot spurred by his mistress, while the sorcerers of Ironwood held her blood." His finger brushed slowly across the base of Miri's chin before returning to the other side. "Then, lo and behold, news arrived that the king of Kirkwall had succumbed to an illness, taken by a sudden, inexplicable decline in his health."

Miri did tense then. Simon's death had come far too soon. The fool must have drowned himself in the doctored tonic the moment he'd first felt unwell.

"Yes," Peter purred at Miri's reaction. "Just as I thought. And what sort of lady, I asked, would we be looking for?" The movement of his finger across Miri's jaw was torturously slow, his lips nearly brushing her flesh as his grip tangled in the silk that hung from mask to neck. "A wound, they explained. A knife point just here..."

Peter ripped the silk free, his mouth suddenly hard. The kingsmen's hands were on Cass before he had a moment to move. A blade was pressed to his ribs, harder than mere threat.

The king shoved Miri toward another kingsman and said, his voice thick with disgust, "Take them to the tower."

※

CASS WAS SHOVED FORWARD and only caught a glimpse of Miri's eyes behind her mask. *The tower!* the look seemed to scream. *The sorcerers.* But she was jerked from his view by another pair of kingsmen as they escorted Cass and Miri across the room. The sorcerers would use Miri's blood to destroy her, draining her of life to summon dark magic for use for the kings.

It might have been best to throw themselves out the window instead of being taken, to end it quickly, but they'd not had the chance for even that. Behind them, the king clapped. His words were muffled by the crowd as revelers gasped and whispered at the pair being hauled through the ball. Peter played the incident off as little need for concern, and his jests were followed by an easy laugh.

When Cass was a boy, he had thought of the lords who'd stolen everything from him a great deal. There was an order to how badly he'd wished them all dead. Peter had been second on that list.

The kingsman at one arm shoved Cass forward roughly, spitting onto the path at his feet. Another held Cass's other arm, and footfalls indicated at least six kingsmen behind them, plus two more with Miri. He could take maybe five of the men and not the big ones, but he had no way to stop them before they decided to run a blade through her side in retaliation. They didn't know who Miri truly was. But it was only a matter of time before they did.

When they exited the ballroom, the kingsmen were joined by four more men, a lead group to clear any trouble crossing the grounds. They would traverse the corridors, cross a high bridge, then start their ascent of the tower, where Miri and Cass could be split from each other, where he might never see Miri again. His mind ran through a dozen scenarios, none of them good. He needed to get free before they reached the bridge, and he needed to do it without getting Miri killed.

Cass drew steady breaths, tracking the footfalls of the men behind him. The bridge was in the distance, its railing lit by lanterns, and the faint outline of the king's banners snapped in the wind. He would have poor footing on the bridge and no room to fight on the stairs. If Cass meant to do anything, it had to happen before they reached the next turn. His foot raised in a step as Cass prepared to move in a swift series of strikes, and a solid piece of blunt metal slammed into the base of his neck.

He felt himself thrown forward, stars bursting in his vision, while his arms were still held by the other men. His head lolled forward, his ears rang, and he was unable to keep his eyes open. Snatches of recognition broke through as he was shifted and lifted. His arms were useless as they hung limp beneath him over the shoulder of a massive kingsman.

CHAPTER 27

Cass woke to the sound of trickling water and flashes of memory of a darkened stairwell, the clank of metal and scrape of stone, and footfalls of the kingsmen as they'd dropped him to the ground and walked away. His head throbbed, his eyes were dry, and thoughts and senses were somehow far away. His hands felt tight and swollen, and when he tried to shift them, they didn't move. He winced as he pulled his eyes open to find a stone floor, his arms draped before him, and his wrists bound.

Then his attention snapped back, alarm roaring through him. He was strapped to a wooden structure and had a rope around his torso, latching him to a bar like some sort of makeshift pillory. But his head was free. He lifted it, wincing at the stiffness and pain, and found the eyes of a sorcerer on him.

Dread rose though Cass, more real since he was fully awake. The man's gaze left Cass as he calmly went back to his work, entirely at odds with the terror and rage coursing through Cass. They were in a tower room, the sorcerer's workspace. Cass had never seen one in person—the queensguard were kept as far from them as possible—but there was no mistaking the implements of the man's craft. Bottles and jars filled the shelves that lined each wall. The space was only broken by tall, narrow windows and alcoves. Tables and contraptions were in the center of the room, and a large fire pit was near an outer wall.

The sorcerer's robe was draped over a rack. His uniform was a tight-fitting, high-collared jacket. He would not need access to his own skin that day, not when he had bodies from which to draw. The sorcerer shifted to set a tool on the table behind him, and Miri came into view.

Cass's throat went thick. She was draped over a rack not unlike his, her head hanging limply over a basin, her body still. Cass's mind supplied a reminder of the sharp metal tools in the sorcerer's grip, an image of just how perfectly the blood would drip from her neck into the basin below. They would empty her of blood.

Cass's gaze went wildly through the room, but there was only one sorcerer present, not a single kingsman or another soul. No one was worried that he and Miri might break free. Assassination attempts had been frequent in the years since the queen's murder. They'd no idea who Cass and Miri truly were. He didn't know if that made it any easier.

Unsure if it was the best path, Cass opened his mouth to speak. He didn't want to give the man information or for the man to realize who Miri and Cass were, but he needed to stop him from draining her before it was too late. His voice was a broken croak. "Don't—" He stopped to clear his throat, but the sorcerer glanced at him.

"Not to worry," the man said mildly. "I've no need for your blood."

Cass swallowed, letting his confusion show.

The sorcerer wiped a cloth over a long, narrow blade. "I prefer the girl's. Hers will be enough. We're well stocked, to tell the truth." He set the blade beside the others, absently straightening each as if running through the procedure in his mind, to be certain everything was prepared.

"What will you do with—" Cass coughed and realized it was not merely a dry throat. Something of a fume hung in the air. A bitter sharpness was on his tongue and through his nose.

The sorcerer waved a hand and said, tone unconcerned, "You'll both be burned, by order of the king." He held a glass vial to the light. "Fortunately, he has no interest in interrupting his celebration with a public display, so he'll never know this one was bled first." He chuckled, glancing sidelong at Cass. "I've a feeling Peter would not approve of the assassin's blood being used to procure his demands."

Cass worked his throat and slid his tongue over his teeth. The king did not want Miri's blood stolen. It was why they were in the tower alone—no witnesses and no reason for concern that a bound girl could escape, not when dark magic was so close at hand.

The sorcerer crossed to the window before opening its shutters wide. Cass glanced down again at the stone ring that surrounded his feet and circled the rack he was tied to. They would be burned upon those racks, sorcerer's fire tearing over them the moment Miri was drained.

The sorcerer crossed to the next window. His features were sharp, and his skin was pale. His short hair was nearly black, his frame tall and lean. Cass did not remember the man from his youth, and the man clearly did not remember Cass.

Cass pressed his booted feet to the floor but was unable to gain purchase. His gaze darted to the open windows, the spiral stair, and the single closed door. "Take me first," Cass demanded. "By the laws of mercy, burn me now."

The sorcerer did not so much as turn.

"Take me first, or I will fight and scream to the very end."

The man gave Cass a flat look. Any number of potions would silence Cass, but he was betting on the sorcerer not wanting to waste stock when his captives would be burned within minutes, regardless. Cass did not let his gaze waver. It was a vow to make the task as unpleasant as possible and drive the meticulous man to vexation by the only means he had. The man gave Cass a measured look, likely deciding whether it was worth the trouble to knock him out or stuff his mouth with a rag, but the sorcerer only sighed and positioned the sharp tool on the table in its neat row.

Cass's chest squeezed, hope thrashing beneath his bonds. When the Storm Queen had taken rule, she'd set a protection to prevent the sorcerers from coming back into power. It was a bond that had helped keep the throne secure. Cass was no mere queensguard. He was bloodsworn.

Inky smoke crawled across the stone floor, spreading from the sorcerer's feet. His thin, scarred hands curled into claws as he reached out. His eyes had gone milky white, and his mouth was hard. The power did not come easily, but it had become their nature to reach for it when other means might be just as quick. The darkness wanted sacrifice, paid in blood. Those who practiced continued to use it, because once they started, they couldn't stop. Magic demanded a price.

The smoke swelled over Cass's body, rising with the sickly-sweet stench of decay. The sorcerer flicked his wrists, releasing the dark energy to do its work with a snap of angry heat, and turned back to his tools.

He had no notion the magic was useless on Cass, less a threat than the tiny blade he held. As the sorcerer's flame erupted, searing and unnatural on the dais, it burned instantly through Cass's clothes and the ropes.

Cass felt the pull of his grim smile. Dark magic was a thing of unmatched power but one that could never reach those bound to the queen by blood. Fire raged over him, but he rose, bare and unsteady. Cassius of Stormskeep could not be burned.

※

CASS BURST from the dais the moment his ropes burned free, launching himself at the sorcerer while flames still licked at the shreds of material that had been his clothes. He was bare but for the pants that had been spattered with blood from a shallow wound over his abdomen. The sorcerer turned just as Cass slammed into him, eyes wide at the realization that Cass had not been burned and that the boy he'd tied to a rack was no mere peasant.

It was too late for the knowledge to be of help. The table crashed to the floor beside them, thin metal tools clattering over stone. The narrow blade he'd held glanced off of Cass's bare shoulder, but Cass snapped the man's neck before he managed another blow. The tool rolled to the floor among the others. Cass's blood dripped from a cut he hadn't felt. He glanced down at himself and the shards of metal beneath his bare feet then cursed, leaving the mess to go to Miri.

He lifted her head gently and slowly, flinching at the sight of her face. She must have fought the kingsmen who'd carried her to the tower, because the coal black she'd painted below her brow was smeared over her features. Her eyes were wide and distant, lost to the call of the dark magic the sorcerers held. Cass didn't need to check the body behind him. The man was dead—which meant the other sorcerer was close, near enough to put Miri into a state of trance.

He carefully unbound her ropes, his fingers slick with sweat. "Miri," he whispered, laying her on the floor beside her would-be pyre. She did not react. Cass checked her for wounds, but she still wore her gown. Her skin was covered aside from her hands and face. He scanned the work table's contents and found a pitcher that seemed to contain only water beside a folded rag. He splashed it over his blood on the floor, cleaned his feet, then, with a steadying breath, stole the dead man's shoes. He grabbed the black cloak from the rack, found his discarded scabbard and sword, and shoved two knives from the table beneath a stolen belt.

Cass knelt before Miri, taking her face in his hand so that she might see him. "I'm sorry," he told her. "I will get us free."

One way or the other, Cass would keep her from another sorcerer's hands. He hoped it would be safely. By the gods, he hoped he could do it. He lifted her body into his arms and ran for the stairs.

CHAPTER 28

Miri was trapped within her body, unable to even scream. A familiar fear threatened to drown her, a feeling she could not separate from the very real danger they were in. She'd felt it before, as a child, when she'd been drenched in her mother's blood.

Cass apologized each time he shifted her and each time he stumbled. Her throat was thick, her chest was heavy, and she had the taste of ash in her mouth. When they'd been caught, the kingsmen had knocked out Cass and thrown him over a shoulder to toss his body into a lift to reach the tower. Miri had tried for her dagger then, but she had lost her faculties and was suddenly being dragged between two men. They'd thought she had fainted. They had laughed. The panic that had seized her had only grown as they'd climbed the tower. Miri was unable to move at all by the time she reached the sorcerer's room. She had wondered if she would soon lose the capacity to breathe, but it had not come to that, even when the man had touched her.

She could still feel the pinch of his icy fingers as they jerked her into place and bound her to the rack. Her mask had fallen off somewhere along the way, but Miri could feel the oily colors that smeared her face. It was maybe all that had saved her. The man no more than glanced at her as she was shoved face down over a basin.

"Leave her," the sorcerer had said, and the kingsmen had done so without argument.

Miri counted the steps, the way she had done on the kingsman's ascent, willing the ability to move into her limbs. But she could not. She was frozen and could do nothing, even as Cass shifted her over his shoulder and ran. She heard the clink of metal, the shouts, and the sound of running boots. Cass spun beneath her, sword in hand, and lunged at two men. One fell where she could see him. The other she only heard. Cass set her down on a step to drag the bodies into an alcove then issued another apology before he lifted her again.

Sorry for what? she wanted to scream. She didn't know whether he was sorry for saving her, for doing the one thing she could never do, or if he was sorry that she was trapped in a hell, helpless to break free. It didn't matter. It only mattered that they got away from there, even if the only answer was jumping from the side of the tower and plunging to their deaths.

Miri would not let them have her blood. It would be the only thing worse than letting them live, the only thing worse than breaking her vow.

"Seven hells," Cass grumbled, spinning to face two more men.

He handled them quickly, even with her body draped over his shoulder, but she could tell the running was wearing him down. He slipped into a darkened corridor, and Miri felt a cool breeze cross her skin as he settled her to the ground. Somehow, beneath the layers of ash and bitter smoke, she tasted fresh air. They were getting away, gaining distance enough that she was not so drowned in fear. But it was not far enough. She heard Cass's breath in the darkness and felt him shifting beside her before he went still. Footsteps echoed down the corridor, nearer then farther away. Cass's dagger slid into a sheath, and he slumped down beside her. His breathing grew steadier before he rose again, taking her in his arms.

She felt as if the high collar of her gown was choking her but could do nothing to rip it free. Her thoughts were clearing, though, and her breath was coming more easily. When they broke through the last doorway and into a moonlit sky, a sigh escaped from her.

Cass's arm was firm across her legs as he strode from the tower dressed in a sorcerer's robe. She could hear the river beneath the bridge and hoped that if they were caught, he would be strong enough to toss her in. If they were lucky, the fall would kill them before their bodies could be fished from the water. If they were lucky, they would be drowned without spilling a drop of blood.

Miri felt the pain in her side once more and felt the movement of her eyelids in a scratchy, horrible blink. She was returning to herself, and her fingers curled into Cass's stolen robe. He jolted, then his head swiveled as he searched their surroundings. He stopped to settle Miri onto the ground and knelt before her to peer into her face. She only nodded. She didn't think she could speak. He shoved aside layers of her dress to check her shoes then slid his hands beneath her arms to raise her to standing. When she didn't wobble, he let her test her steps, and the gratitude was bare on his face.

She could walk. They could run. Cass did not say a word and only shoved a dagger into her hand. He took hold of the other, his palm hot against hers, and turned her toward the path.

Then the bells atop the tower sounded, and a castle full of kingsmen went on alert.

☙

MIRI RAN with Cass toward the cliff's edge, the drop that led to the landing where boats were loaded to haul cargo down the

Maidensgrace. They would never escape. Cass had to know that, and she opened her mouth to tell him so and demand that they should jump. But Cass need not go with her, she realized. He was only a guard. Miri's blood was the true danger, and his vow could not stop him from keeping her out of the sorcerers' hands.

"Cass," she managed, her voice broken and dry, but before another word spilled from her throat, it contracted with unstoppable fear.

He took hold of her, evidently seeing the look cross her face and knowing the second sorcerer must be near. He yanked her from the side of the cliff. Her skirts were a wall of fabric around her, the blood magic a painful seizing of her chest, then they splashed into cool water. Miri's limbs were unable to fight the current, though distance had brought her the capacity to at least not breathe the water into her lungs. She was pushed and thrown in the darkness, cold blackness surrounding her to pull her down, and she was drowning beneath the weight of it for the second time in her life.

Water. Ash. Blood.

Then Cass's arm came around her, and he towed her with him as he swam backward toward the rock wall. She sucked in a breath but didn't struggle, and soon he held on to a mooring as the current tugged at her skirts. Her fingers rose to her neck over his arm, fumbling helplessly over the buttons at her collar. She felt as if she still could not breathe.

Cass's mouth came to her ear, and over the muffled shouts above and sounds of faraway ship work, he said, "I've got you. You're safe."

She let out an incredulous laugh, and her eyes ran with tears as she raised her face to the night sky beyond a cliff wall. Cass held her tighter. She gulped in air, wrapping her arms around his. She could feel the rise and fall of his chest behind her and his legs beneath the current in a stolen ceremonial robe. Miri forced her breathing to calm, pacing it with his, but she could not stop the tears that ran freely.

"You're safe," he said against her neck. "You're safe, and I'm going to get you onto a boat. We're going home, Myrina. We're going to Stormskeep."

CHAPTER 29

Miri spent days in the dark hold of a narrow river boat with Cass, tucked between crates and barrels as ropes and pulleys swayed overhead. Her guard had known men on the river and knew who and how to approach. He'd called in favors, made threats, and handed over the last of his coins and jewels. The first night, they had curled together, soaked in river water and weak from their flight. Cass had loosened the buttons at her neck, which had felt as if they were choking her, wiped the last of the black from her eyes, then returned his arm to its place around her as they listened to the men above and waited for sounds of their discovery.

But the kingsmen had never come. The following day, still exhausted, they sat quietly in the darkness. Miri had relived their escape a dozen times, but that count was nothing compared to the nightmare of being tied beneath the sorcerer's hands, helpless and so close to losing her blood. She was no longer paralyzed by the darkness, but it had become clear exactly how much hold the blood magic had over her.

Queen's blood was the most powerful and dangerous. It was why they hadn't yet killed Lettie. Changing fate always had a cost. The cost of their mother dying had been paid by the people of the realm, thousands slaughtered at the hands of the sorcerers on the kings' commands. They had kept Lettie alive thus far, but it would not last. On her name day, the moment she was a true queen and able to ascend, her sister would be gone.

The magic's hold over Miri was the same as the paralyzing fear she'd felt the day her mother had died. They had stolen her mother's blood, and somehow, it was affecting Miri too.

"I didn't know," Cass said. Dim light shone through overhead, but it barely reached them where they huddled among the cargo. At her look, he said, "I didn't know you were afraid of the water. I should have."

He must have seen the remembered terror in her face, and though Miri could not say she relished once again being trapped in the darkness with the fear, it was not the same. Cass was with her, and she was not alone. She ran her hands over her bare arms. She'd stripped off the dress and draped it in layers so that the material could fully dry, and she sat with him in nothing but a thin shift and her underthings, her mother's pendant safely sewn into the hem. Cass had not done the same, though he'd loosened the neck of the sorcerer's robe enough to reveal that he was bare underneath.

"I'm not," she said quietly. "It's not the water. I thought it was, but all this time…" Her eyes met his again. "It wasn't the water."

It was the magic that had wrapped her in dread and had made her feel as if she would be swallowed by darkness and drowned.

"Do you wonder," he asked, "what would have happened if we'd left on the ship in Smithsport?"

She did not wonder. Miri might have lived, but only at the cost of breaking her vow. Lettie would have died.

"I've thought of a thousand ways in which we might help you," Cass admitted. "Gathering the last of us, storming the castle in the night." He shook his head. "None of it would work.

We all knew it. There was no way to reach her inside those castle walls."

No way to bypass the sorcerers, he meant, and no way to change their fate.

"I didn't know I would react that way," she told him. "I should have. Gods, how could I not have known, but I didn't, Cass. I didn't understand what it would do to me. I never felt tied to it at all."

If Cass had not been bloodsworn, both he and Miri would be dead. And with the blood the sorcerers drained from her—once they realized what they had—they would likely have moved on the kings, taken rule themselves, and destroyed what was left of order in the realm. As it was, only one thing was stopping them.

"We can't let them use Lettie," Miri whispered. "They can never take her blood."

Cass didn't answer, because they both knew the kings would wait. Queen's blood was the only thing capable of dismantling the protections the Storm Queen put in place, and until Lettie's name day, she would not be a true queen. The sorcerers would attempt to take her then. But the kings were no fools. They understood that a queen was the only one who could prevent the sorcerers from overtaking the realm. They would have a plan in place to prevent such a thing, probably to drain her in a public display and let her blood spill over the square. They would be safe from the sorcerers' grasp.

Both sides played a dangerous game. No matter who won, it was the realm who paid the price.

"They'll be watching the ports." Cass sighed, returning to the more pressing issue of their continued escape. "We'll have to swim ashore north of Stormskeep and continue on foot until we can find a safe route in." He did not have to say the rest—that sorcerers would be everywhere and that Miri's face could be recalled by anyone old enough to remember. Stormskeep was her home, its citizens her family. They would not forget. "I'll sneak into the shelter deck and find us some clothes." His gaze raked over her hair. "Maybe see if you can sort that out."

Miri hiccuped a laugh, but it made her chest hurt. "Daring words for a man who's nearly bare beneath a stolen robe."

Cass's expression was solemn, and she had the feeling he was grateful he had any clothes at all. He rose to his feet, muttering, and Miri's smile melted into something more genuine.

※

CASS HAD RETURNED with hard bread and two sets of dusty clothes, and Miri was dressed as a crewman, baggy pants tucked into her boots and braided hair stuffed beneath a worn cap. Cass had tied a block to the monstrosity that was her costume dress and drowned it in the river, in case the ship was searched at dock. They were safe from being reported since the crew had given them passage, because the kings wouldn't care whether they'd intended to help or not. In the days that had followed Miri and Cass's escape, the other sorcerers would have discovered the footprints out of the ash and that Cass had not been burned. The kingsmen would have been questioned and would have admitted that the captive girl had fainted and that she'd had to be carried as they approached the tower.

Traces of their presence and details of the previous assassinations would be tallied. Miri and Cass would be found out.

They leapt from the boat without warning to the captain or crew. Cass had waited for an opportune moment when the crew was distracted so that he could tow Miri with him as he swam toward shore. The fewer who witnessed their departure, the better, and Miri saw none appear to take notice, if they'd seen them at all.

"How long do you think we have?" Miri asked as they walked through the low grass that bordered the river. They would make for the trees and do their best to stay out of sight. Her eyes had not yet adjusted, and the open air seemed too bright.

"Days," Cass said. His linen shirt clung to his skin, his hair was dripping, and his chin was dark with stubble. "It will be much harder, but we will have more help."

Miri's stomach went tight. Terric and the others had been gathering support, drawing together the last of the queensguard and those loyal to the true heir. They would risk everything, all in on the last chance to save the realm. She stumbled, and Cass's hand latched onto her elbow to steady her. His gaze came to hers, searching, and Miri reined in her emotions. "I've got it," she said. "Sea legs, is all."

Cass gave her a look, but she kept on. They walked through thin trees over rolling hills and rich soil and plants greener than anything she'd seen in ages. Familiar scents assaulted her at every turn. Miri's chest swelled in a deep breath, and her fingers itched to touch the trees and the earth and the undeniable sensation of *home*. When she glanced at Cass, his eyes were on the forest, and she could see the change in him as well. They had been dragged as children out of Stormskeep, the only place that had ever felt safe and secure. They were there to take it back.

Cass's gaze met hers, but they didn't speak. They only moved forward, toward the late-day sun. The location of his exit from the boat had not been an accident, and he led them to a small farm that must have been a full day's walk from the keep. It was late summer, warm as the sun set on a field of wheat and the call of goats echoed from their pen near the barns. Miri's thumb pressed against the gold band on her finger, and she reminded herself that she was Bean. They had not a single pack or possession aside from the stolen clothes they wore, but Cass strode forward with a confidence that lent her strength. He left her by the stable while he met with the proprietor and returned by the time the animals had lost interest in their new visitor.

They'd been given a small cabin near the rear of the property, and as Cass fetched water for the heating stove, a woven basket of food and a stack of fresh clothes were delivered.

By nightfall, Miri and Cass were fed and clean and wrapped

loosely in soft blankets beneath thin nightclothes despite the heat. It felt good to be in a bed, over steady planks that didn't sway with the current of the Maidensgrace. The bed was large in the single room, and Cass sat at one end with Miri at the other.

She shifted closer, used to his presence, and leaned her back to the wall beside him. "You've not asked me to tell you," she said. Her voice was soft, and she was hesitant to break the pleasant peace. He'd always asked her before to tell him of the kingdom and the man she would kill and the method in which she planned to do it. But not with Stormskeep and Nicholas.

Cass frowned. "I want to tell you not to do it. After everything, I still want to ask you not to risk it. I warn you that I know it will be the death of you, and my brothers have tried and failed." His eyes met hers. "That I've watched them die trying."

"Why don't you?" she whispered.

"Because I know it's wrong. I understand why you must."

She'd made a vow, a promise that could not be broken. Cass had made a promise, too, one that she would force him to break. He could not keep Miri alive, because Miri was walking to her death and because Miri's vow had been an order by their queen.

Miri swallowed the words that bubbled up, unable to give them voice. She couldn't stomach the idea of losing Cass, but Cass could never be hers. He was bloodsworn. He belonged to the realm. His duty was to protect her, and it was law and his honor that demanded they not be so near. But he wasn't wrong. Miri *would* be gone soon. There would be nothing left to protect.

"Cass," she started, but her voice died away, because in his eyes was an answer to her fears. She leaned forward, watching him as she reached to trace a thumb over the edge of his lip. She had touched him there before, to brush away a spot of honey, and Miri had wanted nothing more than to press her mouth to his.

He did not move to her, but Miri shifted nearer. When she finally brushed her lips over his, Cass's eyes fell closed in what felt like release or surrender. His strong hands slid over the thin shift that covered her hips, and he drew her closer.

The blanket fell away as his warm lips parted beneath hers, deepening the kiss. Her hands went to his chest then his neck, touching his bare skin, and the presence of him flooded her. She wanted to be nearer and to press herself to him and get lost in the comfort that he'd always provided, the relief she'd felt from the constant loss and knowing what was to come. She wanted to let herself fall. But as grateful as she was to be touching him, part of her would not allow herself to be content in his arms—not while Lettie suffered.

Miri drew away, and Cass's eyes locked with hers.

Her chest ached with the knowledge that she could never truly have him.

The understanding passed between them and settled heavily in the pit of Miri's stomach. Resigned, she slid her hands from their grip on him. But Cass drew her to lie down beside him, and he put his arm around her as he rested at her back.

After a long silence, he said, "Tell me about Stormskeep."

Miri felt the squeeze in her chest lighten. His forgiveness was a balm to her tattered heart. She let her breathing steady before she spoke, her words soft. "Beyond the keep is a large courtyard, a maze of gardens and fountains and sculptures of queens gone past. In the center is a walled sitting area that held the Lion Queen's favorite bench. Each afternoon, no matter the weather, she would take her youngest daughter to rest there so they could sit among the gardens and have a quiet moment to themselves." Miri closed her eyes to the memory, hearing the birdsong and the voices that floated over the wall. "The two were not always alone, though, not the only ones hidden beyond that barrier wall. Some days, there was a boy who played at swords."

Cass's voice was quiet behind her. "Was it Lord Ham Hock?"

Miri's laugh was as soft as a breath. "No. This boy was far more pleasant, hardworking, and eager to impress." She smiled to the room beyond them. "Though he was a bit of a glory hound." Cass snorted, and Miri went on. "He would climb the walls that circled the bench, his long sword glinting in the sun. And there he would practice, without a word, as the queen and her daughter looked on."

"Was it to win the favor of a beautiful princess?" he murmured into her hair.

"Impossible to say," Miri answered. "But the queen had two daughters, sisters unmatched in their wit." She felt Cass smile, but her own smile fell. "The princesses were fortunate in so many things, but the youngest took her pleasure not from fancy dress and matters of state but from those small moments in the garden with a mother who loved her. From her lessons with Henry on how to use a sword." Miri's throat caught, but she forced the words. "From running through the courtyard as if it would always be there."

Cass did not offer her assurances that it would soon be returned. They had both lost everyone they had loved that day as well as their very hearts and home. Miri fell quiet, remembering the faces of each of her maids, her tutors, and her friends. She recalled Henry's fingers, calloused from swords, the way her small hand could disappear inside his, and the way a smile could unexpectedly split his weathered face. She remembered her mother's laugh, how it could echo through the garden, and the way the tension seemed to ease from her shoulders each time Miri entered a room. She had loved Thom and Nan, but Stormskeep would always be home. She might not be able to restore their families, but Miri would take back their home—whatever the cost.

CHAPTER 30

Stormskeep had always been wealthy. It was the center of the realm, heavily populated, well-developed, and the worst place Miri and Cass could be. At any moment, they could be recognized or cross paths with a sorcerer. They could be caught.

But Miri could not bring herself to regret it. She stared out the window of the massive second-story room toward the bright and busy streets below. They had traveled into the city under the guise of a local lord and lady, the queen's faithful guard disguised at their sides. Miri had worn a gown and a veil but had changed into slim pants and a jacket, a wardrobe tailored specifically for her coming task.

She had been reminded of her goal and once again embraced her duty. In a thousand ways, outside their window, Miri's people waited for her to fulfill her vow. Her mother's face was carved into the buildings and statues of Stormskeep, staring down at her not with the soft, understanding eyes that had graced her in private but with the uncompromising severity shown to those who opposed her.

The effigies had been chipped and broken, but they remained standing just the same, carved into stone as a reminder of the way things were meant to be. To speak her name was treason, but the kings could not stop the symbolism and subvert icons. The people of Stormskeep carried on. So in Stormskeep, Miri's mother watched her from everywhere and from nowhere.

"Myrina," someone said from behind her, and she turned to face the room.

A dozen men and women surrounded a map spread over the long table. It was a fraction of what was left of the queensguard, each with their own men to command hidden among the city.

"What of the map?" Terric asked.

He'd only just returned to Stormskeep himself, and as the lot of them gathered, Terric had coordinated contacts across the seven kingdoms. The kings had armies, each of which were scattered through the realm. Nan and Thom would cause havoc at Smithsport and Ginger and Hugh at Blackstone. So many others had risen to aid in their plans as well. Riots and rumor, whatever it took. The sorcerers would need to be drawn out, away from the keep and from Lettie, and should the other tactics not succeed, Miri had given the sorcerers cause enough to leave—to find the second daughter of the Lion Queen.

They would scour the land, and all the while, she would be the last place they would expect her and the most dangerous. Miri and her mother's guard would be at Stormskeep, in the den of a bear. They had reviewed the detailed map, including every unmarked passage inside the castle walls, every tactic the kings had ever used, and every favor that might be won. They had a plan. They were ready.

But they were running out of time. Three kings were dead. One sorcerer was gone. They knew that Miri lived, and once they had the second princess, Lettie's life could be forfeit, no need to wait for the end of summer and her name day. Miri's sister could be killed. And now she knew Nicholas, cowering within the keep, had possession of their mother's blood. Miri made another promise. Nicholas would be the next king to pay his debt.

She looked at the map beneath Terric's hand. She knew the layout of the stronghold by heart. "Burn it. We move at dawn."

꧁

Miri and Cass strode through the passages beneath Stormskeep's castle, quietly dispatching kingsmen who stood in their way. They had an understanding between them. Each was aware of the bone-deep knowledge of a place they'd loved as children, and each was deadly and accurate in their work. It was their home. It was their reckoning.

Behind them and in other parts of the city and the castle, queensguard played their parts. Miri could not go near a sorcerer, but instead of dismay, the news had only brought Terric inspiration. He had called it to their advantage, as Miri's reaction would give them the precious warning they needed. Bloodsworn could not be killed by their magic, so the sorcerers who tried could be driven through with a sword. Together, they would stand a fighting chance. Cass had looked on darkly at the idea a princess could be used as bait, but Miri had not argued. She was walking into the keep one way or another. If they could defend her weakness—as significant as it was—she would take all the help she could get.

She had every intention of killing Nicholas, but no version of the plan allowed her to stride into the throne room and announce her intentions to run him through with her sword. They had decided that she would maintain her distance from the keep as long as possible to minimize her chance of running into the sorcerers. So, with Cass and half a dozen soldiers at her side, she traversed the passageways to the only other place that would be worth the risk—to the cells to find Lettie.

Miri pressed down the fear of what she might find and how the years might have worn on her sister, because all of her focus had to be on their task and their last chance to save the realm. The lot of them were dressed in black, their uniforms trim and weapons sparse. They would be fighting in close quarters, relying heavily on stealth. The kingsmen deep within the castle, their forms broad and menacing in the dark, had not been prepared for the attack. Caught unaware, they fell easily, unsuspecting in their duties for an area the court rarely visited—unless, of course, they'd been placed there permanently. As Cass slid a key into the locked gate, Miri recognized what had been once fine clothes on the prisoners in the cells beyond. She suspected the lowborn criminals had been killed to avoid the hassle of providing steady meals.

A queensguard took a torch from the wall and led Miri down the corridor to check each of the cells. Firelight splintered across the stone walls as Cass's gaze made clear he didn't like the possibility of being trapped in a dead-end hall. The others waited on watch in the shadows near the gate. Time was of the essence, but if they could get Lettie free, the king's leverage over the sorcerers would take a solid hit. They passed each cell slowly, Cass on one side of the corridor, Miri on the other, searching the faces of the men and women inside. The farther they went, the heavier the dread settled into Miri's stomach. Lettie wasn't there, her slender figure and lion's-mane hair nowhere among the disheveled forms.

As they reached the last of the line, Miri turned toward Cass, sick as she tightened her grasp on her sword. Her sister's name thrummed with the ragged beat of her heart. But Cass was still. He and the other queensguard were frozen before the opposite cell. Cass fumbled with the key ring as the guard's torch flickered dim light over a square of stone floor with a thin blanket over a prone form. Miri stepped forward, but it could not be Lettie. It was a man, his figure large but worn thin with what must have been years inside the cell. A strange noise came from Cass as he finally released the lock. The ring of keys clattered to the floor in his haste to open the cell door.

He crouched beside the man, while the other queensguard stood frozen in his spot, and Miri stepped beside him. Cass reached for the man with trembling hands. His gray beard obscured much of a weathered face. But the noise from Cass broke, suddenly louder, and Miri realized it was something of a strangled sob. Her hand went to her throat, her knees suddenly weak. On the floor before them, his massive hand held in Cass's, was the head of the Lion Queen's guard—*Henry*.

※

HENRY WAS NOT DEAD. Miri had seen him fall during their long-ago rescue, but she'd been carted away in the fighting. He had lived, injured enough not to evade escape, and had likely been dragged to the cell to be held for ransom should the queensguard or uprisings call for it. Miri, Cass, and the other queensguard went to their knees before Henry. His gaze roamed over their faces with evident awe. Cass put his hands under the man and pulled him to sit, and a realization started to buzz through Miri frantically. She opened her mouth to say so, but the clang of metal rang through the corridor before she had a chance. They were out of time.

Cass and the queensguard pulled Henry to his feet, and Miri took the torch as the two men slipped their arms beneath his shoulders. Then they ran through the corridor. The queensguard at the gate fought off kingsmen with dagger and sword. Shouts rang from a far-off part of the castle, and two of the queensguard at the gate gasped at the sight of Henry as they came into view.

"Go," one of them said. "We'll get him to safety."

Cass hesitated for just a moment, but Henry murmured, "Go, lad." His voice was rough from disuse, but his order was clear. Henry might not know what their plan was, but his eyes were on Miri. He understood they had come to right wrongs. He, above all others, lived by his vow. Miri felt tears well in her eyes, but Henry gave her a solemn nod. "There's work to be done, Myrina. Show her you've the heart of a Lion."

Miri batted away her tears as the sound of approaching boots echoed through the halls. She stepped forward to place a hand on his chest, heartsick at the feel of bone instead of thick muscle beneath her palm. "Thank you, Henry." Fear nearly choked her words, but she had to ask. "What of Lettie? Where are they holding her?"

Henry's brow drew together, something flashing in his gray eyes. "In the tower." He glanced at Cass, confusion clear. "She's in the tower with Nicholas."

A door at the end of the corridor burst open, and half a dozen kingsmen rushed through, swords drawn.

"Go!" Cass shouted, ordering the group with Henry to take him to safety.

Henry's words echoed through Miri's thoughts, but the kingsmen were upon them, and all they could do was fight. There were only four left, Cass and Miri and two queensguard, as the other four rushed Henry to safety. A sword sliced through the air near Miri, barely missing a queensguard's arm. They needed to get back into the passages, staying hidden on their route to avoid facing a larger group of kingsmen. Four was not enough.

Swords clashed, and bodies slid into heaps onto the tiled floor with hands pressed to wounds that could not be staunched. The kingsmen were trained soldiers, brutal in their onslaught, but they met their match in the agile queensguard. Soon, though winded and one bleeding, Miri and the queensguard had dispatched the last of the kingsmen.

They ran again, staggered by the surprise of finding Henry, and Miri's heart seized in the sudden drowning fear within her chest. She stumbled, and Cass's fingers dug into her shoulders as he dragged her into a darkened alcove. He stood at her back, holding her steady as he gestured at the other two queensguard. At Cass's instruction, they crept forward with swords at the ready. Cass's chest rose and fell evenly behind her, his jaw brushing her ear. She focused on his breathing, not allowing the fear to paralyze her further. Miri had watched her mother fight the kingsmen before she had died. Her mother had been under the sorcerer's power—they had her blood—yet she had not been frozen in fear, because she had been a queen and the protections of the Storm Queen had saved her.

Fighting in the room beyond was joined by the muffled sound of a body falling on fabric as the tension released from Miri's chest. The sorcerer was gone and, with it, his effect on her. She nodded, sword in her hand, and she and Cass rushed from the alcove to help fight the remaining kingsmen who had been the sorcerer's guard.

They made their way through the castle, the route painfully familiar. Shadows darkened the stairwell, and they ducked into an alcove, weapons drawn and breath held until footsteps rushed past. As they came closer to the tower, Miri tried to keep her thoughts from what they might find and what the king had done to her sister in the years gone past or why he might want her in the keep so near him. To be certain, it was to make sure she was safe, out of the hands of the sorcerers, surely, something Miri should have thought of before. But a voice deep inside her whispered its doubts. Miri pressed them down, tightening her grip on her sword. Whatever had happened, whatever Nicholas had done, it would soon be over.

An explosion of sound came from a courtyard outside, but the bells had not yet begun to ring. Terric and the queensguard had made certain of it. Cass shoved a massive chest from in front of a library wall then made quick work of the panel beneath. Next, they went down a short set of wooden stairs and ran through the darkness between the castle walls. The queensguard behind Miri held a torch, its flickering light catching on the block walls and the outline of Cass before her. He turned down another passage, and the way became narrower. They froze outside the panel of wood that was their escape, listening for sounds of movement beyond. They were so close to the tower, so close to the worst of the kings and the man who held her mother's blood. She was finally close to finding Lettie, after so many lost years.

Cass glanced at Miri, and she did her best to convey she was well and that she had the emotion and the tingling dread under control. She wasn't certain if she was telling the truth, but she had no choice about it. There was no going back.

He slid the panel free, and they slipped into a sizable bedroom with no evidence of recent use. Beyond its small sitting room would be a door to the corridor that could take them to the castle keep. Cass gave a glance to the men behind them, obviously asking if they were well and truly ready for the sprint through the remaining rooms, for that fight that was to come. At their nods, the lot of them moved forward and came into a sitting room that was entirely bare of furniture. Cass froze near the doorway, his gaze roaming the space. There were signs the room had been charred, though no scent of smoke or hint of ash remained. It had been burned long before, no doubt, but the room had not been repaired. His wary gaze met Miri's. They both knew it had been years since they'd last explored the castle and that any number of things could have changed. Nicholas had been strict about visitors. No one was allowed to set foot in the keep, aside from a small number of servants who'd been locked inside, unable to leave because they had access to his secrets.

It was why none of the queensguard knew much of what had happened inside. Nicholas had been the cleverest and kept himself the most secure. Miri had never wanted a man dead more in her life. Cass gave her one final look before opening the door to the corridor—then an explosion knocked them back into the room.

༄

CASS'S BODY rolled over Miri, knocking her onto the stone as they were pelted with bits of block and ash. Miri's chest went tight with the approach of a sorcerer, and she realized the explosion had come not from them but from kingsmen. It was powder, not magic. The sound of clashing swords broke through the room, and one of their queensguard landed solidly on the floor beside Miri and Cass. Before her ears had stopped ringing, Cass was on his feet, and Miri stood behind him despite the dread building in her chest threatening to drown her. She raised her sword to fend off a blow, but a blast of energy slammed into her, knocking her again onto the floor. It was a sorcerer and too many kingsmen. They rushed forward, swords clashing, bursts of power cracking through the room and over Miri's skin like lightning. Another queensguard's body fell beside her.

As Cass turned to find Miri, his sword flashed, but it was far too late. The kingsmen descended. Miri was frozen by blood magic, her sword limp in her hand, and Cass was outnumbered twenty to one.

He fought on, but it was only moments before Miri and Cass were bound, defenseless, and prepared to be dragged through the castle. The sorcerer's blood ran over Cass's blade. He had not been able to fight them all, but he'd done what he could to free Miri from the magic's hold on her. Blood poured from a wound on his shoulder, a gash on his forehead, and another along his leg. He'd nearly died trying to prevent her capture, and two of his brethren already had.

They had failed—after everything. Cass would be tortured and killed. Lettie would be bled out at the hands of the king. The realm would be lost.

The kingsmen dragged them through the corridors, and Miri realized they were being taken not to the square to be hanged or to the cells to wait. They were going to the tower. The king knew who Miri was. Cass swore and struggled against the soldiers, knocking two from their feet before being subdued by two more. A kingsman slammed his sword hilt into Cass's jaw and was repaid with a fight only that much fiercer. He was outnumbered, and the kingsmen were gathering through the halls. More and more kept coming, and there was less that they could do.

Cass wrenched in their hold, his gaze finding Miri, and she winced at the torment she saw in his eyes. It could only get worse. She gave him a small nod before she was jerked forward again, through a massive arching doorway that led to the tower keep—to the king on his throne.

CHAPTER 31

Miri was shoved to her knees at the base of the polished steps before her mother's throne, Cass beside her. She didn't know whether Nicholas meant to gloat or if he only wanted to witness her death in person. She couldn't defeat him from her knees, but that did not stop her from glaring up at the man with a promise in her eyes.

"Princess Myrina," Nicholas said with a purr. He wore a rich, dark-red, velvet-trimmed suit, a golden crown, and a jeweled chain draped over his shoulders. He seemed to have barely aged. He was the same man in her nightmares, unchanged by years on the throne.

Miri spat. Blood splattered across the steps before her, but none of it was hers.

Nicholas chuckled. "The little Lion still has bite."

Panic was tight in Miri's chest, but the sorcerers had not approached from the back of the hall. She had no idea what was stopping them from closing the distance but was grateful she could manage any movement at all. "You have broken the laws of blood. You betrayed the one true queen."

The king glanced at the kingsman beside Miri, and the man's fist cracked across her jaw. In response, Cass smashed his head into one of the men holding him but was shoved back down in a violent struggle that only left him bleeding more.

The king sighed. "I see you've brought a bloodsworn with you. One of Henry's little brats." His finger waved above the arms of the throne, and his tone bored, he said, "Kill him."

"I wouldn't," someone somewhere behind Miri said. "Not unless you want to lose three more."

The king's gaze shot to the man, and though Miri couldn't see him, she knew it was Terric. He had the sorcerers hostage beneath his blade. It was why the king had not yet acted, why no magic tore through the room. If he killed Miri or Cass, he would lose as many sorcerers as Terric and his men held. Yet Terric could not move on the king without Miri and Cass losing their lives.

She couldn't figure out what Nicholas was waiting for, but she could see that he was buying time. The king had a card up his sleeve, maybe more men or more sorcerers or something worse Miri had not yet considered. Bloodsworn could not be harmed by magic, but they could still be killed.

The door behind the throne opened, and two more figures walked in. Prince Augustus had grown tall, his features as smooth and square as his father's. His dark eyes skirted Miri and Cass, as if the entire ordeal was beneath him. Miri had never wanted a prince dead more in her life.

Her gaze fell back to Nicholas, but the corner of his mouth was pinched in something of a tell. He thought he'd won, yet Miri could not see how. Prince Augustus stopped beside the throne, and beside him stepped a tall woman who curtsied briefly to the king. She faced forward, her golden eyes trailing over the room.

Miri's chest seized, her mind screaming that she had to be wrong. The woman wore a long velvet gown, her hair hidden beneath a headdress that draped her bare shoulders and was woven with red ribbons and jewels. She was older, the soft lines of childhood leaving not a single trace. Her skin was smooth and powdered, not at all the visage Miri had imagined. But there was no denying her sister's face or the familiar expression of both contempt for a prisoner and interest for how the crime would be dealt with. Miri's mouth fell open to speak, but she could not find words.

Lettie stared at her for several moments, and Miri remembered her sister had thought her dead. She wanted to scream at her, to make her see, but Miri's voice would still not come. Then the perfect brow pinched above her sister's eyes, the first hint of recognition coming slowly to her precise features, before it dawned all at once. "Myrina." The word seemed to fall unintentionally from Lettie's mouth, and Miri couldn't make out the emotion that drove it.

Miri's gaze flicked from her sister to the king. His half smile mocked the exchange. It seemed to say that Miri had mistaken everything. Miri's eyes shot back to Lettie. "I thought you were locked in a cell, all these years." Miri swallowed, her breath shallow. "Captive."

Lettie barked a laugh, and the sound sent ice through Miri's veins. She had been shocked, surely, but Lettie did not seem ill at ease that Miri had been shoved to the floor before them, bound and at the sword of a kingsman. Lettie gestured at the throne room they'd spent so many days in as children. "Captive?" Her tone was withering. "I live in the throes of luxury. King Nicholas has been nothing but faithful to my wishes." She shook her head, glancing at the man before her gaze came back to Miri. "The only reason I'm trapped in this keep is because of the threats to my life and my safety. If not for the queensguard wanting me dead, I could leave." She frowned. "You know well I never cared much for travel, but there are so many who still wish me murdered. To end the line. Honestly, Myrina, why go among the rabble at all? Here, I am treated like a queen."

Miri stared at her, the stranger who was no stranger at all. Nothing she said made sense, not the way she spoke or how her hand floated to brush against Augustus's. Nicholas watched, as if the scene were somehow pleasant, and Lettie's words repeated in Miri's head. She thought the queensguard wanted her dead. Her sister, her own blood, had been fooled by a traitorous king. He'd convinced her that she could not leave the keep for her safety and that at his son's side, she would be protected and treated like a queen. Miri's voice came as strong and insolent as when they'd fought as children. "You *are* a queen, Leticia. You are the daughter of the Lion and the last of our blood. You will rule."

"I'll let you make the order, dear princess." Nicholas's voice was low, the words for Lettie nearly sounding kind. "She is your sister, after all."

"Treason?" Miri spat, aware that the entire charade was the king's way of buying time. She could not bring herself to stay silent, though, even if Cass and the others had.

Fury boiled through her, but Nicholas only directed his gaze toward Lettie. "It is unfortunate she's chosen to ally with the men who want you dead."

"They are queensguard," Miri said. "They are sworn to *protect* you."

Lettie scoffed, her gaze trailing over Cass. "You brought a bloodsworn into this throne room, Myrina? After what they have done? And have the nerve to say I am his queen?" Her shoulders somehow became straighter. "If what you say is true, then his loyalty is to me. He owes nothing at all to you." Lettie glanced at Cass. "Kill her."

There was a moment of silence, then she shouted toward the queensguard and the bloodsworn at the back of the room. "Drop your weapons. Let the sorcerers go!"

Miri felt a moment of panic, that Lettie was right, that the queen's word was law. But Lettie was not truly queen yet, not until her name day. Then it would be true.

"Do you see, sister?" Lettie hissed. "They do not follow my command. They never have."

Lettie would not be queen. Nicholas would never let her. But if Cass and the others freed her, she could in a matter of weeks claim her throne. They would be under Lettie's command, whether they agreed with her orders or not. Whether she believed she'd been misled for years, that she was wrong about everything. It would be Cass's duty to follow her word, the same for all of the queensguard and for Miri—except they had sworn a vow and made a promise to a greater queen.

"Our mother is dead, Leticia. At this man's hand." Miri's voice rang like steel through the room, her target clear. Nicholas had orchestrated the death of their mother, betrayed the bonds between sorcerer and queen, and was well on his way to destroying the realm.

Lettie's brow pinched. "No, sister. Rebels killed our queen, just like the men you've brought with you here. Nicholas saved me and rescued me from the same fate." Her tone said *or worse*, but Miri did not argue details. Nicholas's hand had twitched more than once in the moments that had passed. Miri was out of time. She needed Lettie to see.

She tried to shift forward, fighting the grip that held her in place and struggling with her gradually loosening bonds. "They deceived you, Lettie. Killed our mother, the last queen, and freed the sorcerers from her bonds. What do you think they will do to you after the festival of moons, on your name day?"

Lettie's head gave a small, irritated shake. "You know this. The entire kingdom knows this." Her gaze shot to Nicholas, somewhere between apologetic and incredulous. "I'll be presented at the prince's side as future queen."

Miri felt bile rise in her throat. Her sister planned to let Nicholas continue his rule, as if she and Augustus would become king and queen upon his death. As if Lettie would have any power. As if she would live that long. Gods, she thought they would be celebrating her name day with a wedding announcement.

"No," Miri said, emotion nearly choking her. "That's not it at all. They've rounded up the sympathizers to kill on the square. They're in cells just as we speak." Henry was there too. Henry had been locked up beneath Lettie's nose, accused of treason by a man who was no king at all. Miri's tone went hard, her patience gone. "Lettie, they plan to kill you. Before you bear the blood of a queen."

Lettie's breath came out in a huff, a broken laugh, but the confidence she had worn was suddenly thin. Her cheeks colored just the slightest bit, but she did not look at the king or his son. She did not let on that she believed their deception. Lettie was not going to relent before it was too late.

"I watched our mother die," Miri said in a whisper. "I watched these men murder her, watched as her blood boiled from her own body at the hands of the sorcerers."

"No," Lettie said. "That's not true." Her voice was broken, evidence of the panic that rose in her, but she had apparently never conquered her baser instincts. "Do it," she ordered the kingsman beside Myrina. "Kill her now." Lettie stepped forward, her graceful fingers trembling at the end of her slender arms. "By my order!"

Miri closed her eyes and drew in a shaky breath, heartsick. She had lost her sister in a single command. After all they'd been through, she'd lost her to a king who was no more than a treacherous lord. But no, she remembered, Lettie had not been lost. She'd been stolen.

Anger rose in Miri swift and hot, and she bit down hard, jerking her bonds to reach beneath her jacket to the well-worn hem and her mother's locket. She ripped the metal free, the tearing sound loud in the open space, and spread her palm for Lettie to see. "Tell me, sister," Miri hissed, "if this is my lie, then how is it that I hold her locket? How could I have pulled it from her neck after she burned?"

Lettie stared at the locket, her entire body gone still. The expression that washed over her features turned Miri's stomach. She'd seen it before, a thousand times, yet as impossible as it was to believe, it was far more impossible to deny. It was an unbearable truth, the last thing she expected from Lettie.

The locket clattered to the floor. The realization was worse than anything Miri might have imagined, worse than any nightmare.

Miri grabbed the dagger she had hidden at her waist, wrenching her arms free from the last of her bonds with a tearing of flesh to slam the hilt to metal before the guards had a chance to stop her.

The clash was quick and loud and seemed to end all other noises from reaching Miri's ears. Horror flooded her, worse than drowning in a frozen sea. The locket their mother had forced upon her had not been a token at all or a reminder of Miri's vow. It had been evidence against the queen's betrayer.

Miri stared down at the broken pieces, her torn wrist dripping blood where she'd destroyed the only thing she held dear, all that was left of her mother.

Among the bits of busted metal, anyone could see the blood, aged from its time inside. Miri remembered now that she'd not seen her mother remove it from her neck. It had been given to her by Henry when he'd found out and he'd come to warn them.

All she could think of was the fear that had crossed her sister's features at the sight of it. It was fear that said she knew where the locket had been and how it had been taken from her mother's neck. It was fear that said Lettie was guilty of more than falling for sweet words and empty promises.

"Lettie." Miri's word was only a breath, the tone one of mourning and of a final, unchangeable regret.

Her mother's words rang in her ears. *You will come back, Myrina of Stormskeep. You will earn your name. I command your vow that you will end the traitor for good. Only a true Lion will hold the throne.*

The Lion Queen had known all along. And Henry, when they'd found him in the cells, had known too. *Show her you've the heart of a Lion.* Myrina had never suspected or considered such a thing of her sister at all, even when it was clear she'd been misled by Nicholas. Lettie had given them what they could never obtain on their own, even if she didn't realize the weapon it would become. The doors to the throne room burst open, and the king shouted an order at his men, but Miri could only hear the rising of her blood. Lettie had betrayed them. The heir apparent had killed the queen.

Miri's fingers curled into a fist, but the king's game had run its course. Their time was up. Myrina would watch Cass and the queensguard be killed. Lettie's eyes strayed to Prince Augustus, her face pale as realization dawned. He was the prince she'd given the locket to and who had tricked her into falling for their ploy. Miri could nearly read the revelations that flitted over her sister's face. How many must have been sacrificed to perform such magic, to cause a death that would twist the fate of so many. Lettie hadn't just killed the queen. She'd killed thousands.

Miri's heart pounded, but her chest had eased in the strange drowning sensation from the presence of sorcerers. She was aware of the fighting behind her, the flare of heat and magic and the clash of swords. The sorcerers were not dead, yet their effect on her seemed to be broken. She stared down at the locket, a token she had carried with her everywhere. Every time a sorcerer's presence had frozen her, she'd been carrying it. And how much worse it had been when she'd been soaked in her mother's blood. It had been the blood in the locket all along. Miri was free of their hold.

Her gaze shot back to Lettie, but her sister's realizations had shifted into a familiar rage. Her eyes swam over Nicholas and the chaos of the room before they stopped on Miri.

Miri was still on her knees at the hands of the kingsmen, but her answer was steady. "He doesn't have the power, Lettie. He never has." Her tone rang with the promise *You are a Lion.*

Lettie's jaw went tight, and her hand moved swiftly to the dagger at the prince's side. She shoved it into Nicholas's neck, straight and fast and deep. Then she ripped it free at an angle, the king's blood spraying over the throne. Miri shouted, trying to jerk free from her captors, but her warning came too late.

Lettie turned into the prince's arms, his blade spearing through her gut as her mouth opened in a gasp.

The betrayal in Lettie's eyes was the worst, not because she had trusted the bastard king and his wicked son but because Miri had seen the look before from their mother. The Lion Queen had died knowing she'd been betrayed by her own daughter. As Lettie's expression melted into pain, Miri forgave whatever rage that might have followed. The prince dropped her body to the floor as queensguard rushed the dais. They took down the prince but were too late to save Lettie. Her blood spilled over the steps of the throne, pooling before Miri and the locket.

Lettie's beautiful face had gone slack, and as the last bit of breath left her sister's body, Miri felt the jolt of ages-old magic rush into her.

The hum of it rose inside her, biting within her veins. She threw her head back in a scream, and the room fell still as if it were the roar of a lion. Magic cracked through the air, a singing pulse that snapped taut against the bonds of the sorcerers. "Stop!" she commanded. "Kneel."

Miri could not see the men behind her, but she more than understood. She was no true queen yet, but inside her rested the power of the queen's blood. Her sister had been young and foolish and had released the tethers that bound the magic through her. Her mother's had been stolen, used against her by men who wished her ill.

Miri was untainted by betrayal or fear. She was done with being trapped, bound before a stolen throne. Her next command was a whisper, and it echoed through the room. "Kill the kingsmen."

Sorcerer's fire tore through the throne room, searing death to each of the king's armed men. Swords clattered to the floor, and the room was scented with bitter smoke and ash. Her queensguard stared for only a moment before they moved again and had surrounded Miri and untied her bonds. She watched in silence as Terric approached the throne and his booted foot rose to shove the body of Nicholas to the floor.

Terric's eyes met hers, showing a promise fulfilled. Then he knelt slowly before Lettie with a reverence due a queen.

"Burn her," Miri said. "Take her ashes to the courtyard." *For our mother.*

Hands came to Miri's arms and helped her gently to her feet. It was over. She'd made it, surrounded by queensguard in her home at Stormskeep. Still, her mouth tasted bitter with smoke and blood.

EPILOGUE
SHADOW QUEEN

Miri stood near a window, high in the keep, staring out at the kingdom of Stormskeep below. Weeks had passed, and with them had come the first cool days that marked the end of the season and Lettie's name day. On the wall beside her rested a newly hung map carved with the rivers and forests of the seven kingdoms, once again whole. The soldiers of the queensguard, Cass and Terric with them, had been gone for weeks as they removed the last kings from their stolen thrones. Miri had not needed the kings' justice dealt at her own hand. Her vow to her mother had been fulfilled. The betrayal had not come from the kings at all. It had been her sister. And Lettie was gone. She had been misled by a handsome face and promises that played to her darkest fears, and she had paid for it with her life.

Miri spun the gold band on her finger, its weight somehow heavier than the crown. Henry sat on a cushioned bench in the room behind her, deftly managing matters of state. He would be named regent once he was returned to health for the nearly two years until Miri's name day, the start of her twentieth year. He still seemed so frail but only compared to her memories. Henry had weathered the time locked away well enough. He was strong, and his mind was still sharp. His heart was ever true, faithful to his duty to the realm.

The castle had been filled with uncountable visitors in the previous weeks, each offering support or resolving business that Miri's counselors had seen to on her behalf. They'd left her to decide larger matters, and though she'd been taught as a child and schooled since by Nan and Thom, Miri leaned on the knowledge of those who'd remained in Stormskeep and understood how things had changed. As it was, only a few dozen members of court milled about the room, their presence a strange comfort—so like her memories as a child—and a stark reminder that she was no longer the girl she had been. Miri would be queen.

She swallowed the nervousness that swam up with the thought. She had time, two years to prepare. But it felt like a new vow she'd never meant to take. She did not want to do it alone.

The tall doors opened across the room, and Miri glanced over her shoulder absently at the newcomer. Her chest squeezed at the sight of Cass. His shoulders were straight beneath the fine black coat of the guard, his steps purposeful as he crossed the space to address Henry and the members of their council. He handed over a scroll, likely a report that detailed that their work was done, then his shoulders squared once more. Miri turned to face him, and as he approached, her bloodsworn gave a small bow. It was not required of his post. There was a moment of hesitation before his face rose again.

His eyes found hers, and he said, something tremulous beneath his tone, "You look well, Your Majesty."

Miri felt the words more than heard them, somehow entirely too aware of the lavish gown she wore, the delicate curls a maid had tucked beneath her crown, and the thin gold band she'd left upon her finger. "Cassius." She might have said more, could she only trust her voice.

"My duty as queensguard has been fulfilled. The lords of the realm no longer call themselves king." He was being kind, because the lords of the realm could no longer call themselves anything. They were dead. Cass pressed his lips together, and Miri had the sensation he wanted to glance around the room, but his gaze did not leave hers. Despite the time they'd spent together, this was how court business was conducted. He'd no right to ask for an audience alone. "As such," he said, "I am here to ask of you a favor."

"Anything," she started, but her response fell away at Cass's expression.

His hair had been freshly cut, revealing a faint line that marred his brow from their fight with the kingsmen. He seemed otherwise in perfect order, but his finger twitched at his side. "I ask that you release me from my duty."

The words were like a blow to the chest. Miri's fingers clenched where they rested before her waist. He understood he never should have allowed her to kiss him, because he was blood-sworn. He could not do his duty to protect her—to be so near without breaking his vow again. His honor demanded it. There was no way to stop him, no other answer she could give. The words tasted of ash, and her voice was not her own when she finally uttered, "Of course."

Cass's brow shifted at her expression, his neck heating in a flush of red. His gaze darted momentarily sideways, but no one could see his face but Miri. They were as alone as they would get, and it felt strangely like Cass wanted to drag her away from the others. *What is it?* she wanted to whisper, but she couldn't. So she waited, silent and still, until Cass spoke again.

He cleared his throat, but when he spoke again, his voice was low. But that didn't matter, because all other discussions in the room had come to a halt. "It is not that I have any desire to acquit my duty, Myrina. Only that..." His throat bobbed, his hazel gaze seeming to beg for her understanding. "Henry has seen fit to offer me his name, officially, so that I might be welcome among the court."

Miri's breath seized in her chest as Cass's confession fell so unexpectedly into place. A quiet murmur went through the room as people realized that something far more unusual had happened than a queensguard retiring from his duty. Miri's gaze snapped to Henry, whose expression was serene aside from a small twitch at the corner of his mouth. Gods, they had played her. Henry gave her a wink and turned back to his fellows, and any outrage she felt was washed away by the utter disbelief that came with the impossible.

Miri's hands slid to her sides. "Clear the hall!"

At her order, Henry stood, leaning heavily on one hip as he waved his cane at the stunned counselors. "Go," Henry said. "All of you."

As the bodies filed from the room, Cass's discomfort seemed to increase tenfold. Miri did not know whether he was expecting a dressing-down or that she might rebuff him, but she had only one reason to get him alone, and it was nothing of the sort. Henry gave her a smile, one she remembered so well, before he turned to leave as well. Cass and Miri were truly alone, court gossip be damned, for the first time in weeks.

She faced him and said, her voice quiet in the massive room but steadier than it had ever been, "You were raised bloodsworn. Duty above all. You're willing to sacrifice that to become a lord?"

Cass twitched as if he might move forward but was restraining himself. "My loyalty will not be diminished by the loss of those duties, Myrina. I will always be faithful—"

She raised a hand, cutting off his vow. "The question is, will you be satisfied instead with duties of state?"

He blanched. "I would never presume to ask for court favor."

"Of a king, Cassius. Not a lord." She stepped forward, close enough that she could touch him, should she only decide to do it. "In two years' time, I will be queen."

Cass had thought her angry and was clearly agitated his plan had gone nothing at all how he'd wanted, but suddenly those emotions fled from his face. Shock had replaced it instead. He had known she would be queen. He had only wanted to be near her, not to be a fisherman's grandson who might someday be king. It was clear he'd thought nothing of the sort. A new emotion, one she could not quite identify and had not before seen, passed over his features, and Miri thought it was possibly hope.

Cass bowed low, his knee to the rich tile floor, his hand over his heart as his face rose to hers. "By my honor, by my soul, I swear to serve this realm with loyalty all the days that I live. May the gods grant me strength so that I may remain ever vigilant in my duty, the maiden wisdom so that I remain ever faithful in my cause. I vow to you, Myrina of Stormskeep, by my heart and my blood. I am yours."

Miri swallowed back the urge to sob, a ridiculous hiccup of hysteria wanting to escape. She forced her emotions to steady and her voice not to tremble. "Then rise, Cassius of Stormskeep." She felt her lip twitch into a smile. "A king of the realm will not be brought to his knees by anyone."

Cass stood to face her, taking her trembling hands in his. His breath was a whisper over her skin, his eyes on nothing but her. His mouth had twisted into that lopsided grin, his expression one of wonder. "Only you, my queen." He leaned closer to brush his lips against hers. "Only you."

ALSO BY MELISSA WRIGHT

- **STANDALONE FANTASY** -

Seven Ways to Kill a King

Between Ink and Shadows

- **SERIES** -

THE FREY SAGA

Frey

Pieces of Eight

Molly (a short story)

Rise of the Seven

Venom and Steel

Shadow and Stone

Feather and Bone

DESCENDANTS SERIES

Bound by Prophecy

Shifting Fate

Reign of Shadows

SHATTERED REALMS

King of Ash and Bone

Queen of Iron and Blood

- **WITCHY PNR** -

HAVENWOOD FALLS

Toil and Trouble

BAD MEDICINE

Blood & Brute & Ginger Root

Visit the author on the web at

www.melissa-wright.com

CPSIA information can be obtained
at www.ICGtesting.com
Printed in the USA
BVHW081243060223
657825BV00024B/1228/J

9 781950 958108